NONE SHALL SPURN

'Your grandparents have never seen you, Tim. When their son John – your father, that is – married your mother he was made an outcast from his family. They had nothing more to do with him. When he was killed on active service . . . well, they just didn't bother. Twelve months after your father's death, your mother died.'

'What did she die of?'

Tom looked at the anxious questioning face. 'A broken heart,' he said.

NONE
SHALL SPURN

Jane Kingsley Barratt

A STAR BOOK

published by
the Paperback Division of
W. H. ALLEN & Co. PLC

A Star Book
Published in 1985
by the Paperback Division of
W. H. Allen & Co. PLC
44 Hill Street, London W1X 8LB

Copyright © Jane Kingsley Barratt, 1985

Printed in Great Britain by
Hunt Barnard Printing Ltd, Aylesbury, Bucks.

ISBN 0 352 31593 8

ONE

PROLOGUE

The big gas lamps lit the railway station in pale, wavering light. Little serpents of naked flame crept from the charred burners and a ballet of tangerine shadows pirouetted on the whitewashed walls.

The dark beast shape of a locomotive stood bleakly in the platform bay, its boilers cold and dead.

An army private belching resonantly after drinking strong ale lurched unsteadily along mumbling and grumbling as he picked his way between porters' barrows, oil lamps and dumpy milk churns.

A waiting train with crimson fire in its throat panted like a stallion which has run long and far.

In his arms she felt warm and the fragrance of lilies-of-the-valley came from her hair.

She smiled at him, her upturned face tear-stained hiding the torment she felt because he was leaving her.

He looked elegant in the superb fit of his officer's uniform and he knew that she was being brave for his sake.

The station was crowded and yet they seemed remote from all the people around them.

'Have courage,' he murmured. 'I shall be with you again before long.'

She clung to him without speaking, her body tense and arched. Soon she would be alone – and yet not alone, for she had the child from whom to draw comfort. Their child. 'Goodbye, my heart,' he whispered gently, kissing

7

her on the mouth. 'Take care,' and then turning he walked quickly to the waiting train.

Steam blowing suddenly across the platform hid him from view and when next she could see him, the train was on the move.

She waved and then there was nothing save the blankness where the train had once been.

He had gone and now her life would lie in shadow until he came back to her.

Four months later it appeared in the Gazette: *Lieutenant John Farley, 17th King's Rifle Brigade, killed in action, Mafeking, May 15th, 1900.*

1

The boy stood alone on the hill, grubby hands clenched with excitement, small, puckered face turned expectantly to the bird hovering at the edge of the nest. Fascination glowed in his eyes as he watched the fat worm struggling in the bird's yellow beak, and the gaping, upturned mouths of the squawking fledgelings.

Quickly, the sharp beak segregated the worm and the brood were suddenly hushed. The watching boy moved, and the bird hopped in stricken panic. 'Nice bird,' he murmured soothingly, 'nice little bird.' But the thrush only bobbed in terror, shaking the twigs with nervous movements of its feet.

The boy lifted his hand in a gesture of comfort, and the bird, with a last despairing glance at its young, took wing, and vanished.

Disappointed, the boy walked slowly to the nest and examined the chattering inmates who peered at him with bright beady eyes.

'What are you up to, little boy?' a girl's voice suddenly piped at his elbow: 'and aren't you dirty?'

The boy turned sharply, his brow creasing into a frown at the interruption, and with solemn eyes assessed the intruder carefully.

She was small and pretty, with dark shining hair.

'Who are you?' he asked at the end of his appraisal, 'I haven't seen you before.'

'Nor I you.' There was a certain insolence in her voice.

'I'm Timothy Swaine. I live in a cottage at Worley.'

The girl shrugged. 'You must be one of the people my father told me not to play with, then, if you're a cottager. I'm Nancy Weston, and my father is Mr Douglas Weston: he's very rich you know.' The patronisation was completely unconscious. The boy thought for a moment, attempting to measure this in his mind. Riches were foreign to him, a symbol of something of which he was not quite clear. 'Oh! Well,' he said, shrugging his defiance, 'what are riches, anyway?'

Nancy sniffed at this careless dispensation of her claims. 'I live in a big house,' she said impressively, 'and we have lots of servants. My mummy's a beauty, everybody says so.' This latter was in patent mimicry of her elders.

'I don't care,' declared Timothy, still on the defensive, 'I know all the nests around here anyway, and I know where there's a secret pool, too.'

Nancy considered this statement carefully. 'Where?' she asked, with womanly cunning. Timothy frowned, and unable to resist the challenge hitched his shabby trousers a little higher and said gruffly, 'I'll soon show you. Follow me.'

Nancy followed him along the path, eager for adventure: finally they came into a clearing, where a pool, shadowed by willow trees, glinted in the sunlight.

The water, crystal clear, was fed by a bubbling spring, which in turn gave rise to a tiny brook, whose sandy edges were a thread of bronze in the emerald blaze of the undergrowth.

'This is *my* pool,' the boy said with possessive satisfaction. 'I don't show it to everyone, you know.'

'Is it deep?' Nancy peered into the glassy surface: 'it looks deep.'

'I've often paddled, it only comes to my knees, but it's muddy at the bottom, and awful cold.'

'I'd love to paddle now,' the girl exclaimed excitedly: 'shall we?'

10

Timothy looked doubtfully at the expensive clothes of his new companion. 'You'll get muddy,' he warned, 'your dress will be spoiled.'

'I don't care,' she said defiantly: 'I'm eleven, anyway.'

The boy shrugged, and sitting on the grassy bank drew off his boots to reveal socks badly in need of mending.

Nancy's shrill laughter mocked him, and crimson faced he dragged them off and hurriedly lowered himself into the water.

'Ooh!' he spluttered: 'it's cold.'

'Do you think it's too cold?' the girl was anxious, half scared of the expected chill shock.

'Not when you get used to it. It takes your breath at first.' He moved out a step and the water became murky where his feet disturbed the mud.

'Don't move, you're making the water dirty,' Nancy cried.

'I can't help it, there's a lot of mud at the bottom.'

'Don't go any further, wait for me. I'm coming in.' Seating herself on the bank she hurriedly took off her shoes and stockings, wriggled her toes in fearful anticipation, and made to follow. The bank, steep and moist, yielded unexpectedly to her slight feet. 'I'm slipping,' she squealed, 'Timothy, Timothy, hold me.' And then she hit the water with a splash.

'Ooh! Ooh! Ooh!' Her cries, high pitched, suddenly ceased and she sat on the muddy bottom of the pool with the water lapping placidly just beneath her chin.

Timothy, too frozen with horror to find voice, squelched towards her. 'Oh! my goodness,' he croaked, 'now you've done it! What will your mother say?'

'Help me up; don't stand there. You just help me this minute.' She was near to tears.

Desperately the boy groped for her hand, tugged for all he was worth in a supreme effort to justify himself, slipped, and with a terrific splash sat beside her.

They sat looking at each other, until Timothy, churning

and splashing, scrambled to his feet. 'You can get up yourself now,' he snapped angrily, 'it's not deep, and I'm all wet.'

Nancy suddenly saw the humour of the situation, and she laughed until the tears rolled down her cheeks.

'It's no laughing matter, I can tell you,' said Timothy now more angry than ever, 'my Dad will tan me for this.'

With a flurry of miniature waves Nancy stood up, and after a crestfallen glance at herself, made for the bank, Timothy following.

'What shall we do?' she asked, with chattering teeth and utterly at a loss for any solution to a calamity of this magnitude.

Timothy sneezed violently. 'We'll catch cold standing about: better put on our shoes and keep moving.'

He squeezed as much water from his clothing as possible and pulled on his boots.

'Ready when you are,' he said, 'and I think we'd better run.' Nancy hastily put on her shoes and they tore off down the path like a couple of young hares, trailing water behind them, before panting to a halt at the place where they had first met.

'Shall I see you again,' the boy gasped.

'I don't know. My governess will be awfully annoyed, and I'm not supposed to play with people.'

'Will you get into trouble?'

'I expect so.'

'I'll come with you. I feel quite dry now, and I can say it was all my fault.'

Ten minutes later they came to Nancy's home, and Timothy fell back a step when he saw that it was the old squire's estate.

'I didn't know that you lived here,' he said, awed.

'I told you that we were rich.'

'Yes, I know you did, but I thought you were joking.'

'My father has lots of money.' She said this with her old air of hauteur. 'Look! There's my dog.'

A fat spaniel trotted down the drive, but before Timothy could even stroke it, a heavy hand, striking his left ear, almost lifted him from his feet.

A voice shrill with indignation penetrated his numbed senses, and he found himself peering at a tall thin woman with a long, horsey face. His eyes, smarting with tears, were some time in focusing, and when at last he was fully able to see, he knew that he was facing the outraged governess of his new friend.

'You dirty little urchin,' rasped the voice, 'what have you done to Nancy? Wait until her father hears of this. Look at her: soaked to the skin, and all your fault.'

'But – ' stammered the hapless boy.

'Silence!' stormed the woman.

'But – ' ventured Nancy.

'Silence, and go indoors at once. I shall have words to say to your father about this conduct; I can't let you out of my sight for a minute.'

The spaniel, aware that things were not all that they should be, plumped down despondently on fat haunches, while Nancy, on the verge of tears, faced her tormenter defiantly.

'Don't you dare shout at me,' she cried, 'or I'll never speak to you again.'

'What!' The governess flushed crimson. 'Go into that house at once, change yourself into dry clothes, and then report to your father's study. I shall be waiting for you there.'

Nancy burst into tears, and Timothy, his young heart melted by her utter dejection, suddenly lowered his head and, darting forward, butted the irate governess in the stomach.

He looked but once to see a pair of black stockings poking from beneath a frill of white petticoats as she collapsed to the ground and then he fled as fast as his legs would carry him.

2

On a fine day, with the sun throwing bronze streamers on to the earth, the Swaines' cottage looked a very pretty place.

It was an authentic structure of brick and timber, with roof tied and thatched, and a whole acre of land. Rambler roses clung in profusion to the lower walls, and in bloom, the sea of dazzling pinks made a wonderful sight.

Thomas Swaine farmed the holding, and despite the rich, brown soil and the row upon row of cultivated vegetables and flowers, only he knew just how hard a pinch it was to make both ends meet season in and season out. But even with all the pitfalls that beset a market gardener, the acre produced a justifiable amount of return for Thomas in the summer. And with early morning mushroom gathering, and the preparation of plump, table birds for folks with means above the average, he could steer a fairly safe course in the bitter winter months, when the earth refused to yield anything save greens and leeks.

Pausing in his digging, Tom ran a practised eye over the level lines of his produce with satisfaction. This summer promised him reward enough to look after the winter, and possibly save a bit into the bargain. Spitting briefly on his earthstained palms, he once more began to dig, considering in his mind what would most likely happen if ever he became ill. He thought for a moment of the boy Timothy – not his, not his wife's, and far from sturdy enough to tackle the land.

Tom wished the missus would keep him a bit more tidy, and supervise his washing more closely. There were times when the lad looked ragged and grubby as any city urchin. Mary had become slack somehow: the house was going downhill. It looked much better from the outside than it actually was: the roses on the wall gave it that pretty, postcard look, but Tom knew how different the reality was. He shrugged, and felt the keen bite of the spade slice into the brown, moist earth.

'I've fed the chickens,' said Timothy at his elbow, 'and cut twelve dozen tulips as you told me. I wonder if they can feel it when you cut them?'

Tom paused in his efforts and gazed at the boy in wonder. 'Wherever did you get that silly notion from?' he said, and spat disgustedly. 'You get some peculiar ideas in that noddle of yours, don't you, young 'un?'

'I only wondered,' the boy ventured.

'Wondered my foot. Go and ask your mother if she's a decent pair of trousers for you to put on. Those are the raggedest I've seen yet.'

Unabashed, Timothy turned and left him to his spade work. Passing the chicken run he cast an appraising glance at his charges before entering the timbered doorway of the cottage.

Once inside, the sunlight was cut to a minimum, and the red-tiled kitchen looked dark and forbidding. A few brasses badly in need of a clean lined the mantelshelf, and a middle-aged woman idly watched a panful of stew simmering on a wood fire.

'Father says have I some better trousers to wear,' Timothy informed her, at the same time peering to examine the stew.

The woman paused in her activities. 'You tell your father that your other trousers are for when you go back to school at the end of the holidays, and if he's feeling generous-like then maybe he'll take you to market in the morning and buy you a pair.'

'Yes'm,' said Timothy, further examining the stew.

'What's wrong with you lad – hungry? You've all but put your nose in the pot.'

'I'm fair peckish. Mom, how do people become rich?' The woman straightened at his question, her mouth open a little. She was fiftyish, with greying hair, a pink, smooth face and friendly, brown eyes. At one time, she had obviously been good looking, but now there was an air of neglect about her, just as there was in her untidy kitchen.

'Where did you get that question?' she enquired, as though Timothy had been prompted to ask her advice.

'I just thought of it.' He did not tell her of his chance meeting with Nancy Weston.

'Well, best forget it. It's not for the likes of you and me. It certainly doesn't come from hard work: your father will testify to that. God knows he's worked hard enough for little.' She examined the stewpot, and began laying a red and blue squared cloth.

'Tell your father dinner's ready.'

Timothy ran out calling, and very soon all three were seated at the table eating.

'You're as good with a stewpot as ever, Mary,' praised Tom, smacking his lips with relish after he had eaten. 'I'll just have a pipe before turning over that last corner. We might put down a few fruit trees next year. The stuff's coming on grandly.'

His eye roved over the dark furnishings of the kitchen, the faded prints, the unpolished brasses. Yes, Mary was a good cook, but she had let the cottage slip.

'By the by,' he went on, 'there's some new people taken on the old squire's place. There's four fat pullets ready dressed to go over tomorrow and you'll be taking them, young Tim, so be on your best behaviour.'

Timothy's heart plummeted into his boots. 'To the old squire's place?' he faltered in dismay.

'That's what I said; and what are you so scared about? Look at him mother.'

'I can see. Strike's me he's been up to something: maybe broken a window. Have you?'

'N-no. Course not; it's just that it's so big.'

'You'll be all right,' his father reassured him, 'take the birds to the back entrance. They'll mayhap have stuff from us regular. Jeremy Streten recommended me to the cook.' He chuckled to himself, and then went off to his work.

The sound of a linnet, a gay sweet lilt, greeted Timothy next morning as he walked unwillingly up the slope to the great house. The mullioned windows, liquid gold in the sun, smirked down at him, as warily he trod the curving drive. Massive oak doors with great shining brass knockers seemed to know that he came at his peril, and leered at him with their shiny, polished surfaces.

Apprehensively, Timothy scudded round the granite buttresses of the wall, crept beneath the huge, flat windows, and scampered to the little green door of the tradesman's entrance. He gulped his relief as he knocked: he had seen no one.

A plump, pleasant-faced woman in a starched overall opened the door to him and enquired his business.

'I'm Timothy Swaine,' he said, panting, 'and I've come with the chickens you ordered.'

'You're all out of breath: what have you been doing – running?'

'Yes'm,' said Timothy.

'Better come inside and I'll see if I can find you a slice of plum cake.'

'Thank you ma'am.'

Promise of cake had already dispensed Timothy's forebodings but, as he made to enter the huge kitchen, the further door swung open, and in marched Nancy Weston's governess. Timothy's mouth gaped, as the woman's eye fixed him icily. Too horrified to move, he could only stare like a stricken animal as she pounced on him and fixed his ear with merciless finger and thumb. 'Hah!' It was a grunt

17

of triumph. 'So we meet again. This way if you please.' Tottering in fearful anticipation Timothy was led away from the amazed cook and steered firmly down carpeted corridors smelling faintly of musk. Without easing her grip by so much as a fraction of an inch, the boy's captor led him to a large panelled door gleaming with beeswax, upon which she knocked sharply.

In answer to the response from within, she opened the door and dragged Timothy before the man seated behind a huge, walnut desk in the centre of the room.

'Mr Weston, this is he: this is the little wretch who struck me and who caused Nancy to get wet through and catch her dreadful cold.'

'Oh! indeed.' The man looked up, and Timothy, his ear now relaxed from the grip which had all but torn it from his head, gazed into a pair of gimlet eyes.

'Well, young man, give an account of yourself, or haven't you anything to say?'

Timothy swallowed hard, ready to deny anything and everything.

'Well?' said the voice.

'Well,' stammered Timothy.

'Is Miss Ciceney's complaint true?'

'Y-yes sir,' confessed Timothy in a small voice, and the governess smiled triumphantly.

'Do you usually go butting people and pushing small girls into pools of water?'

'I didn't push her,' Timothy reproached him stoutly. 'We were only paddling, and anyway, she fell in.' He had not imagined anyone like this to be Nancy Weston's father – such a small man, with such a large head.

Gold *pince-nez* hung from a velvet ribbon at his lapel, and his hands, stubby fingered and strong-looking, were covered with tufts of glistening black hair which fascinated the boy. His face, unlined, was very determined, and his hair, black and thick, shot straight up from his forehead.

'What are you doing here now?' asked Mr Douglas Weston.

'I brought the chickens, sir.'

'The chickens, h'mm.' That appeared to have been an order from the kitchen, which his wife dealt with. 'Why did you strike Miss Ciceney?'

'Well sir, it-it just happened. First she boxed my ears, and then she shouted at Nancy, so-so I just butted her.'

'Just like that; didn't you run?'

A slow flush of shame crept over Timothy's face. 'Yes sir,' he breathed. 'I ran.'

Mr Weston's eyes half closed as he assessed the small boy who seemed so badly in need of a wash and a hair cut. At length he said: 'I have instructed Miss Ciceney to see to it that Nancy does not mix with – with let us say children who haven't the same position as she. It's all a question of breeding. You are much too young to understand. It's a matter of social values – snobbishness, some people call it.'

'What's snobbishness?'

Mr Weston closed his eyes. The boy was beyond him. By now he should have been abject in fear and trembling. He had fine hands, too. The finest hands he had ever seen in anyone of any age. They were slim, wonderfully balanced hands – grubby, but shaped with great artistry, and certainly not to be expected in a cottager's boy. The flexing and reflexing of the fingers as the child spoke in passionate protest or plea fascinated him.

Miss Ciceney, grown bored with the proceedings, said, 'Mr Weston, it's time for Nancy's medicine: shall I see to it?'

'By all means, Miss Ciceney, by all means.'

Douglas Weston was tired, but he felt the boy refreshing. It had always been a strict rule that Nancy should be brought up with the best. He was a self-made man with vast properties and large blocks of capital invested in most parts of the world. His fortune had long since passed the two million sterling mark – and he had bought society too.

He had virtually bought his wife, daughter of a peer and as thoroughbred as his finest racehorse. Her love had been a cool thing, even their child hadn't sprung of passion. Clare had loathed her disfigurement and the child within her. Had he made a mistake after all, despite his wealth and huge ambition, his financial genius, his courage which had won him everything save his wife to love? And Clare insisted that Nancy should be unflawed and strictly guided, mocking his parentage as he was all but mocking Timothy's.

The boy's compelling grey eyes regarded him seriously. 'I'm still here Sir,' he ventured.

'Yes, Timothy, you're still here. I like you Tim, ask the cook for a piece of cake and come back here. While you are gone, I shall write a note to your father. I want you to deliver it for me.'

Timothy was sorry to go. What had promised to be adventure in the depths of terror had turned out to be something of a pleasant experience. When he had eaten the large slice of plum cake which the cook gave to him, he went back to the study, there to receive a thick, yellow envelope with his father's name on the front and the flap securely gummed down.

'Don't open it,' said Mr Weston sternly, 'it's private. You know what that means, don't you?'

'Yes Sir.'

'Right. Off you go then before I alter my mind, or before someone alters it for me.'

And with this strange remark on which to ponder, Timothy left the Weston's house and thoughtfully made his way back to the cottage.

3

Next day, Timothy, bewildered by instructions from his father that he should put on his best suit, wash thoroughly, and go to visit the Weston's, trod the slope to the squire's mansion with misgiving.

No friendly linnet piped to him this time, and he felt uneasy in his unusual scrubbed cleanliness; with his new haircut which his father had given to him personally, and rough tweed suiting which smelled of mothballs.

The front of the house loomed up and the mullioned windows peered at him blankly. There was no molten gold today.

The boy, a strange feeling of trepidation in his heart, reached up to the brass bell-pull of the front door, and jerked hard. The clang-clang far away inside sent a peculiar chill up his spine – and then the door opened to reveal an egg-bald man-servant, with nose and eyebrows elevated as though in perpetual disagreement with the world in general.

'Please, sir,' began Timothy. 'I'm Swaine – Timothy Swaine. Mr Weston asked me to call.'

Half hoping that he would be told to go away, the boy stood waiting until the butler in a sepulchral voice bade him enter.

Left to his own devices in the hall, while the servant sought his master, Tim gazed at the faded oil paintings in their heavy gilt frames, the armour breast plates and the shiny surface of the waxed mahogany panelling.

High up in the timbered ceiling a chandelier sparkled, the cut glass reflectors hanging like a bunch of transparent grapes. Timothy stood in uneasy awe and jumped at the voice of the butler saying smoothly that Mr Weston would see him now if he would please to follow.

Nancy's father sat at the desk where Timothy had seen him the day before.

'Ah, young man,' he said, benevolently. 'I hardly recognised you – so clean and spruce.'

'It's my best suit, sir.'

'Good. Very good indeed.'

Mr Weston smiled, and then the smile faded.

'Timothy, my plans have gone awry. I wrote to your father asking you to come here as a sort of guinea pig. I thought that you might be good for Nancy, who is not really leading a child's life. You see, Nancy's mother and I disagree on certain points concerned with her upbringing. My wife was away in London, and I thought the time ripe to try out my experiment. Unfortunately, my wife returned last night, although I was not expecting her, and she thoroughly disapproves of the idea. You do understand don't you?'

Timothy didn't, and wondered about the guinea pig, but he nodded his head all the same. Douglas Weston smiled kindly at him, and with a short stubby forefinger touched a bell.

The butler appeared almost at once.

'You rang, sir?'

'Yes, Edward. Please ask Mrs Weston to spare me a minute.'

'Very good, sir.'

'I am asking my wife to look you over,' Nancy's father said. 'Perhaps she will change her mind, and let me go ahead with my idea.'

Mr Weston smiled again and then his brow corrugated in perplexity.

He was a man approaching fifty – a highly successful

22

man, rich, powerful, a financial genius. His marriage had been a partial failure, but apart from that his judgement was acute. His assessment of new acquaintance was always shrewd and accurate, and yet this child Timothy – a lowly cottager's son, an outcast as his wife would say – somehow eluded his judgement, and perplexed his incisive clever mind. He could not make him out.

Further conjecture was prevented by the sudden entrance of Mrs Weston, who came in so softly that Timothy was not aware of her at once. When he did see her he was enthralled.

She was the type of woman of whose existence he had no knowledge. To him a thing was beautiful if it pleased him. A piece of cold granite could be beautiful when the sunlight caught the crystals – his senses responded and he knew that it was beautiful. To him, beauty was pleasure. The face of a puppy dog was beautiful, the tapering wing of a starling, the mist on the hills, half opened buds, the fragile ear of a rabbit. He had never before related beauty to people, and he had not even been conscious of its existence.

He knew that Nancy Weston was pretty because she was clear skinned and round faced in a nice way. He knew that Mr Weston was rather funny because his head was large and too big for his body. But when he saw Mrs Weston he actually felt beauty for the first time. He was enchanted, as only a child could be.

Clare Weston, who had been the Honourable Clare Duquemin, slipped into the room with an easy grace. Her hair shone with the softness of new silk, her dark blue eyes like the sky clearing after a storm. Her face, pale ivory, was softly rounded, with etched cheekbones faintly pink as though an artist had carefully tested the weight of colour on his brush. Lips red as any cherry Timothy had ever eaten, were parted the merest fraction and her smooth neck had the grace and carriage of a swan. Timothy felt the impact of her beauty and his senses reeled.

Mr Weston was aware of the impression which had been reigstered on the child's mind.

'Clare,' he said. 'This is Timothy, the boy of whom I told you.'

'Well?' The cold hauteur escaped Timothy as did the quick narrowing of the eyes. 'You know my views, Douglas.'

'Yes, Clare, I know them well enough but I thought perhaps if you saw the boy you might reconsider.'

Even Timothy could not miss the curling of her velvet lips and the shock hit him like ice water on his back.

'Douglas, the child is a cottager's boy, an urchin – do you seriously expect me to allow Nancy to mix with – with . . .'

'It's for her own good.' Weston cut in. 'She's spoiling I tell you – spoiling.'

'I know better.'

'Yes, Clare, you always know better, don't you? Always.'

'Where the upbringing of the child is concerned, I do.'

'But my dear it's 1912 now, ideas of the blood ring are finished – they went out with the old Queen.'

'You're so wrong. There are so many things of which you know nothing.'

'I know that your ideas, and those of your friends are bad.' Douglas Weston's mouth was a grim hard line. 'I am not an aristocrat, Clare. Your father was a peer, your friends are lords, baronets and right honourable gentlemen, yet I could buy and sell all of them, including their landed acres, and ancestral homes. You're a fool, Clare . . . you're . . .'

'Please, sir, I'm still here, sir,' interrupted a small voice. 'I thought perhaps you might have forgotten me.'

They had forgotten him.

Clare Weston wheeled, her cold beautiful face pallid with emotion, her lovely blue eyes burning and angry. 'I think,' she said, 'that you had better go.'

'Stay where you are, Timothy.' Douglas Weston's voice was gruff with emotion, possessed as he was with near violent rage. His eyes, hard as agate, looked into those of his wife, until she could no longer meet his gaze. All the determination that had made him the man he was had been unleashed, and he was in the rare mood that Clare knew to be indefatigable.

Her own blaze of anger died abruptly.

For decency's sake, at least, she should behave before the child – and even though she sometimes despised her husband she had to admit that he commanded respect.

She thought that as he was now, she could almost find room in her cold heart to love him. Her breeding and family background were a flimsy excuse for what she actually knew to be hardness. A flaw in her beauty which over-rode an intelligent outlook. She was a Duquemin – and Nancy would be a Duquemin – an aristocrat. God knew she had never wanted Nancy, but now that she had her she intended that the jewel should be polished her way, and not the way of her husband.

If Douglas had some cranky idea of mixing Nancy with the serfs it was high time that she went to the seminary, and then to a Continental finishing academy.

'The boy might stay for a while today, but after that I shall have to consider the matter further.' This much she unbent, but her husband knew that although he had tasted victory, it would be short lived if he did not stand firm.

'I don't really want to stay if you don't think that it would be right,' said Timothy, addressing her.

He could not follow the precise logic of their argument, but he knew well enough that this beautiful woman objected vehemently to his contact with Nancy.

'You may as well spend an hour or two with my daughter now that you are here.' Clare's eyes on him were consuming. There was no warmth, not even a little compassion to soften them.

Timothy sensed the protest within her. Quite obviously

25

he would never see Nancy again after today, other than by his own devices.

'You'd better go out on to the lawn. I'll send Nancy to you.'

'Yes'm.' He shrugged. Folks were funny. After all, Mr Weston had asked him to come here.

Out on the lawn he surveyed the wide expanse of parkland with a practised eye. The trees doubtless harboured countless nests, and even as his mind absorbed the possibilities of exploration he saw one, and then two grey squirrels climb swiftly the straight trunks before peering at him from their safe vantage point, bushy tails held stiffly to attention.

As his face lit up with pleasure he remembered, with dismay, that he was wearing his best clothes, which dashed any ideas he might have had about the inviting trees ahead.

Nancy, looking none too pleased, suddenly joined him, and he felt peculiarly embarrassed.

'My mother's home.' She pouted. 'That means I'll be indoors for goodness knows how long. A new tutor arrives on Monday, won't that be pleasant?' She pulled a wry face. 'And Miss Ciceney has been told to box your ears if you come around here after today. I heard my mother tell her. She doesn't like cottage people and I've got to be kept away from you for my own good.'

'Why?' asked Timothy bluntly.

'I don't know why.'

'Your father wrote a letter to my father asking me to come. He seemed to think I'd be good for you.'

'Well, my mother thinks otherwise, and there's a whole crowd coming here at the weekend, including my cousin Evelyn Duquemin. He's a pig! He eats too much.'

'Well, what are we going to do?' the boy asked, brushing the whole affair aside. He had lost interest in the ways of the Westons.

'Let's go to the pool.'

'Not likely. I've got my best suit on, and anyway, your mother would stop you. I expect that Miss Ciceney has told on us.'

'She's an old cat.'

The expression quite shocked Timothy, coming as it did from this fragile little person.

'Timothy, what's it like at school?' Nancy asked unexpectedly. Surprised, the boy gestured with his hands. 'It's all right,' he said.

'What do you learn?'

'Oh, 'rithmetic, geography . . . I like geography.'

'I wish I were like you.'

'Why?'

'To go to school with other people. I get so lonely.'

'I don't think you'd like our school,' he said gravely. 'I don't think you'd like it a bit.'

'Why not?'

'Well, you just wouldn't,' he replied firmly.

This meeting left Timothy at a loss. It didn't seem natural – and knowing the storm that his presence had produced over the house, he just wanted to get away. Now he had the uncanny feeling that the eyes of Nancy's mother were watching him. He felt her presence somehow, and knew that he was unwelcome.

'I won't stay,' he said. 'Your mother doesn't seem to like me. I'll go now, but I hope that I shall see you soon.'

She watched him trot down the drive, a short little figure with a shock of dark chestnut hair, and she felt that in her loneliness he was her only friend.

4

When Timothy arrived home his father had just finished sowing the late peas.

'Well, young fella me lad, how was it?' he asked with interest.

Tim shrugged eloquently in answer.

'Like that, eh? Oh well, how about feeding the chickens?' Tom was careful not to press the matter.

Timothy ran into the shed and filled a bowl from the cornbin. As soon as he entered the big chicken run the plump birds flocked about him chattering. Flicking out handfuls of the grain his eyes checked each of the birds for sign of defect. There was nothing amiss. He assured himself that the water supply was adequate, and closed the pen carefully. Upstairs he had an injured fieldmouse in a box he wanted to get to urgently. Replacing the bowl in the shed he flew up the creaking stairs of the cottage, opened the door of his minute bedroom and withdrew the fieldmouse, stroked the quivering whiskers, and slipped it into his pocket.

Outside again he took out the mouse, examined the damaged hind feet in the bright sunlight, satisfied himself that it was all right, and released it. The mouse scurried away, stopped for a moment to regard him gravely, and then vanished.

Part of this pastoral scene was old Walter Barnaby, piddling in the hedgerow as he did regularly after a heavy bout of cider drinking. He was there now and Tim regarded the stooped back reproachfully for a moment. Suddenly he heard his mother calling.

His father was just sitting down to tea as he entered the cottage. Tim was pleased to see that the meal was ready, for he was hungry. He had rushed up to his bedroom before going into the kitchen and his mother looked at him suspiciously.

'What have you been up to?' she asked.

'Nothing,' said Tim evasively. 'I went for a box.'

'Like as not there was something in it which hadn't ought to be.' She was always wary of his boxes. 'Salad for tea, you like that don't you?'

Timothy inclined his head in assent and sat down next to his father who was already eating.

'Well, Tim, aren't you going to talk to us about the big house?' his mother asked curiously. 'We'd like to know.' Timothy sliced a firm red tomato in half.

'Don't suppose I'll be going again,' he said with conviction. 'Mrs Weston doesn't like me. I don't seem to fit in somehow. She said so.'

'Oh,' said Tom with disappointment. 'Well, don't let that bother you. I was being selfish and hoped it would bring us in a bit more trade, you know, chickens and the like.'

'I didn't do anything to anyone.' Tim was defensive. 'The cook likes me, I think, and so I expect she will still want to buy from us.'

'Good, good.' Tom applauded for he was a firm believer in making the most of contacts. New opportunities were too infrequent to be overlooked or lost through carelessness. He had counted on better news from Timothy, but if it was not to be then no amount of fretting would alter anything. He hadn't, at the outset, imagined Timothy merging into any scheme which the grandiose occupants of the big house may have had.

'Tell him after tea, Tom' said his wife as if she had been waiting her opportunity. Tom grunted assent.

Timothy paused in his eating. Tell who, what? He looked at his father, who in turn was looking at his plate. There was something coming, Timothy sensed it.

He was having a second cup of tea when his father spoke.

'Timothy.' Tom's pipe was going well, and blue smoke hung heavily in the kitchen.

'Yes father.'

'You know something of history, don't you? Have you covered the Boer War yet?'

Timothy had not. He knew that the climax of the Boer War had come some twelve years back, but the details of the event had not been discussed by Miss Grosvenor, his school teacher. They were doing Lord Nelson at the moment, which was ancient history compared with the Boer War.

'Timothy, we've had you with us for close on twelve years and the missus and I have decided to acquaint you with some important information.'

Timothy suddenly became all attention, possessed as he was with the intense curiosity of youth.

Tom smiled at the sudden concentration which had fixed itself on the unhandsome face with the level grey eyes.

'You know me, Tim, as your father. Mary as your mother. Actually, neither of us is your father or mother. You're coming twelve now, Tim, and it's time you knew. Your real father was a lieutenant, a commissioned officer in the army. He was killed at Mafeking in 1900, the Boer War which I just spoke of. Your mother, Tim, was a lady's maid. Don't misunderstand me, she was properly married to your father.' This meant nothing to Timothy, less than nothing in fact. But it was exciting.

'Your father, Tim, was John Farley, and your real name is Timothy Farley. Your grandparents are the Farleys of Bath, a very rich and well placed family, almost aristocracy.' Timothy's interest grew.

30

'Your grandparents have never seen you, Tim. When their son John – your father, that is – married your mother he was made an outcast from his family. They had nothing more to do with him. When he was killed on active service . . . well, they just didn't bother. Twelve months after your father's death, Tim, your mother died.'

'What did she die of?'

Tom looked at the anxious questioning face. 'A broken heart,' he said.

'Oh,' said Timothy. It was beyond him how anybody's heart could be broken, it was so well hidden. She must have had a very nasty fall.

'You came to us then, Tim. Your real mother and the missus were cousins. Before she died your mother asked us to have you. We agreed, and you've been with us ever since.' Tom's eyes had gone very moist. Mary dabbed away a furtive tear, her head bent resolutely over the mending.

'We thought it best that you know the truth just in case anything happened,' Tom went on. 'Your birth certificate's in a box upstairs and your mother left two hundred pounds for your keep. It was everything she had. We tried to keep the two hundred intact for when you grew up, Tim, but there were some lean years. The land wouldn't produce. We had to eat. There's about a hundred left, and it's yours to do with as you will when you're of age.'

'Mind not and waste it now,' said Mary, looking up for the first time. To her Tim was already of age. In a little over two years' time he would have left school – and then what? A hundred pounds wouldn't do much. It would be the land for him, because there was nothing else.

'There's plenty of time for that,' said Tom, kindly. 'Plenty of time.'

'Not so much time. What shall the lad be put to when he finishes schooling?'

'He could do worse than wi' me. What else, anyway?' Mary shrugged. There was nothing else, she knew – not in this area.

31

'We could develop more on blooms. It would suit young Tim. He has the hands for it. He might even be a green fingers with hands like that.'

Tom had his doubts, however. In fact on looking back he remembered well that all Timothy's efforts at growing in the past had come to nothing.

Anyway, with the boy with him full time he wouldn't have to harness up and go to market so often. Tim was adept at learning, he could teach him to do the job.

Outside in the bright sunlight Timothy sat on the rough wooden seat and surveyed line after line of healthy crops.

The flowers were a blaze of colour, reds and yellows, purples and blues. Flowers were such wonderful things. Tiny seeds growing inch by inch until the full glory of the final bloom resulted. Gardening wasn't so bad really. You could watch results daily, you could check the living growth and savour the pleasant feeling of a good yield, or a blaze of flaming colour.

As he sat he pondered the things that had been told him about Lieutenant John Farley, his real father. It left him in some doubt as to the relationship which now existed between himself and the people whom he had supposed were his parents, but who lawfully were not his parents. He had known them as his father and mother for as long as he could remember. They had cared for him, fed and clothed him. His instinctive feeling was that of a son. This new information made very little difference to his feeling for Tom and Mary. He had rich grandparents at Bath, apparently, but he seemed to be as unwanted at Bath as he had been by Nancy's mother at the old squire's place. To his immature mind life was peculiar. People wanted you, or people didn't. If you were a bit ragged-looking mostly people didn't.

Anyway, he was Timothy Farley and his real father had been a commissioned officer and killed at Mafeking. Exactly what a commissioned officer was he had no idea.

32

As far as he was concerned, things were exactly as they had been. It seemed very much as though he should go full time with Tom when he left the village school. That would be to his liking. To grow flowers, to harness the mare and go to market – he couldn't think of anything better. And a whole hundred pounds, too.

Perhaps he shouldn't have the money. There might be more lean times – and then what would Tom do? In any case, he knew that coming of age meant being twenty-one: he had a lot of time to wait, and probably the hundred pounds wouldn't wait quite so long. He knew that Tom had ideas about growing under glass. He had talked of it often, but the expense seemed so much. With a hundred pounds, surely they could have all the glass in the world?

A swallow flashed across the sky, wheeling and soaring, a thing of grace and beauty. Birds fascinated him. In fact all life fascinated him. At heart he was least interested in people. He liked birds, animals and flowers best – even chickens had intriguing characteristics.

The sun resting on the hills had changed to a deep vermilion and the purple tendrils of dusk were hovering when the boy rose and went into the cottage. It was almost nine, and supper time. Timothy could always be relied upon to be present when a meal was due – it was his bedtime in half an hour anyway.

Timothy Swaine; Timothy Farley; killed at Mafeking; grandparents at Bath; Miss Grosvenor and school; Nancy Weston and her mother and father. Everything went through his mind as Timothy lay in bed before sleep finally claimed him. Even in sleep his subconscious recorded the incidents of the past days, again and again until at last he passed into a deeper sleep which shut off his mind from everything.

On Wednesday an event occurred at the cottage which created a minor sensation. A motor car arrived at the front door. Tom Swaine had never seen a motor car close to, let alone have one call upon him, and he was agog with wonder.

It was a large handsome car driven by a chauffeur in a green uniform. The chauffeur climbed down from the high front seat, opened the rear door of the vehicle – and out stepped Miss Ciceney.

Timothy had observed everything from the kitchen window, and he was aghast. Now what had he done? The very presence of Miss Ciceney was frightening enough, but to have her call in Mr Weston's chauffeur-driven car was past his comprehension.

Tom Swaine unlatched the front door before Miss Ciceney had time even to knock.

'Mr Swaine.' Miss Ciceney's gimlet eyes settled unwaveringly on Tom.

'Yes'm.' Tom gulped in Miss Ciceney's somewhat forbidding presence.

'Mr Weston sends you this letter.' Miss Ciceney addressed him imperiously. 'Read it if you please.'

'Yes'm.' Tom gulped again, by now thoroughly overwhelmed. He tore open the expensive grey envelope and perused the missive slowly.

'Well I'm blowed,' he ejaculated at last. 'Well I'm blowed. They wants you at the big house regular, our Tim!' He called to the cowering Timothy. 'Who'd have thought it. You must have done all right then old lad, after all.'

Having now received the blessing of Nancy's father, Tim's association with Nancy grew into a warm comradeship in defiance of Clare Weston's philosophy of social segregation.

Nancy was rarely permitted to leave the grounds of the estate itself, but there was much for the children to occupy themselves with. Despite his own school activities and his work on the small holding, Tim always managed to squeeze a little surplus time so that he could spend it with the girl.

Clare Weston, Nancy's mother, was a figure he seldom

34

saw and Douglas Weston never. He did not know that his friendship with Nancy proceeded unhindered thanks mostly to Douglas Weston, who crossed swords time and time again with Clare over the matter – and won each time.

Tim was an outdoor boy, and although they were confined to the grounds of the house these were at least large and full of various forms of wildlife. Occasionally he and Nancy would walk the dark corridors of the great house looking at the paintings which Douglas Weston had acquired, and examining elegant bedrooms which Clare Weston had expensively furnished for the benefit of her many weekend guests. Hand in hand they would gaze at sumptuous brocaded hangings and peer at themselves in gold framed mirrors. They grew close in their mutual loneliness – but over the months of friendship with Nancy the naive Timothy failed to see that his companion was fast maturing. She was no longer a child, but a darkly pretty young girl. Timothy was younger than she – and as innocent as the day.

One Wednesday over the Whitsuntide period with holiday time from school, Timothy and Nancy were driven in-doors by sweeping rain and time began to weigh heavily as a result. In an effort to keep Tim amused Nancy suggested a game of hide-and-seek, and to this Tim readily agreed. It was his turn to hide and he raced up the winding staircase to the first floor and made his way to the far side of the big house. The many bedrooms offered plenty of sanctuary to anyone who wanted to hide, but Tim was not unmindful of the fact that they were forbidden. He made his way, therefore, to a remote corridor he had not been down before, and cautiously opened the first bedroom door he came to. This chamber was on the east side of the house and smelled of mothballs and disuse. Satisfied with his hideout, Tim looked around for further cover amongst the darkly expensive furniture and chintz-covered bedroom chairs. A large gilt framed mirror on one wall reflected the whole of the bedroom as if it were a series of conical shaped pyramids. Tim pulled a face at himself and wondered if he were not too far away for Nancy ever to find him.

In the centre of the room stood a magnificent four poster with fine lace drapes gathered back to the corners. Fluffed up pillows at the head of the bed were squared invitingly, and Tim marvelled at such luxury. Deciding now that he was too far from the main part of the house for Nancy to have a chance of finding him he was about to open the door and return down the corridor when he heard voices. They were fast approaching. Timothy froze in horror. He knew that he shouldn't be there, just as he knew that one of the voices was that of Clare Weston, Nancy's mother. He was petrified. Without pausing to think he hurled himself under the great bed and lay in panic just as the door opened.

Clare Weston and Nigel Thorpe, a visitor to the house, slid into the room conversing quietly. Timothy recognised the handsome Thorpe immediately, for he had seen him from time to time arriving for Clare Weston's many functions. He had always seemed to Tim to be at the house much more often than other people. Now he peered from underneath the high bed – and saw Nigel Thorpe's polished shoes and Clare Weston's elegant slippers close up. Then they suddenly moved, he caught a fleeting glimpse in the mirror of Clare seeming to fall into Nigel's arms – and he was unable to see more.

Unaware of Tim's presence and secure in the knowledge of their isolation, Clare looked into the face of the young Adonis who was her lover, and sighed deeply. If only she could have Nigel permanently instead of the ungainly Douglas – then perhaps her life might take on a new purpose. But it would never be. Douglas Weston was rich and powerful – and Nigel Thorpe had nothing. It was best, therefore, to make the most of what she had while she had it.

She murmured urgently into Nigel's ear and clung closely to him. A kiss or caress from him served only to inflame her and they had chosen this safe and remote part of the house because they both knew what the outcome of their clandestine meeting would be. Clare's breathing had become very rapid, her fantastically blue eyes dilating with passion as she eased off Nigel's jacket and plucked hungrily at his shirt buttons.

Within seconds he was half undressed, struggling to take off his trousers whilst Clare with deft movements had removed every single one of her garments so that she stood naked and trembling in the faint chill air. Without effort Nigel Thorpe scooped her slim shape into his arms and fell with her onto the inviting bed. His embrace and flaring desire devoured her, and she cried out with a pleasure so sublime that Timothy trembling beneath the bed thought indeed that Nancy's mother was being murdered.

He could see nothing. He could hear the threshing and heaving as though two people were fighting. Then suddenly Clare Weston said, 'You darling, magnificent animal you!'

Timothy looked cautiously out, and in the mirror was shocked to see the naked rump of Nigel Thorpe moving rapidly. Then it became very still, with a kind of sobbing from Clare until that too became still. All was very quiet. To the boy the fight seemed to be over. He was wondering how long he would have to stay there until they went away when suddenly in the mirror he saw Clare Weston looking back at him with eyes that were dilated and unbelieving. She screamed and Tim cowered in terror. A large strong hand urgently groping under the bed seized him and then yanked him out from his hiding place in trembling disarray.

Tim was looking fully into the belligerent face of Nigel Thorpe! The glowering Thorpe stood over him, his snatched shirt covering his nakedness. Tim scrambled to his feet.

'Please sir, I'm sorry sir. I was only playing hide and seek.' The words tumbled out.

37

'You wretch.' Clare Weston stormed at him. 'You absolute wretch.' She had climbed from the bed and wrapped a sheet round herself, her white legs glistening in the half light.

'What did you see us doing?' Nigel snarled.

'I don't know, sir.' Timothy gulped. 'I couldn't see, honest, sir. I thought that you were fighting.'

'Fighting,' echoed Nigel. 'Good God.' Words seemed to fail him.

'Yes, we were fighting.' Clare Weston seized upon the suggestion in anxious disbelief. 'We had been quarrelling. Of course I don't want Nancy's father to know or there will be more fighting. Do you understand?'

'Oh yes, ma'm.' Timothy said fervently although he hadn't the faintest notion of what she was talking about.

'Do you think he is as stupid as he sounds?' Nigel asked Clare with scepticism. 'How old are you, lad?'

'Nearly thirteen, sir,' Tim responded, unhesitatingly, desperately anxious to be dismissed.

It was not to be so simple however. Nigel Thorpe could scarcely believe that a thirteen-year-old could not even guess at the sounds he had been listening to; and even Nancy's mother, much as she desired it, found it difficult to accept the boy's innocence.

However, more rough questioning from Thorpe failed to shake Tim in the slightest. Finally they could do no more than believe Tim. Conspiratorially Clare warned him again of not involving Nancy's father, and silently prayed to God that the boy had indeed been telling the truth. In the palm of that slightly grubby hand now lay the whole of her marital future.

She need not have worried. Free at last, Timothy fled down the corridor, his only concern that of getting as far away from her as he could in the shortest time possible.

5

And so the trauma of the bedroom seemed to fade into the background, although Tim always had the uneasy feeling that Nancy's mother was constantly watching him, despite the fact that he rarely saw her in person.

Only once did he encounter Nigel Thorpe again, who gave him half a crown for no reason that the sublimely innocent Timothy could think of.

The weeks slipped gently by, and Nancy was growing restless with the prohibitions which lay on her as to where she could and could not go. She had private schooling within the house, but she knew that her mother was far from satisfied and was even now pressing her father to send her to a finishing school – Switzerland had been mentioned.

'I have a feeling that I shall be going to boarding school before long,' Nancy announced to Timothy gloomily.

'She's nagging my father all the time and I think he's about ready to give in. I shan't be seeing you then, and I shall hate that.'

'If you do have to go there'll always be holidays,' Tim said by way of comfort. 'But I shall miss you.'

'Let's go to the pool,' Nancy suggested. 'Your pool where I first saw you.'

'But you can't leave the grounds!' Timothy protested. 'And there's always someone watching.'

'Never you mind,' the girl said boldly. 'I know where

there's a way out. Now about tomorrow after you leave school?'

'We-ll.' The boy was doubtful.

'Oh come on, Timothy.' Nancy sounded vexed.

'All right then,' he agreed, eventually giving way to her.

'Just after four o'clock tomorrow afternoon. I leave school at four. Is that all right?'

'Of course.' She tossed her head delightedly.

'If ever your mother or Miss Ciceney find out there'll be trouble. You know that, don't you?' Timothy warned.

'They won't find out. I'll be ever so careful.'

'If you're sure then. I must go now. The chickens will need feeding. See you tomorrow.' He smiled and she smiled back, both enjoying the secret they had between them.

Next day Timothy left for school in the highest of spirits. The day wore on slowly, punctuated by the dinner bell at twelve o'clock, and at half past one for recommencement of classes. This particular day seemed interminable, and Timothy was on edge thinking about the pool, and Nancy Weston.

The whole business was fraught with danger. He would be late for tea, which would want some explaining since he was never late for a meal, and if ever Nancy's mother or governess found out, the consequences would be dire.

At four o'clock he shot through the gate, and ran as hard as he could down the road. The pool fortunately lay between the school and the cottage, which meant that he had less than a mile to go. Very soon he was out of breath and his pace a mere crawl. When finally he mounted the hill where he had met Nancy on that first occasion so long ago, he was compelled to rest a while. From then on he walked.

The pool lay still and clear in its leafy bower. The brook bubbled ceaselessly, and the shade was restful after the impact of the hot summer sun. But Nancy was not there, and the boy felt keen disappointment. She must have gone, he thought: it must be long past four o'clock. He was hot and tired with running, the pool beckoned, slivers of sunlight reflected through the branches lay on its surface in shimmering silver. So, removing his shoes and stockings he relieved his aching feet in the cold embrace of the water.

He was proud of this pool. An accidental discovery when looking for nests, he regarded it as his own personal property. It had about it a quietude which soothed him and a pleasing secretness.

Suddenly the peace was broken by the snap of twigs and then a voice calling urgently, 'Timothy, Timothy.'

He sprang to his feet and turning saw Nancy Weston leaning for support against a tree. Her eyes were wet with tears, and the fine stuff of her dress torn and bedraggled. Without waiting to put on his shoes the boy ran to her, a hundred questions crowding into his mind.

'Oh, Timothy,' Nancy sobbed. 'I fell. I was running and my foot caught in a tree root.'

Timothy's heart sank. 'Are you hurt badly?'

'My ankle's twisted or broken or something.'

The boy went taut with dismay. Now there would be trouble.

'Let me help you to the bank.' He slipped his arm around her waist and helped her hobble to the side of the pool.

'I was late, Tim. I thought that I should never get away and I was running hard when it happened. I shall never be able to get back. My ankle hurts terribly.'

Timothy, looking into the big tear-stained eyes of the girl, knew despair. Nancy's ankle was hurt, her clothes torn, and she was playing truant against the express wishes of her mother. How would he ever get her home – and how would she ever explain?

'You'd better take your shoe off,' he suggested: 'and soak your foot in the pool. If there's any swelling the water will help take it down.'

41

Groaning with agony Nancy undid her shoe and eased it from her foot a fraction of an inch at a time, emitting loud 'ooh-oohs' of pain as she did so.

At first Timothy thought that she was acting, she made so much fuss, until the sudden paleness of her face warned him that she was about to faint. He steadied her with his arm and made her lie at full length on the grass for a minute while he removed her stocking.

His mouth formed a soundless Oh! of dismay. The damage much exceeded his worst expectations. Nancy's ankle was an ugly blue-black in colour as the angry bruise formed, and it was swelling almost before his eyes.

'Put it in the water quick,' he said, horrified, as though the water of the pool was endowed with magical properties.

Nancy slid along the bank and plunged in her foot.

The water, deliciously cool, soothed the aching burning pain.

'Its nice,' she said. 'So nice and cold.' She beamed at Timothy, who showed no great enthusiasm.

'How do we get back?' he enquired in a troubled voice.

'You can carry me.'

'What?'

'Piggy back.'

The idea appealed to him. He could probably do it in easy stages. Now that Nancy had suggested a solution the problem of transporting her seemed the least of his worries. The gravest issue was that of satisfactorily accounting for their meeting which had been so emphatically forbidden.

He looked at the girl half lying, half sitting, with her leg dangling in the water. Her deep blue eyes were fixed on him affectionately, and he felt himself blush.

'I do like you, Timothy,' observed Nancy softly.

The blush receding from Timothy's face sprang up anew. This sounded soppy talk to him, but nevertheless it was impressive.

'Time to get started,' he said gruffly. 'If I've got to

piggy-back you it will take hours. Lift out your foot, and I'll wet my handkerchief and tie round it.'

He knew the simple curatives, and was anxious to help Nancy as much as he could because she had said that she liked him. That had been a proud moment. No one ever before had said such a thing to him. He liked Nancy too.

Obediently she removed her foot which started throbbing anew, and Timothy examined the swelling with the tenderness he lavished on injured animals.

Delicately he fingered the puffed flesh, and at his touch the violent aching receded so much that Nancy's first pleasurable reaction changed to a frown of perplexity. Something seemed to have slipped from Timothy through his fingers and into her ankle. Nothing tangible, a queer kind of vibration which made her suddenly frightened.

For his own part Timothy knew nothing of this. He fingered the bruise with care, averting his eyes steadfastly from the marble whiteness of the girl's firm leg which embarrassed him. With his left hand he wrapped the soaked handkerchief around the swelling and tied it.

As soon as his fingers released the bruise the aching violence returned and Nancy's eyes grew puzzled. Covertly she examined Timothy. He was rather an untidy boy with a nondescript little face, but nice eyes, the sort of eyes she liked. She shrugged.

The boy sat down and replaced his footwear. Time now to put himself to the crucial test. He flexed his small muscles, and slipped Nancy's shoe into his pocket. It had been impossible to put that on and her stocking, only half on, hung forlornly from the end of her toes.

Gently he helped her to her feet and crouched waiting for her to jump on to his back. She was much heavier than he had anticipated and he staggered forward several paces before regaining his balance.

Hitching her close to him and gripping her thighs as comfortably as possible with his arms, he set off slowly down the path. Her weight grew heavier as he went on,

43

and the conversation she continued in his ear didn't help, since it required valuable breath for replies.

He made three hundred yards before he set her down, puffing and blowing.

Resuming after a short rest he made a hundred yards less than his first effort, and so on until his last attempt was only a meagre forty yards.

Exhausted, he sat her down for the fourth time, and collapsed full length completely winded.

Nancy sat comfortably by him, face serene and confident. Timothy had nagging worries. It was growing late, much past his teatime and he had a long way to go yet, including a fair stretch uphill. He would soon be in dangerous territory too, and dreaded an accidental meeting with the fearful Miss Ciceney. Nancy had no such fears. She was thrilled and excited at the adventure, although the throbbing of her injury had not diminished in any way.

The sun was fast dying in the sky when finally he staggered into the drive leading to the great house with its trim lawns and sentinel oaks. The windows seemed to look at him accusingly as he set his companion down gingerly.

'I'll leave you to hobble up the drive now,' he whispered, as though innumerable ears were waiting to catch sound of his voice.

'All right,' she whispered back, and pressed her soft lips to his cheek in a token kiss.

For the third time that day colour flamed into his face, and he was so surprised that for a moment his jaw hung loose. The kiss seemed to burn and linger as he watched the diminutive figure of the girl hobble down the drive. Furtively he waved a hand and she waved back before quietly slipping out of sight.

For a hundred yards or more he fingered his cheek where Nancy's mouth had lain briefly, before the urgency of his own situation suddenly took hold of him and he began to run hard.

Dusk had fallen when panting he reached the cottage.

There seemed a strange air hanging over the place as he pushed open the door and he was surprised to see Mrs Lomas, one of the older village women, sitting in the chair by the fire. The table was part laid with his favourite salad tea, but of his father and mother there was no sign.

Mrs Lomas rose to her feet as he came in. Her face, brown as a berry with a hundred tiny wrinkles, tried to smile reassuringly, but the strain and obvious effort alarmed the boy.

'What's wrong?' he burst out. 'Where are they?'

'It's all right, Tim boy, they're both upstairs. That father of yours has been taken a wee bit ill. Your mother's with him. The doctor's just left, everything's all right, don't fret yourself. Your dad'll be fine.'

Timothy felt his heart change to ice.

'What's wrong with him?' he asked shrilly: 'I must see him.'

'Better not, Tim boy.' She placed a friendly arm about him. 'Don't see him tonight, Tim, he's got to rest, tomorrow perhaps, see him tomorrow.'

Her seriousness upset him and he felt the tears sting his eyes. All this time he had been away and his father ill.

'Don't cry, lad, come and have a bite of tea.' Timothy snuffled, hurt by his own conscience, but nevertheless hungry. He sat down to his tea.

'You're a might late, Tim lad,' Mrs Lomas said kindly. 'Your mother's been expecting you for hours.' Timothy gulped his shame. 'I went to my pool and someone got hurt. I've been till now getting her home.'

'Her?' Tim saw Mrs Lomas's eyes kindle and felt strangely embarrassed.

'She's my friend,' he said. 'I couldn't leave my friend with her ankle hurt.'

'Of course not, Tim.' He was a strange lad she thought. Always had been. She felt sorry for him, knowing the seriousness of the situation. His father had had a stroke, came on him sudden, like they always did. It was a bad business. She shook her head.

'Eat hearty,' she said. 'I'll just slip upstairs and tell your mother you're here.'

Her feet were noiseless as she trod the bare boards. A candle flickered in the bedroom throwing bouncing shadows. Mary Swaine sat motionless at the side of the bed.

'The lad's come, Mary.'

'Where's he been?' She lifted her head.

'Down at some pool or other. A wench he was with hurt her ankle and needed him to get her home. He's a queer 'un, no mistake.'

'Does he know about Tom?'

'I told him that he'd been taken bad. I didn't say how bad.'

The breathing from the bed was heavy. Tom Swaine lay inarticulate, and almost unconscious, his eyes staring, a vein on his forehead twitching convulsively.

'Sit with him, Anna, while I go to Timothy.' The older woman nodded and pulled up a chair without a sound. Mary Swaine went downstairs.

'You were late, Timothy.'

The boy stopped eating and looked at her. She was dry eyed, but there was a glassy fixity about her stare. Her hair, never tidy, shot out in tendrils of disorder.

'I went to the pool and Nancy Weston hurt her ankle.'

'Nancy Weston! I thought – never mind . . .' She broke off. 'Your Dad's a very sick man, Timothy.'

'Mrs Lomas wouldn't let me go up, but she didn't seem to think he was very sick.' He felt frightened again.

'He's very ill, Timothy. The doctor's been. Your father's had a stroke, came on him sudden. He may never work again, Timothy, he might even – even die.' Her breath caught, and then she steadied herself. 'Have you had enough to eat, Tim?'

Her concern for him, this woman who had mothered

him, who he loved with all his heart, touched him queerly. His face twisted and he began to sob quietly at first, and then loudly, as though he knew a strange terror.

The woman not his mother, and yet who had every right to the claim, placed an arm round his thin shoulder, her brown eyes humble and troubled. She hugged him to her breast and he heard her use the word darling. He had never heard it from her before, and he clung to her closely, his breath coming in long shuddering gasps. She knew that he was terrified. Through her contact with him she could feel his fear. His sensitivity was such that his emotions were transparent, and the shuddering abjectness of him stirred her to great pity. He was so weak where pain or suffering were concerned, and with death hovering in the air his maturity had slipped away, and he was only a child, such a small child, and so ill-equipped to leave her shelter.

'He won't die, will he?'

'No, Timothy, I'm sure he won't die.'

'I'll pray for him so hard.'

'I'm sure you will.' She was crying herself now: softly, so that he would hear nothing. But the tears which rolled down her cheeks had touched his forehead and he knew.

6

Winter came with snow and bitter wind. The countryside was a mantle of white, the trees cradling snow with their naked arms in piles, like the ripe bursting of cotton.

A letter had been delivered to Tom saying that Nancy

Weston had now gone away to boarding school and that Timothy's services as a play companion would no longer be required. Clare Weston had lost no time.

Following the snow and wind came hard frost which froze the wells and pumps, and suspended the atmosphere so that even the fires in the cottages refused to draw.

The Swaine's cottage, coated like a cake with sugar icing, bore an air of desolation. The smoke from the chimney was the faintest haze against the leaden grey of the sky. On one particularly cold day the bread refused to bake, and Timothy, his fingers numb, had to poke at the water pump with an iron bar in a vain endeavour to release the frozen mechanism.

Tom Swaine crouched over the reluctant fire. The whipcord figure of the ardent gardener was broken wreckage. His pale face, thin to decimation, twitched painfully and his left leg had a dragging limp. Over him hung the ever-likely fear of another seizure.

Mary, looking ten years more than her age, had given up any attempt at baking. Her animated chatter to Timothy as he came in for a fresh tool with which to attack the pump concealed a secret fear. Their future was in jeopardy. Tom would never work the land again, the cottage would have to go. Then what? Village help had pulled him through the summer. It had been help well meant, but half hearted in its application. What had promised to be a good season had soured on them. They had missed markets and Timothy had had advantage taken of his youth in the selling of the flowers. She heard the door open and close as Timothy came back again. There were two chickens ready plucked for the Weston's at the old squire's house. It was called *The Gables* now that the Weston's had it, but somehow she preferred to think of it by its old familiar name.

'It's no good,' complained Timothy. 'I can't get it to go.'

'No use if you did,' said Tom. 'The water hole's frozen.' The boy nodded miserably. He couldn't bear to see his father as he was. He'd been frightened lest he die, now he was more frightened of the ravages he had suffered.

'The two birds are due at the Weston's today, the cook specially asked for them.' Timothy noticed the drawn pinched look of his mother's mouth as she spoke.

'I'll take them right away; it's not too bad outside if you keep on the move.'

'Mind and wrap up warm now.' She reached for the coat made from a blanket which hung on the door. 'Put this on or you'll be catching a chill.'

Out in the snow, the chickens secure beneath his arm, Timothy had much to occupy his mind. It was Saturday and no school. Get the winter and spring over and it would be time for him to earn his own living – 1913 would soon be out. 1914 would be his year. He would have the responsibility of a worker with an invalid father. Even his own enthusiasm was appalled by what this meant. He intended to have a go at the holding. Young as he was, he knew about crop rotation and Tom could teach him more. He hadn't done over well at the market with his selling, but he was willing to learn.

Suppose he failed, suppose the money ran out, or Tom got worse – just suppose. Maybe he could get a job at Bassington, there was the chandlers, or maybe Wixson would give him an errand boy's job in his butcher's shop. Wixson already had an errand boy, so did the chandler. Tim's shoulders drooped.

He was in the Weston drive now. The huge mansion loomed up, glittering in its casing of white like a marble palace. He could see the ruts cut into the snow by carriage wheels and the occasional blob of footprints. He cupped his hands and blew them. He felt wretched with all his family's troubles and worries.

His feet crunched on the drive. He hadn't seen Nancy Weston since the advent of her twisted ankle. He had heard from one source and another that she had been sent away to a ladies' school somewhere in London. It was strange, the impression she had made upon him in their infrequent meetings.

The cook opened the side door for him as he knocked. 'Please, I've come with the chickens.'

'Aye, lad, and you must be frozen stiff.' Her quick eye took in the pinched troubled face, the home-made blanket overcoat.

'Come inside and warm yourself, there's a nice fire, and there's a slice of meat pasty for you, all hot and crisp.' She examined the chicken carefully while Timothy sat in the fire nook. Pine logs blazed and threw off a sweet scent. There were big black ovens, shelves full of bottled preserves and a whole ham hanging from the ceiling.

Opening the oven nearest the fire the cook took out a savoury brown pasty and cut a large slice.

'That'll keep you going for a bit.' She slid it on to a plate and handed it to him.

Timothy munched contentedly. 'What do you use all those ovens for?' he asked curiously.

'Baking bread and pies, and cooking for all the guests that come and go. You're the youngster who used to play with our Nancy aren't you?'

Timothy nodded.

'Did you have anything to do with our Nancy hurting her ankle bad?'

Once more Timothy nodded. 'She didn't tell, did she?'

'No, but I guessed, and the mistress did. She was that annoyed. Nancy's gone away now.'

'I know. I haven't seen her since that day. We had a letter from Mrs Weston.'

'Nancy was fond of you. It's a shame, I say. The master's all right, but the mistress – ' The cook threw up her hands in despair. 'He has a dog's life, that's what, and to cap it all he's just found out that my fine lady and Nigel Thorpe have been having an affair. There's been ructions I can tell you, ructions.'

Timothy although he did not realise it, was seated in a

50

hotbed of gossip. In fact all the gossip of the house had its source in the kitchen, either from the cook or the maids who helped her. A little fact and the cook's imagination went a very long way indeed.

'What's an affair?' asked Timothy innocently, pricking up his ears at the mention of Nigel Thorpe's name.

The cook was taken aback. 'You're too young, my fine lad, much too young. Had enough to eat?'

'Yes thank you, ma'am.'

'Want to know something?'

'Yes please.'

She leaned toward him confidentially. 'Miss Nancy comes home tomorrow for a holiday. I heard that Ciceney woman say so.' Timothy listened eagerly. 'Do you think that I could see her?' he asked anxiously.

'There's no telling, but mistress is in London and I know what for, if master don't; but if you'd like to leave a message . . .'

Timothy calculated rapidly. Today was Saturday, Nancy arrived tomorrow, Sunday. 'I could see her tomorrow afternoon at three o'clock on the hill. She knows where that is. Perhaps she wouldn't want to come though.'

'I'm sure she would. I'll tell her anyway, and if she's not there at three you'll know why.'

'Thank you, and thank you for the pasty, it was nice.' He stood up, and the cook laid an affectionate eye on the diminutive figure with the large serious eyes.

'Hurry off now, and if I get a chance I'll tell Nancy, she and I are good friends.' Timothy waved as he slipped through the door. 'I'll see her somehow,' he promised, and then with head down trod purposefully out into the snow.

Nancy came next day.

Tim waited on the hill adjoining the trail leading to his pool until he saw her in the distance. She looked like an Eskimo in a short fur coat with calfskin boots almost to

51

her knees. Her face was pink with the wind, her blue eyes sparkling. She seemed older somehow, and more mature.

'Hello, Timothy.'

'Hello, Nancy.' He felt embarrassed. 'How did you manage to get away?'

'It was easy: my mother's in London, and Miss Ciceney had migraine. I think she'll be leaving soon now that I'm at boarding school. Remember my hurt ankle? Mother suspected, although I denied ever having seen you. She sent me away. I cried, but I had to go – father was upset too, but mother had all her own way. Mother's are a nuisance, aren't they?' Timothy didn't think so but refrained from making any comment. Instead he told her of the troubles that had beset him since he had last seen her. Nancy was sorry for him and held his hand.

'What will you do, Timothy?'

'I can work. I leave school at the beginning of next year.'

'I shan't see you very often, shall I Timothy, now that I'm at boarding school?'

'You'll have holidays, lots of them, and in summer time I'll show you my special nests.'

'Oh, lovely,' she clapped her hands. It was cold on the hill, and a crisp wind skirmished the snowflakes.

'I mustn't stop long because I only arrived this morning, and my father will miss me. Cook told me you had been yesterday.' They walked hand in hand, their feet crunching in the snow. A robin piped a tune, and they listened to the remote sweetness on the freezing air.

Still holding her small hand in his, Timothy walked almost to the drive with her. She waved to him, and then sadly he stood watching her until she disappeared from sight.

7

Winter's farewell was black frost in early March. Spring arrived with cold rain and gales, followed by pleasant sunny weather which brought forward the hedge buds, and dusted the fruit trees with blossoms of pale pink and white.

On the last day of December 1913 Tom Swaine had a second stroke from which he never recovered consciousness, and Timothy understood what heartbreak was. In April of 1914 he left the school of Miss Grosvenor and was faced with the immense task of working the holding.

Mary Swaine had become a changed woman since her husband's death. She had always been untidy, but now she went to pieces completely.

Timothy concentrated on the poultry, of whose care he had expert knowledge; but there were plenty of birds in the area and the prices were margin level.

Transport was of little use with nothing to sell. They sold first the horse, and then the cart. The vegetable growing slipped away altogether and that part of the holding was let for a pittance. This left flower growing, which was seasonal, since they had never been able to afford glass.

Timothy, diminutive at fourteen, worked vigorously. Care of the chickens was transferred to Mary, and he tended the flowers.

A sudden sharp frost was his first setback. The new shoots of the less hardy plants withered and died, and unexpected changes in the weather put paid to all hopes of early blooms.

One night he sat down and cried, a thin, emaciated figure with dark shadows under his eyes from too much hard work, and too little sleep.

His foster mother's meagre store of money was very low, he knew that well enough, but always she managed to raise a smile for him. Of Nancy Weston he had heard nothing, nor had he seen her.

Occasionally, he would walk up the hill, but she was never there.

The Weston's hadn't had chickens from them since January, and the cook hinted darkly that it was the mistress's doing.

One morning the postman called with a letter, and Tim watched Mary, old looking and troubled as she read it. Unaware of his eyes following her she slipped the envelope behind the clock. When she was out he removed it, and read the contents. It was from Mary's sister at Droitwich, and its portent plain. They were crowded, but no doubt could fix up Mary if she were willing to share a bed with Dolly. Timothy wondered who Dolly was, for he had never heard mention of her name. The letter went on to say that it would be impossible to have the boy – that must mean himself – so if he could find a station now that he had left school Mary would be welcome. A station obviously meant a job which included somewhere to live.

'Don't worry Timothy, I'm not leaving you.' Mary had come in by the back door and observed him reading the letter.

'Yes, I wrote,' she said in answer to the accusation in his eyes. 'It's silly for you to go on trying to work the land, you're a Farley: the land wasn't meant for you, you're worth so much more.'

'We must eat,' he said quietly.

'We have sufficient money for quite some time, and there is always the parish.'

The parish. That was the lowest level one could reach, a standing joke in the district.

For most of the day Timothy wandered around Great Bassington asking for a job at the various shops, but the answer was always the same. 'Too small.' 'Not strong enough.'

He thought of the steel mills, but knew from others that there was nothing for boys. Rumours were circulating in Bassington that a war was on the way, and he wondered about it. His understanding of war was limited to history lessons and vaguely associated with an unknown father.

Back at the cottage, he selected in his mind flowers for cutting in the morning. There were pitifully few, but already tourists were passing through the village on their way south, and he could offer them for sale at the gate.

Inside the kitchen he found a half written letter on the table. It was to someone in Bath. It was to his mysterious grandparents. Mary must be desperate; and then the idea struck him, and for the first time in weeks he actually smiled. The letter went into the fire, and he began laying the cloth for tea, whistling tonelessly.

Next morning he was up at daybreak, and crept downstairs quietly. With the stub end of a pencil he wrote a long letter, and placed it prominently beneath the corner of the clock.

Selecting a large paper bag he filled it with a loaf, a slab of cheese and one or two onions. There was a shilling belonging to him on the shelf and this he slipped into his pocket. Opening the back door soundlessly he tiptoed down the path, and walked quickly away, setting his course for Melchester, sixty miles distant.

He had been gone for an hour when Mary, awakened by twinges of rheumatism in her arms, decided that it was time to get up. Heavy with sleep she blundered downstairs and had lit the fire before catching sight of the letter hanging from beneath the clock. Fear caught her, and she clutched the paper with a force that almost upset the timepiece.

The writing was large and legible, but the woman was a laborious reader, and it was some time before she understood the message.

Timothy had bequeathed the trust of his hundred pounds to her, if there was any left. Also she must sell what she had to sell and go to her sister at Droitwich. He would be all right. He had gone north to seek work, the holding was doomed, and so it was no good carrying on.

He sent her love and kisses, and said not to worry as he would write in about a month's time. He had her sister's address, and he had taken a shilling from the mantleshelf and plenty of bread and cheese. She had been good to him, and this was the best way out of their difficulties. God bless her, and P.S. Don't worry.

Mary blinked tears, and then laying her head on her arms sobbed bitterly.

The morning which had promised brightness changed to leaden grey before ten o'clock, and the dusty road beneath Timothy's feet stretched endlessly.

A wagonette carried him for six miles, and then he had the luck to be picked up in a motor car. He felt wonder and a sudden sense of joy, perched on the dickie with a foul-smelling exhaust beneath him and a crashing engine in front. The driver, a redfaced man, goggled and waistcoated, fought with the machine for mile after mile and Timothy watched in fascination the spirals of escaping steam which plumed from the brass-topped radiator. His luck was such that his benefactor released him safely to the earth's comfortable solidness barely a quarter of a mile from Melchester. He expressed thanks gravely and continued his way munching dry bread.

Melchester, in comparison with Worley and Bassington, was grimy and squalid. The shops had a battered soiled look, and a row of giant chimney stacks belching unsavoury blackness into the firmament overshadowed the town. It was three in the afternoon when Timothy finally entered the public library and with extended forefinger perused the classified newspaper advertisements in search of a job.

There seemed little or nothing for lads such as he.

Queer meaningless words were open for his examination: canvasser, collector, agent, coster, moulder, lathe operator, and numerous offers for people to sell things on a commission basis.

He slept that night hidden under a dark bench behind the locked doors of the library reading room, the last crumbs of his dry slices of bread sprinkled around him.

8

'Dibbern, Dibbern, oh! My poor pansies.' The vexed tones of Charlotte Bemmington suddenly ceased and she wrung her gnarled old hands in despair.

A clump of brilliant blue pansies lay with broken heads where some dog had placed a careless paw.

Old George Dibbern, the gardener, bowed his rheumaticky legs and coaxed the sagging flowers with horny fingers.

'It's no use, Dibbern, no use at all,' the bent old figure in the wheelchair wrung her hands once more.

'Don't vex so, Miss Charlotte, 'tis a pity I'm sure, but they'll come again next time brilliant as ever.'

'Next time, next time, Dibbern. I may not be here next time.' Dibbern averted his head. The old lady was working up into one of her turns. 'You shouldn't be moving your hands so or you'll have the "aches" again,' he scolded. He hated these times when he had to wheel his mistress into the gardens to inspect the flowers. If so much as a petal drooped she spluttered with annoyance, and even with the high wall and the iron gates dogs managed to break in somehow – blast their flea-bitten hides. He was old himself, and touchy with rheumatics. His knees creaked ominously when he bent; but bend he must if ever a flower was disturbed. 'I like to look into their faces' Miss Charlotte would say, and Dibbern had to lift their faces so that she could.

A ponderous cloud slowly covered the sun, and Miss Charlotte exclaimed in annoyance. She shivered as though the sudden change of light had frightened her, and instinctively Dibbern moved behind the wheelchair.

'Take me to the house, Dibbern, take me to Alice, it's gone cold.' She had forgotten her flowers, and her gnarled old hands lumpy with arthritis gestured impatiently. The house she was so intent on reaching was Georgian, a perfect example, following the classical tradition transmitted through the Renaissance with Greek portico and simplicity of plan and elevation.

Tended lawns lustrously green and perfectly cut swept in two immaculate lines between sturdy oaks and sentinel poplars. A carved statue here and there amongst the rockery looked housewards, and the scarlet flash of geraniums glinted from the glasshouses. In all of the little world she queened, nothing lay so dear to the heart of Charlotte Bemmington as flowers, and trees, and the bounteous profusion that nature offered so willingly.

Almost broken by cardiac disorder and the crippling agony of osteo-arthritis, she hoarded the pleasures of sight. The beauty of growth, the unfolding of vivid petals, rose, begonia, columbine, the dignity of stately trees and well-kept lawns.

Dibbern pushed his charge towards the concrete slope-way especially laid so that the wheelchair could be steered right into the house itself.

Miss Charlotte began to move her hands again, but this time in little agonised gestures. Dibbern pushed harder for he knew all the signs. The doors were open and he shouted 'Alice' at the top of his voice. A girl quickly appeared, a lovely girl, long limbed, and graceful, her eyes a startling blue.

Dibbern dithered with exertion. 'It's Miss Charlotte, Alice,' he panted. 'She's got the "aches" again.'

The girl, obviously capable and well used to the ritual, knelt beside her mistress with soothing words and gently stroking the gnarled and twisted legs as the beady brown eyes fixed on her.

'A drop of brandy, George Dibbern,' Alice ordered. 'You know where it is – and I know just how much is in the bottle so don't try any of your tricks.'

Dibbern creaked away, mumbling under his breath. Always the same that Alice was, suspecting him of stealing the brandy, when it was that old fatheaded professor who was the culprit, if anybody.

Alice was still calming Miss Charlotte when he returned. He handed over the liquid, and the girl stood up and gave it to the old lady in sips.

'That's better, my dear.' The dry, whimpering voice was husky with pain. 'You do me a world of good. I'll go into the drawing room now.' Alice nodded, and wheeled the chair into the big drawing room where a log fire burned.

'I'll bring your dinner, now sit quietly until I come back.' She was capable and confident. 'Would you like Dibbern to bring in a fresh bunch of flowers?' Miss Charlotte nodded, and the girl conveyed the information to Dibbern, who silently expressed his disgust and regret at the constant ill usage of his person.

He was still mumbling to himself as he cut the last bloom when a voice at his elbow said with startling suddenness. 'Please, I've come for the job.' Dibbern almost dropped the scissors in astonishment as he turned to face the diminutive untidy figure with the serious grey eyes who regarded him gravely.

'Please, sir, I've come for the job,' repeated the voice.

'Job, job?' Dibbern was flustered. 'What job?'

'The job in the paper for a gardener's boy.'

'Oh, that! You'm a mite on the small side.'

'Yes, sir, I can't help it, sir, but I know all about flowers and things. My father was a gardener.'

'Was he now? Well, it ain't me you'm to see, it's the mistress and she wunt have you because you'm too little.' But the weariness of the waif softened the old man's heart, and he patted the boy's head. 'We'll see, we'll see. Come along to the house and talk to Miss Charlotte, you might look better scrubbed – and if she does take you on, scrubbed you certainly will be, and by Alice.' He said this forbodingly, and the boy following the old man up the pathway envisaged in his mind the ogre, Alice.

They entered through the still open front door, went down a short corridor and into the drawing room where Miss Charlotte was just finishing her soup.

'I've brought you fresh flowers for the vase, mistress, and this here.' Dibbern jerked a thumb in the boy's direction.

'He's applied for the job of gardener's boy.'

Miss Charlotte patted her lips with a napkin and fixed her beady brown eyes on the trembling waif. She saw a youngster of at most only fourteen, terribly ragged and dirty with a fine line of worry already chiselled on his brow. She saw also a face that was almost ugly except for the superb grey eyes which gave it a subtle air of distinction.

She spoke softly. 'What's your name, boy?'

'Timothy, if you please ma'am. Timothy Sw – , that is, Farley. Timothy Farley.'

'Timothy Farley.' She mused on the name. 'Are you hungry?'

'Yes'm.'

The old head nodded. 'Dibbern take Master Farley to Alice, have him fed and scrubbed and when he's clean bring him back to me for a little chat. Tell Alice also to find him something to wear. Anything will be better than his present rags and tatters.'

'You'm for it now,' said old Dibbern with feeling, as he lead Timothy away. 'When Alice has finished with the carbolic there'll be none of you left.'

At the gardener's words Timothy was strongly tempted to run, but he was hungry and aching from his hard night of trespass in the library. He saw some faint prospects, too, for the old bent lady in the drawing room might keep him on. Surely, if she had no such intention she wouldn't be sending him off to Alice like this?

He was already frightened of Alice, for in her he saw another Miss Ciceney. His heart sank to his boots and he licked lips dry from dust and exposure.

'I've brought you something, Alice,' said Dibbern with relish, pushing open the kitchen door. 'You'm to scrub him, feed him, and clothe 'im – them's mistress's orders. What you'll clothe him in goodness only knows, unless you finds 'im a fig leaf.' And he went away cackling.

Timothy's fear oozed away when he saw the lovely country girl with the smiling mouth and blue eyes. The old gardener had been pulling his leg all along.

'Please, miss, you're to do what Mr Dibbern says, then send me into the old lady in the drawing room. I can scrub myself if you'll show me where the water is – and the soap,' he added as an afterthought.

'I doubt,' said the smiling girl, 'whether you'll make such a good job of it as I shall. I suppose you're the new gardener's boy?'

'Not yet, miss, but I hope to be.'

'Come along to the bathroom and we'll see what can be done for you.'

To the bathroom they went, and there Timothy suffered the humiliation of having to undress in front of the exacting Alice, after which he was plunged into hot water and scrubbed as he had never been scrubbed before.

The shame of the thick film of soap and grime which settled on the surface of the bath water was insignificant compared with the shame of the revelation of his early adolescence before Alice. Taking no notice of his confusion she soaped and poked him mercilessly, before finally rescuing him from the water and leaving him with a towel to dry himself while she sought out clothing for him to wear.

When next he appeared before Miss Charlotte he was shining clean, amply fed and wearing an open-necked blouse of Alice's, a tawny man's waistcoat several sizes too big, and a pair of cutdown trousers.

'That,' remarked Miss Charlotte, 'is decidedly better. A good girl Alice, now come and sit here beside me,' she patted a cane stool. 'And tell me something about yourself.' Timothy obediently sat down on the stool.

'Now, where do you come from boy?'

'Worley.'

'Worley? – Worley? Never heard of it.'

'No, ma'am it's a long way from here,' – and Timothy related his story.

The beady eyes softened as the boy told of his heartaches.

'And you came here all by yourself?'

'Yes, ma'am.'

'Timothy, why when you talk do you move your hands so?'

'I didn't know that I did, Miss Charlotte.'

'Let me see your hands, Timothy.' Obediently he held out his hands, and she took the slender wrists in her own twisted swollen fingers. 'You have beautiful hands, boy, has anyone ever told you that before?'

'Not that I can remember, ma'am.'

'Do you draw or paint well?'

'No, Miss Charlotte, very badly. It was my worst subject at school.'

'I see.' She lingered over the fragile delicacy of the boy's hands, the perfect fingers so like porcelain in appearance.

'Miss Charlotte, why are your hands so funny and why do you sit in a chair with wheels on?' He fixed her with his serious grey eyes.

'An inquisitive boy, too. I'm a cripple, Timothy, and very, very old. My joints have a rheumatoid infection and I'm unable to walk.'

'Does it hurt?'

'Sometimes it hurts very much and then Alice has to rub my poor old joints. What age do you think I am, Timothy?' The boy eyed the twisted old figure speculatively.

'A hundred, maybe.'

'A hundred.' She laughed drily. 'I'll never reach a hundred but I'm eighty-three, and I trust that you will respect my years.'

'I can stay then? I've got the job?' His eyes lighted up and the old lady's lips trembled into a smile at his eager willingness.

'You've got the job, Timothy. A few shillings a week for your pocket, a good bed, and as much food as you can eat.'

'Oh, thank you, Miss Charlotte.' He was overwhelmed.

'Dibbern will put you to work, but if Alice wants you for anything you must go to her first.'

'Yes'm.'

'There is no one else here except for Professor Bernardt, an old friend of mine who has lived in this house for a good number of years. Occasionally, I shall want you to talk to me: it gets very lonely at times. And look after the flowers, Timothy, they are my special friends.'

She signalled for him to go and he went lightheartedly to inspect the house.

That night he wrote of his good fortune to his foster mother, and also a long detailed letter to Nancy Weston.

He wrote to Nancy three times in all, but never received a reply. He finally concluded that his letters were kept from her.

As the days progressed the old Georgian house and its inmates became very dear to Timothy. He liked crusty old Dibbern and idolised the efficient Alice who ruled his ablutions with a rod of iron. In Miss Charlotte he recognised a kindly old woman whose occasional sourness was caused by the pain she suffered. He cringed when she had the 'aches' and would run in wild terror for Alice who seemed to know just what to do and just what to say.

Dibbern chided him good-naturedly and complained endlessly, but Timothy was obedience itself: following the rheumaticky old man about the garden helping to roll and mow the lawns; pushing Miss Charlotte around her favourite flower beds; cutting roses and running errands as he was required.

He had a huge bedroom all to himself, and a big double bed into which his small body disappeared completely, and Miss Charlotte allowed him to bring grasshoppers and other insects into the house. Beneath the bed he had a menagerie of field mice, which he fed until they could scarcely move before setting them free again.

Miss Charlotte's house was much smaller than the Weston's, but nevertheless it was on a grand scale. He loved the walk along the balconies and down the massive winding staircase to the polished reception hall with the brass and copperware ornaments.

He was allotted the task of cleaning the brass and copper, much to the disgust of old Dibbern who complained that he ought to be helping him in the gardens. Melchester, ugly and industrialised, was only a few miles away; but the Georgian house was set in country untainted by the hideousness of belching chimneys or the acridness of town air mixed with the waste chemical vapours of the factories.

* * *

On the fifth day after his arrival he was weeding in a corner of the rose garden when he observed a quaint old man in a moth-eaten frock coat regarding him severely from the wooden seat upon which he sat.

A slim volume lay loosely in the stranger's hands and a thin forefinger remained lifted as though about to turn a page.

'You must be the new gardener's boy,' the old man remarked suddenly, nodding his head bird-like so that the black ribbon of his *pince-nez* fluttered.

'Yes, sir,' said Timothy nervously.

'I am Professor Jules Bernardt. I trust that one so young as yourself will not become a source of annoyance to one so old as I,' he said with dignity.

'No, sir, I'll try not to sir.'

'Good, good, very good.' And he commenced reading again, ignoring Timothy's presence from then onwards.

At supper in the kitchen Timothy mentioned the incident to Alice.

'The Professor.' She laughed. 'He's a queer old bird. Some mystery about him all right. He was living here before I came, a naturalised Austrian whom I think was a lover of Miss Charlotte's long, long ago. Sometimes we don't see him for days and he never seems to eat at all. He and old Dibbern are always bickering: the gardener hates the sight of him.'

'Why is he called the Professor?' Timothy enquired.

'Because he is, or was, a Professor, I suppose. Always reading queer books, and Miss Charlotte says that he's clever, got lots of degrees or something of the sort but I personally think that he's a bit cracked in the head. Sometimes he says the most extraordinary things. After today you probably won't see him again for a week. He hides like a dormouse in the attics reading, reading always reading.' And she touched her head significantly.

At the end of the month Timothy had a letter from Mary giving him news about herself. She was pleased that he had done so well and from the scarcely legible scrawl he gathered that she was quite comfortable with her sister.

Now that his mind was released from worry he became a boy once more, and put on weight with all the good food he was eating. Alice insisted on feeding him up, and already the pinched drawn look had left his face. Sometimes the girl watched him curiously. The eloquent way he moved his hands when he spoke drew attention to a beauty of form which fascinated her, and the grey heavily lashed eyes always so serious in expression were magnetic. She couldn't quite make up her mind about him; he was just a child a little over fourteen and yet there was something peculiar about him, something fine and unconsciously hidden, which her shrewd sensitiveness faintly registered.

August 1914 brought world war and in the same month Timothy received notification that Mary Swaine had died. She had already been lain at rest three weeks when the grubby ill-pencilled letter arrived from Droitwich.

He had grown far apart from Mary in the months he had been with Miss Charlotte, but this sudden news vividly brought back to him his life at Worley. The cottage, Tom and Mary, the good, kind people who had reared him. The Weston's and Nancy. Somehow it all seemed so very long ago.

At the time of his fifteenth birthday in the following January the war for which the prophets had forecast a quick end, was plainly destined to be a long job; and a steely tension settled over the country, reaching as far even as the old Georgian house at Melchester. Factories were in full production, and the towering chimneys of the town vomited black smoke ceaselessly day and night in writhing compressed clouds.

But the multiple crises which followed quickly one upon the other did not to any extent disrupt the placid fundamentals of Timothy's life. At fifteen he was still little more than a boy, and the household he lived in had received the shock of prolonged warfare and comfortably absorbed it. They were too old – and too young – for serious perturbation. The flowers still bloomed, Dibbern still grumbled, and Alice remained as efficiently capable as ever.

Timothy tried his first cigarette, truant fashion, and was ill. He remained without friends of his own age, but his respect for Alice and Miss Charlotte deepened.

Chocolate bars grew fewer and Melchester was almost stripped of its youth. Next year it will end, next year. The Kaiser's shot his bolt, we'll soon be laughing again.

During one of Timothy's tours of the garden with Miss Charlotte, in which with much pride he was pointing out his own particular achievements, his mistress was suddenly shattered with an attack of her increasingly frequent arthritic pains. The boy, not ten yards from the house, left the chair and ran in terror, calling for Alice at the top of his voice. From Alice there was no response, nor did his frantic searching reveal her. Panic-stricken he shouted and shouted, growing more fearful every minute as Alice did not come.

Blind with tears, he stumbled back to Miss Charlotte, who twisted in agony, and vainly tried to smile at him.

'I can't find Alice,' he panted desperately. 'She just isn't anywhere.'

'Rub my legs, Timothy,' gasped the old woman. 'The tips of your fingers at the – joints like Alice does. Take my mind off – the pain. Kneel . . .'

The boy, eyes swollen with tears of pity at her aged helplessness, her deformed, diseased body, knelt on the damp turf beside her and grasped the thin legs hidden beneath the thick black skirt. His slim fingers felt the knotted deformities of her knee joints and with a natural sensitiveness his fingers explored the structure as though he sought to find and tear out the thing that was hurting her.

Miss Charlotte sat hunched, her mind shadowy with the needle agony, wishing that Alice were there to talk to and comfort her; to bring a small glass of brandy, to stroke her old legs and deflect the pain. And then quite suddenly the pain began to recede. She felt it diminish as though it were being rubbed away, withdrawn from her. It drained from her racked body like water from a leaking vessel. The effect was so startling that she straightened suddenly in the chair, senses keen and alert, seeking to fix her reaction as an hallucination.

She looked at the dark tousled head of the boy bent over in concentration, unaware of her watchfulness. She observed closely the long fingers touching her, and then the head suddenly lifted and she looked fully into the grey depths of his eyes, a film of tears adding lustre to their intensity.

On seeing her recovery the wide full mouth of the boy slipped into a smile, and a lock of hair fell over his forehead. The lined face of Charlotte Bemmington quivered, and tried vainly to smile back, and then she was crying quietly.

When Alice returned with her shopping basket, Timothy was struggling to push the wheelchair indoors. She ran to help him, and as the lissom grace of her touched him he knew an unfamiliar sense of pleasure.

'Miss Charlotte would like a glass of brandy, please Alice. She's had an attack of the "aches" but it's better now. I wish you'd been here.'

'I had to fetch the groceries. Quite sure you feel better, Miss Charlotte?' She bent over her mistress.

'Quite better, Alice, thank you.' Her voice struck the girl as being a little strained.

'Dr George is due here next week.'

'Yes, but he can do nothing, we both know that.'

Alice, instead of answering, went off to fetch the brandy. When she returned, Timothy had gone, and her mistress was sitting in front of the window.

'Alice, has anything about Timothy ever stood out in

68

your memory as unusual?' Miss Charlotte asked as soon as the girl entered.

Alice answered without hesitation. 'His hands, Miss Charlotte. I've never seen hands quite like them before, so perfect and so . . . so . . .'

'Mobile, Alice.'

'Yes, mobile.' She passed the small measure of Napoleon to the old lady.

'He's a strange boy, Alice.'

'But nice. He's kind, and very generous.'

'You've no need to defend him, I do not intend to dispense with his services.' She made no mention of the incident in the garden. 'Alice, when did you last see the professor?'

'A week or so ago.'

'I want you to ring the bell for him. I must speak to him at once.'

'Very good, Miss Charlotte.' Alice slipped away wondering at the suppressed excitement of the old lady.

From the linen cupboard she withdrew a large brass handbell and standing at the bottom of the attic stairway clanged it with all her might.

The terrific echoes swept through the house, and Dibbern, pollinating in one of the glasshouses, pricked up his ears.

'There's the bell,' he said to Timothy. 'Mistress wants to see the old crackpot.'

Timothy, who had been helping with the operation, raised his head.

'Who's the old crackpot?' he asked curiously.

'The professor. Him who sits in the attics for weeks on end. Off his chump he is, nosey old b – . Actually came in here once and tried to tell me my business.'

'And did he?'

'I told the varmint his.'

Timothy smiled, and blew a little pollen with a tiny bellows from one stamen to another.

'What do they ring a bell for?'

'So that the old fool will know he's wanted by Mistress Charlotte. He'll come down fast enough if he thinks delay will be the means of his getting chucked out of here on his neck; been living on the mistress for years . . . and a danged furriner, too.'

'When does he eat?'

'Comes down at night and takes lumps of bread and cheese. He's barmy.'

'Alice says that she thinks there was a love affair a long time ago.'

'Surprisin' what love will do, ain't it?' Dibbern cackled until he almost choked.

Timothy, failing to see the joke, was about to question it when he saw Alice waving.

'Alice wants me for something, I'll be back shortly.' Putting down the bellows, he ran to her.

'Miss Charlotte wants you,' Alice said. 'And the professor is with her. What's in the wind I don't know, but something most definitely is.'

'What have I done?' He knew a sudden fear; perhaps he wouldn't be wanted any more.

Alice smiled and patted his cheek reassuringly. 'Everything will be all right, don't worry.'

Trepidation eating at his heart, the boy went into the drawing room where he had last left Charlotte Bemmington.

The professor turned round as he entered and fixed him with a speculative, faded eye. Timothy noticed that he was still wearing the same old frock coat stained here and there with food. The yellow skin of his face was stretched tightly across the cheek bones in a skull-like effect. *Pince nez* hung at ribbon length and there was about him a faint odour of decay.

'This is Professor Jules Bernardt, Timothy, whom I believe you have met once before?' Miss Charlotte introduced the old man.

70

'Yes, ma'am,' said Timothy, wondering what was coming next. The professor bowed mockingly, and Miss Charlotte frowned and raised a finger in a gesture of command. The old man stiffened immediately.

'Professor Bernardt,' said Miss Charlotte, 'is a very old friend of mine, and very distinguished. He has academic degrees, both in the sciences and the arts, and I have asked him to tutor you.'

Timothy guessed that there had been no asking; that the professor had received positive orders. He waited.

'You are spending a good deal of time helping Dibbern, which would be better spent helping yourself,' Miss Charlotte pursued.

'Professor Bernardt needs an outlet for his creative knowledge, Timothy, and I think it best in your own interests that you should learn from him as a special pupil. He will instruct you on Monday, Tuesday, Thursday and Friday of each week, for the rest of the time you will carry on as before.' Timothy's jaw dropped in dismay. For four full days a week he was virtually to go back to school. 'But . . .' he began.

'No buts, Timothy,' Miss Charlotte's voice was very kind, but very firm. 'You will commence next Monday, with the library for classroom.' Her eyes twinkled at the boy's obvious dismay. 'You will find the professor a very clever man, and perhaps one day you will thank me.'

'Yes, Miss Charlotte.'

'That will be all, Timothy.'

He fled, and seeking Alice, poured out his woe. At supper, seated around the kitchen table they discussed the matter. Dibbern was of the firm opinion that the old lady was going as barmy as the professor.

Alice didn't quite know what to think. She fixed her blue eyes on the dejected Timothy and said nothing.

She was shrewd, but this move of Miss Charlotte's was too complex for her.

9

Monday loomed forebodingly, and with its coming Timothy's worst fears were more than realised.

The professor had drawn up a curriculum for a three year programme which included meaningless names like Algebra, Trigonometry, Physics, Biology, Geometry, Latin, French, and Chemistry. Timothy's head reeled. Miss Grosvenor's teachings were a drop in the ocean compared with all this.

Professor Bernardt seemed to be enjoying himself. The new interest derived from having a pupil whom he could use as a guinea pig brought a sparkle to his eye.

The day wore on, to be followed by other days which in turn became weeks and then months.

Miss Charlotte's decree of four days a week tutorage soon became five, and then six, leaving a bare Sunday for idleness and leisure.

Dibbern, the gardener, grumbled and complained at the loss of Timothy's useful assistance, but it had no effect.

As the finger of time moved the professor grew sprightlier and sartorially more careful. He pushed Timothy hard, offering his vast knowledge simply and efficiently, so that the reluctant pupil, by no means a dullard, soon became a willing eager scholar.

Hours of private study for consumption in the evenings were added to the programme and Timothy wrestled with Pythagoras, Homer, and a variegated assortment of weird chemical equations. The smooth, brilliant tongue of the old man fed his young receptive mind unstintingly and soon the boy's own latent talent stamped him as a scholar of promise.

The professor reported to Miss Charlotte, who was immensely pleased and complimented Timothy on his ability.

The old lady was slowly growing worse with time, and Dr George had warned them that her complaint would bring the end at any moment. Whenever her pains were bad it was Timothy who was summoned now, and the fragile hands brought relief that was both amazing and frightening.

'Is this,' she chided herself often enough 'the imagining of an old woman? Am I the subject of hallucinations?' And yet when the pains came and the kneeling boy placed his hands on the afflicted part, the pain would dull and vanish.

Timothy, grasping the essentials of his new subjects, recognised with the acquisition of fresh knowledge the academic brilliance of his teacher. Not only had the professor a thorough insight but also an ability to convey learning to his pupil in a manner which enabled the boy to store away each piece in his mind for future reference.

By Timothy's sixteenth birthday, the war which was strangling all Europe had taken on an even grimmer bloodiness. It sucked up British manpower and smashed it piece by piece. Reverses were heavy, and the air full of gloomy foreboding.

In July of 1916 came the first battle of the Somme on a twenty-five mile front, with the French taking six thousand German prisoners. In the same month the second battle of the Somme was launched and the Allies succeeded in making further small advances, though at great loss.

At this period the professor developed a grim satisfaction in working his pupil, and Timothy grew thin and pale under the pressure. At the same time he fell violently in love with Alice, a passionate, idyllic affair common with the calf stage of youth.

The professor had been particularly biting in his criticism of Timothy's failure to absorb a complex mathematical application and the boy, weary from a long day of mental toil, staggered to the bathroom determined to soak the weariness from his mind by lying in steaming water.

He swung the bathroom door inwards and then stood transfixed, mouth open. He knew little of women, and the actual physical structure of a woman was a shadowy uncertainty in his mind. Now he was seeing the revelation of a woman for the first time: Alice, who had forgotten to secure the door, had just stepped from the bath.

The magnificent ivory length of her, glistening with water, struck him into immobility. Alice, equally shocked, stood rooted – blue eyes wide with horror.

Timothy knew that he should withdraw immediately and his mind kept telling him to run, but his legs refused to move.

He had formerly held a vague and naive belief that the human adult female was somehow constructed in the fashion of a marsupial, into whose pouch a Divine hand popped an infant from time to time as required.

The creamy hue of Alice's unblemished skin glowed with vitality, throwing into sharp relief the tight curls of hair.

He watched the gentle swaying of the girl's rounded breasts, the pink flushed tips lifting and falling, until the demands of his brain at last infused life into his fixed legs, and he fled.

When Alice finally emerged she found him in the kitchen alone, head bent in preoccupation over a bowl of soup. He heard her come in but his head remained bowed.

'Timothy.'

'Yes, Alice.' The head did not lift.

74

'I know that the whole thing was an accident. Please promise that you won't tell anyone, ever, then I won't scold you.'

The boy's head lifted, his face ardent. 'I promise, Alice, honest I do, I'm sorry. It never entered my head that you might be in there.'

'I forgot to lock the door.'

'I know now.' The grey eyes fixed on her adoringly, and colour slowly flowed into the girl's face. She turned away abruptly. 'Don't look at me like that, Timothy.'

'No, Alice.' He lowered his head, and made great play with the soup.

After this incident, despite the intensity of his studies Alice occupied his mind continually. He loved her with a violence which threatened to suffocate him. He brought her flowers and helped her whenever he was able with flushed face and glowing eye. He had awakened, and his subdued instincts released. The pale vision of the girl's naked loveliness haunted him to a degree which prevented him sleeping well at night, and within a week his own mental turmoil and constant overwork erupted in a fever, and the doctor had to be called in.

He was confined to bed for a week and ordered complete rest – much to the professor's annoyance.

Miss Charlotte, now wasting more rapidly than ever, became much concerned, and especially indignant at the impossibility of her wheel chair being conveyed upstairs so that she could constantly be near the patient.

Alice was the chief ministering angel, pouring out the bitter medicine at the prescribed intervals and creating tempting delicacies with her culinary skill. At night she tucked him in and wished him well before turning out the light.

On one such occasion as she was putting the finishing touches to arranging the coverlet he suddenly threw his arms about her neck and fastened his mouth on to hers wildly. She made no move to restrain him, for she had

75

long known of the springing of his youthful love. Instead she let him have his fill of her lips, and then patting his hot forehead went downstairs without a word. She was worried at his preoccupation with her: this sensitive strange youth with the fine eyes shining in such unconcealed adoration.

She was an intelligent girl versed in the complexities that lay around life's innumerable corners, and yet this situation had her at a disadvantage. Obviously the sixteen-year-old Timothy was going through an adolescent crush. She herself was almost nineteen and understood his feelings for what they were – and yet his devotion had a strangely disturbing effect. It had been foolish not to have locked the bathroom door with the possibility of someone unwittingly entering so obvious. She knew that the sight of her pleasant nudity had stirred the innocent youth with a shock so profound that the reaction had been quite alarming.

When Timothy had lain his lips on hers and she had left him so quietly and had been so passive at his action he lay curled in shamed despair at his offensive audacity. Perhaps in that moment he jumped the span youth to man because on the next day he was full of humble apologies.

On his return to health he avoided the generous Alice with hurtful obviousness, nursing his shamed pride until the wound had healed and by degrees he became normal again. He still adored her, but without demonstration and gradually was able to talk to her without embarrassment.

Her understanding tolerance of him during this period of storm brought a warmth between them which became a steady bond of comradeship, and had he been a little older the strange bud of true love would surely have opened and flowered.

As it was he went forward with his studies in a way which gratified the professor, who had now shed all eccentricity in his eagerness to impart learning to the youth.

In the following September the third battle of the Somme began, in which the British used tanks for the first time with devastating effect on the enemy. By November the fighting subsided into grim trench warfare.

At Christmas time snow lay thickly around Melchester, and the Georgian house was transformed into a delicate ivory carving.

Alice decorated a fir tree with silver tinsel and coloured glass balls. Holly and mistletoe were scattered about the house and they made as much of Christmas as they could, for Miss Charlotte had grave misgivings as to whether she would survive another one.

Timothy and Alice sang carols and the ancient professor unbent his staid personality sufficiently to applaud with enthusiasm. Dibbern told a ghost story which the professor pooh-poohed with scientific explanations, much to the old gardener's disgust.

At seventeen, Timothy had grown in stature and found it necessary to shave regularly. Miss Charlotte raised his wage a few shillings, but as he now had to clothe himself this did not go very far.

In March arrangements were made for him to take his matriculation in London, and he was packed off for a first ride ever on the steam train.

Backed by the professor's brilliant teaching he matriculated with ease, winning a distinction in all subjects.

Miss Charlotte, who was now permanently confined to bed, so that even her garden was lost to her, was delighted.

In the kitchen speculation ran rife as to what was behind it all. Timothy himself had no solution to offer, for the professor still worked him mercilessly, even after he had taken his examination. On his frequent visits to her bedroom Miss Charlotte told him little or nothing of the future. She was slowly becoming paralysed and would sit holding his hands in hers, stroking and admiring them as though they were separate personalities.

Dibbern, now that the mistress was bedridden, relaxed his grip on the garden which began to lose its trim well-kept look. He was too old a man to give it the attention it actually needed, and now that he was released from Miss Charlotte's goading he grew leisurely, as befitted the dignity of his age.

Charlotte would not take on any additional staff, hinting that she was unable to afford further expense, which indicated plainly enough to Dibbern that the old lady hadn't much money.

For hours in the evenings Timothy pored over large volumes on Physics, Chemistry, Botany, Zoology and Higher Maths. He had developed into a brilliant pupil, and to the professor he was a gem to trim and polish. The boy's brain was receptive and quick to absorb and the old man crammed everything into it that he could. He had become a strict disciplinarian: there was none of the musty decay about him that there had been when the boy had first seen him reading in the rose garden. He was the distinguished scholar again, and he had a pupil that would be the envy of teachers over the world. He revelled in it.

Timothy could talk on almost anything, and Alice had developed an awe for him as he would sit praising the professor, or explaining some thesis with quick movements of his striking, mobile fingers.

'Let's go for a walk,' he suggested one evening. 'There's almost an hour until dusk.' And so they walked until finally they sat down on the crest of a hill and looked into a shallow wooded valley.

Melchester was on the edge of the industrial area, and the southerly direction led into patches of pleasant countryside.

'It's good to be alive, isn't it Tim?' said Alice, drinking in the fresh cool air.

'I suppose it is.'

'You don't sound very sure of yourself.' She looked at him sharply.

'I'm worried about Miss Charlotte.'

'She'll die soon, you know that, Timothy, don't you?'

'Yes I know.' He was pensive.

'She's had her life, Tim.'

'Yes, but this business of the professor coaching me day after day is so queer.'

'I've an idea she's fitting you out so that you can fend for yourself when she's gone.'

'Do you really think so.' His eyes grew soft. 'She's been so good to me, Alice.'

'And she wants you to make her very proud, knowing well enough that she will never live to see it.'

'If ever I get the chance I will, Alice, I promise.'

She patted his head, and the touch of her hand gave him pleasure.

'You've come a long way, Tim, from the ragged waif. You're the educated young master now, and quite handsome.'

Tim smiled at her flattery. 'I'll never be handsome, Alice, I know that well enough, and as for growing into a young beau about town I have no knowledge at all of dress. There's the war too, I may have to go to that yet.'

'Hush, you're still too young at seventeen, and anyway, no one knows of your whereabouts.'

'And so you would make me a coward?'

'I certainly would. I think too much of you to want to lose you, Tim.' Her blue eyes rested on him affectionately.

'I think an awful lot of you too, Alice.' He whispered. 'I know that you're older than I am but some day . . .' She placed a forefinger on his lips, silencing him.

'A lot of things will happen before someday. There are other people to meet. You've met none yet.'

They strolled to the house hand in hand as would brother and sister, or youthful lovers, quite unconscious of the possible comparisons.

Alice had a head buzzing with thoughts. She must be

fair to Tim; he was only a boy still. She was three years older, a woman fully mature. No, it could not be, the whole thing was quite impossible. And yet, perhaps, in a year or two – she sealed her mind, refusing to dwell further on a situation that seemed to be a little ridiculous.

Next day Timothy was surprised when his tutor, reclining in an armchair, informed him that there would be no further lessons.

'But I have much to learn,' he protested.

'And much you have learned, my boy.' The old parchment-like face was serious. 'No one can learn all, nor is it possible for you to put so much into your work any longer. Your health would suffer. Partly under duress I have compressed into three years, studies which an average person would not absorb in ten. You are well above average, Timothy, and I am as proud of you as it is possible for a teacher to be of his pupil. Charlotte is proud of you too.'

'But I owe you so much more than I can ever repay.'

'You owe me nothing. I had gone to seed when I undertook this job, and it has brought me back to reality. I feel almost young again.' He smiled warmly, and held out his hand, Timothy shook it firmly.

'You are very kind, sir, I feel so embarrassed.'

'Do not be, there is a great future in store for you, Timothy.'

'Doing what, sir?' The question came eagerly.

'We'll see, we'll see. Next week you go to London again to sit for your Higher School Certificate. That you will distinguish yourself I have no doubt. Your future will then be in the hands of Charlotte.'

'You think highly of Miss Charlotte, don't you, sir?'

'I love her, Timothy.' It was a strange and incomprehensible statement for one so old to make, and about Charlotte Bemmington who was older still. Incomprehensible to Timothy, at least, because of his youth.

'When I was a young man,' said the professor. He left

the statement unfinished, and the boy observed a moistness of the bright old eyes. 'There was a child, too,
Timothy, but he died.' He threw up his hands. 'I gave up
my career, gave up everything, the scandal you know. I
left Austria and came to England, but Charlotte would
never marry me, although I became naturalised. Oh well,
time has helped, but the past is not dim, at times it is
bright, my boy, over bright.' He shook his head wearily,
and Timothy felt a great pity for this brilliant man who
had so little of life left to him.

'I'm sorry, sir.'

'You have small need for sorrow. Charlotte has been
most gracious and kind, but do not push into life headles-
sly, my boy, there are many snares. You have wisdom,
now, the wisdom of learning, but you have very little
experience. As you live your life so will you gain experience. The futility of experience is that it usually comes too
late, the event is passed and often regretted when more
wisdom of life's treachery would have warned you to
bypass it. Often these mistakes are irreparable, particularly when they destroy happiness. That is why we look to
older people for advice. Not because they have learned
more academically, but because they have grappled with
the world, and know things that it takes a lifetime to
know. Experience, Timothy, experience – and always
beware of women.' He wagged a warning forefinger and
walked away leaving the youth in a state of bewilderment
by his remarks.

As the professor had forecast, Timothy took 'Higher'
and passed with ease. In the same year he took a minor
professional examination in which he distinguished himself in Physics, Chemistry, Botany and Zoology.

Success did not disturb him and he was bewildered by
the particular trend his life had taken. He was a boy
utterly sincere, and the opportunities that had been made
available for him left him very humble and very grateful.

As for any idea of what Miss Charlotte intended for

him, he had not the remotest knowledge. He was completely nonplussed and she had not been at all forthcoming in the gratification of his curiosity.

He visited his benefactor in her room on the day news reached them of the examination results. She was too weak to respond overmuch, but he knew by the sudden spark of light in the fast fading eyes that he had pleased her.

'You've worked hard, Tim, very hard. I've been told all about it, and I'm very proud of you.'

'I want to thank you, ma'am, most sincerely.'

'Nonsense, Tim, nonsense. The talent was there, the professor simply put it to its best usage: as a teacher he is excellent – is he not?'

'Yes, ma'am, I cannot put into words my appreciation.'

'You don't have to Tim, you don't have to.' Her old, gnarled hand grasped his, tightly.

10

On the 6th June, 1918, Miss Charlotte died.

The funeral took place quietly without fuss or ostentation. There were no friends – just the professor, Timothy, Alice and Dibbern, the professional executors of the arrangements, and Mr Mathew Spry, Miss Charlotte's solicitor.

Alice prepared the customary meal and they chatted in undertones as though the close proximity of death forbade any raising of voices. The girl busied herself unnecessarily in an effort to contain her troubled emotions.

Mr Spry, finishing an egg sandwich hungrily, cleared his throat and wiped bony fingers with a snowy linen handkerchief. The professor, who had withered noticeably, looked at him as though he were a new found botanical specimen.

'Miss Charlotte,' said Mr Spry to his fidgety listeners, 'instructed me to read her will immediately after the internment. That had been her wish for six or seven months past. She bade me advise you not to mourn her passing. She has lived a full life . . . er . . . humph . . . yes.' Mr Spry's prepared rhetoric failed him and he wiped his fingers once more on the white handkerchief.

'Have any of you any objections to me reading the will now?'

Old Dibbern the gardener seemed about to say something. His mouth opened and closed in agitation but no sound came.

'If you will accompany me as far as the library then we will go through the formalities.' He stood up. A bent stick of a man, leading the file awkwardly from the dining room to the library.

Timothy sat near to Alice, who was still a little weepy. He had no expectation from the will, and neither could any of the others, save Alice. The professor and Dibbern were very old, and not likely to survive for many more years. He felt Alice's warm hand steal into his.

'Hrrmph,' grunted Mr Spry, clearing his throat again, and rustling the papers. 'Hrrmph.'

The tick of the clock on the wall was like a drum-beat and it seemed as though Miss Charlotte was actually in the room with them. Timothy was convinced that he could feel her personality.

'The last will and testament of Miss Charlotte Bemmington deceased' began the solicitor without further delay. 'There is no provision concerning anyone save for the four of you here. Perhaps you were not aware of it, but Miss Bemmington was far from being a rich woman –

in fact her capital had been ebbing quite seriously for the past six years. No, she was by no means rich. In the figures quoted and with precision may I say, allowances have been made for anticipated death duties, and also for the expectation of life of the beneficiaries.

'The will . . . hrrmph . . . I, Charlotte Bemmington, being in sound mind . . . to my old trusted comrade Jules Bernardt the sum of five hundred pounds annually so long as he shall live, together with permanent residence at my house and the use of any of its amenities. To George Dibbern, gardener and friend, though wont to grumble, the sum of three hundred pounds annually for so long as he shall live, together with permanent residence at my house and the use of any of its amenities, particularly the garden.' A tear escaped and rolled slowly down the old gardener's weather-wrinkled face. The solicitor coughed again.

'Hrrmph . . . To Alice, my dearest Alice, the interest from my debentures about six hundred pounds per annum together with ownership of my house which she must never offer for sale. My solicitors are instructed to pay particular attention to this term and condition.'

Mr Spry paused and cleared his throat loudly.

'Hrrmph . . . to continue. The calculated residue of my estate, allowing for the beneficiaries so far enumerated, is the capital sum of four thousand five hundred pounds, which is bequeathed to dear Tim Farley and is to be administered immediately by Professor Bernardt as I have instructed him, namely that it shall provide the necessary fees for entry of Timothy Farley to the Queen's College of Medicine at Caldmorley, Edinburgh. This sum will pay for all necessary tuition, and I have seen to it through my solicitors that there is a vacancy for the boy's inclusion at the next current term. I have had special guidance in this matter and feel sure that Timothy will bring great honour to all of us, to the profession of medicine, and to the country.'

As Mr Spry broke off and began to collect his papers Tim emitted his breath in a low whistle.

'The Queen's College of Medicine' he whispered perplexed. 'I don't understand it.'

'That must have been Miss Charlotte's idea all along' said Alice looking at him. 'A college of medicine. She wants you to be a doctor.'

TWO

1

Kiledin Manor, once the home of Scottish lairds and one of the oldest inhabited buildings in Morayshire, dated back to the Stuarts and before. It owed its long life to the three foot square slabs of granite, shale mortar, and steep solid buttresses which compounded to form the main structure. Narrow latticed windows sprinkled frequently in its grim, bastion walls peered like watchful eyes as though perpetually segregating friend from foe and trusting no one. The manor had survived storm and pestilence, it had withstood seige and attempted burnings; cracks which boulder cannon had hammered into its thick walls, had been resealed and in the year 1918 it was good for another five or more centuries.

The present owner of the Manor, Mordrake McAlister, sat in a deep leather armchair in the massively furnished drawing room, his slippered feet resting on a low stool.

His son, Neil, at ease on a damask sofa with a book propped in one hand, indolently turned a page and then tossed the volume to one side. He yawned.

The weather outside was heavy as the first edge of a gale hissed round the battlements. A log fire roared in the huge grate. It was December and the Great War had been over for almost a month. Snow was in the air.

'Looks bad outside,' Neil remarked. 'Big storm brewing.'

'Kiledin can stand it,' his father grunted. He was a large man with bright blue eyes, plump face and a paunch which owed its generous contour to rich living and fine malt whisky. He was a man who in youth had been wild and tough. He had roughed it, made money and spent it, mixed with the best and the worst. Over indulgence had dissipated him early and then an American ancestor had obliged with a considerable legacy. Now he was master of Kiledin, unemotional, unhurried though forceful, enjoying comfort and a background which wallowed in history.

Neil at twenty was his father all over again, wild, loving life with his father's shrewdness and heavy wit, but creative in his desires and academically clever. He was not sitting back waiting for his father's money, he wanted to know things and had an overwhelming desire to accredit himself.

He had chosen medicine for a profession and his father warmly approved the unexpected selection of such a difficult and onerous calling.

Without warning a heavy door banged, feet pattered on stone flooring and a girl, flushed and breathless, sped into the room, two springer spaniels at her heels snuffling and barking excitedly.

'Must ye make that row?' Mordrake snapped irritably, 'I'm trying to rest.'

'Sorry. It's going to snow. I've raced the dogs over Glen Tor. Settle Pancho! Settle Jan!'

With lolling tongues and eyes bright the spaniels lay down near to the hearth, forepaws extended, heads cocked and listening.

Stella McAlister looked scornfully at her indolent brother. She was alive with life, flushed and pink, dark eyes sparkling. Neil was her senior by a year, but where he was inclined to chubbiness, she was straight-planed and slim, with handsomely curved legs and high jutting breasts.

Both of the McAlister children had been born in Italy, where they had lived for three years before Mordrake's itching feet had taken them to new places. Neither Stella nor Neil had a trace of Scots in their speech and the girl, wildly lovely with rich tawny hair, had the smooth creamy skin of an Italian signorina. She was a passionate slip of a girl, violent in rage and love, tempestuous, respecting neither conventions nor personalities. She was cruel with men, gentle as a kitten with animals, a wild harem-scarem child who swam in the adjoining sea when rain poured in torrents and the waves threshed and roared on the shingle.

'Mercer is looking in later,' she remarked. 'He's got a new car, a Ford.'

Neil's lip curled, for he disliked Mercer Grant intensely.

Stella tossed her head defiantly at Neil's obvious contempt.

'I'm going up to change,' she said. 'Pancho, Jan, fetch 'em! Go fetch 'em!'

Her father cringed as the dogs, howling delightedly, chased the girl, and then settling back into his chair closed his eyes with relief.

Neil watched a bubble of resin seep from one of the sizzling logs and began to fill his pipe carefully. It grew darker outside: snow was definitely on the way. He thought of the barmaid in the neighbouring village of Blairgowie and then of the slim, sexy Lois Gunter, whom he'd met in London the year before. All that had got to change. He was going to be Doctor Neil McAlister in six or seven years time, provided that he had the perseverance. It was an achievement that he particularly wanted, although he could have lazed for years on his father's money.

Stella, who had changed into an elegant black dress, opened the door.

'Brr,' she complained, shivering. 'It's gone chilly. Wake up, Popsy!' She tickled her father under the chin.

Outside could be heard the chug-chug of a motor car on the drive, the rattle of lamps and mudguards.

'That's Mercer,' Stella said.

Neil groaned. Stella pulled a face at him.

They heard the car stop and the servant cross the hall; there was the click of the door opening and then Mercer Grant strode into the room.

''Lo all,' he greeted. 'Snow's on the way.'

Neil grunted and Mordrake opened sleepy eyes.

'Whisky's right beside ye,' he wheezed huskily. 'Help yourself.'

This was another young puppy upon whom his daughter was exercising her wiles, and a banker's son at that. Mordrake hated bankers.

Mercer's sharp eyes flickered over the desirability of Stella, and he felt the quickened coursing of his blood.

'Is that yours?' Neil asked suddenly, jerking his thumb towards the window through which he could see Mercer's car.

'He knows quite well it is,' Stella said angrily. 'He's just trying to be funny. Let's go into another room.'

Neil laughed wickedly to himself as the door closed, the sudden draught of air carrying the elusive fragrance of her perfume to his nostrils.

Neil left Kiledin on 18th January, 1919 and Stella drove him in the dog cart as far as the tiny station of Blairgowie, where she mocked him cheerfully until the train arrived.

From Blairgowie he changed at Elgin and thence to Edinburgh, where a ramshackle steam-bus with solid bone-jarring tyres connected him with Caldmorley. He found the Queen's College of Medicine with very little trouble and rang at the janitor's gate.

Queen's was smaller than he had anticipated. It was a long narrow building of grey brick, with a series of oblong windows running in parallel. A dormer crossed at right angles so that the whole structure looked like a letter T, with smaller buildings grouped about, long green lawns – now frost-covered – a few glasshouses, a

Macadam drive and open air squash courts. There was also an indoor gymnasium.

The steps to the main entrance were long and wide with polished black pillars on either side. Neil felt very noble as he walked up, the porter carrying his hand-sewn leather travelling case.

There were one or two other people lounging around inside the hall and his suitcase was dumped with several more in a corner. Neil tipped half a crown, slid out a silver cigarette case and lit a cigarette. He looked about him with interest.

A large marble bust of Louis Pasteur looked him squarely in the eye from the centre of the hallway, and a smaller one of Lord Lister stood in an adjacent corner. There were Latin inscriptions in gilt on two wall tablets and the founder's date, September 28th 1895, which he remembered was the date of Pasteur's death. Queen's was one of the most modern medical schools.

One or two more students chatting in loud whispers came up the steps and then there was a hush of expectancy as the Registrar, a long thin man with a completely bald head and faded drooping moustache, shuffled from the farthest corridor and cleared his throat noisily for attention. Neil McAlister glanced at his companions-to-be. There was a stout youth with bright red hair and a scrub of wild beard; several pale, waxen-looking city dwellers; a distinguished-looking young man with a diamond in the knot of his tie and a youth with grey eyes, a shock of dark hair and thick tweeds which fitted appallingly. Further scrutiny was curtailed by the Registrar's reedy voice suddenly informing them that class would commence on Monday next, in 'A' lecture room of the West wing under Mr Adam Hepplewhite, who would advise what books would be required. Owing to limited accommodation for boarders it would be necessary for the private quarters to be shared by two people. The Registrar then called the study numbers and the names of the occupants.

Neil had study six but missed the name of the person with whom he would be compelled to share. Carrying his own suitcase he climbed the stairs with the others and sought his room number.

'Hello,' said a voice behind him as he entered. 'I'm in with you. It's exciting, isn't it?'

'Is it? Oh, yes, I suppose it is. Come inside and look the place over. I'm Neil McAlister.' He held out his hand to his new room mate.

'I'm Tim Farley.' Neil saw that it was the youth with the grey eyes and badly fitting tweeds. He gripped the slim pale hand with his own strong brown fingers.

'What are you after?' Neil asked, turning out his suitcase. 'Made up your mind at all?'

'Not yet. It was a bit of a shock to me coming here anyway. What's your particular sphere?'

'I'll settle for Conjoint, if needs be,' Neil grinned. 'I'm not planning anything too ambitious.'

Tim nodded in agreement, looking his new companion over carefully and unobtrusively. Then he busied himself turning out his possessions and stowing them away in the wall cupboard and locker provided.

There followed weeks of lectures and study on human anatomy and physiology. There were long hours in the dissecting room with the senior professor, working methodically through the human body.

The curriculum split the year into four terms covering Leg, Arm, Abdomen, Thorax, Head and Neck with special lectures on Embryology, Neurology, Biochemistry, Organic Chemistry, Histology and Pharmacology. It was all very perplexing to Tim at first – and Neil became pessimistic over the whole business.

The class came under the jurisdiction of Adam Hepplewhite, a long, cadaverous second professor with black-rimmed *pince-nez* precariously balanced on the end of a narrow, pointed nose.

'The Stomach,' he would say in a dry, bored voice, 'consists of the omentum, colon transverse, jejenum mesentery, ileum, caecum with appendix, colon descending and rectum thus.' Dramatically he unfolded a coloured chart and emphasised his remarks with a wooden pointer. 'You are here for second MB which will graduate you on your next stage towards your final degrees. I trust that none of you had the idea of becoming comic doctors,' he coughed wheezily. 'Because in the lecture papers here,' he pointed to the pile on his desk, 'there are a good many comic answers. In fact, Mr Farley has the somewhat irregular idea that the organs of the abdomen are also to be found in the thorax.' Tim squirmed under the sarcasm. 'And Mr McAlister's abdomen apparently is deficient of at least four major organs. How he survives I do not know. Mr Carter and Mr Ferguson appear to have no stomachs at all and very little for work either.' He grinned at his own pun briefly before his dry precise voice rolled on and on and on.

The friendship which had grown between Neil and Tim developed solidly. The Scot was a bulwark upon whom Tim leaned, and they shared many a confidence together.

Tim explained to Neil how he had come to be at Queen's. He talked about Alice and Charlotte Bemmington, about Professor Bernardt and the crucial changes which had occurred in his life during the past years. He talked of the will and the insight of Charlotte: now that he was at Queen's he felt that he belonged here, that it was as it should be, and that somehow Charlotte had known that this would be so all along.

For his part Neil extolled the virtues of Kiledin and the glory of its isolation.

'In good weather the scenery is magnificent,' he enthused. 'And Queen's is not so very far away. In fact this is the nearest medical school to Kiledin in the whole country.' He paused for a moment as if considering this statement. Then he thought about Tim Farley. He liked the chap, something deeply sincere about him. He knew that Mordrake, his father, would like him too. 'I have a sister,' he said one day. 'Stella. We get on all right when we're together although she can be a bit unpredictable at times. She does what she wants to with people and there's been many a broken heart at Kiledin, I can tell you.'

'She sounds a very interesting person,' Tim said.

'Interesting,' Neil laughed. 'Oh yes Tim, lad. Stella's interesting all right.'

From time to time they took walks into the city of Edinburgh, keeping up a ritual of outdoor exercise which revived the flagging brain and re-oxygenised the body cells. The studies were very demanding, the professors exactingly absolute and the atmosphere one of complete concentration. To visit St Giles or John Knox House, or any other of the fine edifices of the city, provided a safety valve for their pent up energies. It was fast approaching the end of the second term with a month's holiday to consider, and Neil in a burst of characteristic generosity invited his room-mate to Kiledin. Tim was overwhelmed. 'Thank you,' he said. 'You're very kind but . . .'

'You have to see Alice and the folks?' It was a question.

'Yes. It wouldn't be very fair if I didn't, would it?'

'No, I suppose not. Anyway, there'll be another time,' Neil said.

'I'd like to ask you to come home with me except that . . .' began Tim. Neil cut him short. 'I know how it is, old chap.' He smiled, not a little embarrassed and took one of the cigarettes from the crumpled packet which Timothy offered. They smoked in silence for several seconds, and then the Scot opened his despatch case and drew out a thick wad of papers.

'No time to lose,' he said. 'I must rub up on Biochem. You might ask me a few questions from the text book when I'm ready. Must say I'm looking forward to term holiday next week.'

He bent his head to work and Tim, after several seconds of pensive gazing through the open window, went to his own books.

Silence settled.

2

Alice was waiting for Tim at Melchester station on his arrival, and she hugged him to her, eyes bright with affection.

It was late spring and once outside the grimness of the town the hedgerows were a riot of colour. All was green and new, bursting with life, birds chirping, nature emerging fresh-faced after the sharp bite of winter's snow and frost.

'How do you like it, Tim, how is it at Queen's?' Alice was eager for news as they tramped the lanes towards the Georgian house.

Tim told her. He told her of Neil McAlister and the bond that had sprung between them.

Alice squeezed his hand. She was attractive in a blue summer dress which matched her eyes, and the grace of her body had a lissom fullness about it, her lips soft and cherry red and her cheeks tanned to the colour of bronze.

'The others are longing to see you, Tim, especially the professor. He's a sick man now that Miss Charlotte has gone, and Dibbern's rheumatics are terrible.'

The Georgian house looked magnificent in the sunlight. The lawns were still lustrously green and perfectly groomed, but he saw with dismay that the rest of the gardens were in a bad state.

'Dibbern can't manage them any longer,' Alice said, shaking her head regretfully. 'When Charlotte died it seemed as though the spirit of the house went with her.'

It was obvious to Tim just how much Dibbern and Professor Bernardt had succumbed to time when he shook hands with them.

Over tea he told the professor of all that he was learning at Queen's. They talked again later on, and Tim was amazed at the vast knowledge of his friend. The old man spoke succinctly on histology and embryology.

'I'm rusty, Tim,' he said. 'But I think that I could have taken you to second MB, but I'm old, Tim, now, too old.'

'Did you qualify in medicine, Professor Bernardt?'

'I have the Viennese Royal which is equivalent to the Bachelor, and several other qualifications. My life has been a peculiar mixture, Tim.'

The youth looked at the professor with awe. 'No,' he said. 'Your life has been wonderful.'

'Perhaps,' the old man smiled. 'You will go farther in medicine than ever I did, and you have a gift of which as yet you know nothing. You have the gift of God.'

Tim looked at him from narrowed eyes, wondering perhaps if his aged friend had suddenly gone senile.

The old man, reading his eyes, smiled.

'The brain is still active, my boy,' he said. 'It's the body which has failed. I've never mentioned this to you previously, Tim, but if I die before you are at the top, I want you to follow these lines for your future conduct. You must not fail at the examinations because there will not be sufficient money to put you through again. Of all things, Tim, avoid women, because if you have the choice of a lovely woman and an hour's study you will choose the woman. I know that well enough.' He smiled and the youth remembered that Jules Bernardt had told him of this once before. 'When you have passed second MB, boy, you will be drafted to a hospital for further study. I want you to go all out for your bachelorship in both medicine

98

and surgery, with the diplomas of the Royal Colleges as a second string if by any wickedness of the devil you should fail. Exercise your body well, Tim, or you will falter under the strain. Go out, have leisure, play games, mix with people and eventually you must become a surgeon. You must specialise for primary FRCS and then finally, the Fellowship itself and any other honours you can collect on the way. I'm telling you this early, Tim, because I might not be here to advise you next time you come and you must be a surgeon, Tim, understand, you must be a surgeon. Orthopaedics, that's a fine branch, you'd like that.'

The youth was overwhelmed, perplexed lines furrowing across his brow.

'I think I understand, sir,' he said, protest in his voice. 'But you realise what you are asking me. Why, the Queen's men speak of the surgical Fellowship with bated breath, the unattainable.'

'There are a great number of surgeons in the world, Tim, many of them bad ones.'

'Yes, I know, but am I equipped for all this? Have I the brain, the – '

'Don't worry, boy, just try. If you don't succeed – ' he shrugged. 'Charlotte wanted it, Tim, and she was very special to me. You understand, don't you?'

'You know I understand, professor.' His eyes were moist. 'I'll try for both of you. I'll try my hardest.'

He talked it over next day with Alice as they sat together in the tangle of thorns which was all that remained of the rose garden.

The girl failed to understand what the greater part of it was about. The degrees and honours and the innumerable stages confused her.

'Don't worry, Tim,' she said, taking his hand in hers. 'Don't worry.'

'How does it feel to own the house?' he asked, changing the subject.

99

'Just the same – and it will always be waiting for you, Tim, you know that.'

Her lips were a little parted as though she wanted him to kiss her.

'How are you for money, Alice?'

She shrugged. 'There's not a great deal, but enough. I don't spend much on myself. How are you finding it?'

'I smoke, that's about all; but the fees are heavy. Neil McAlister embarrasses me sometimes by insisting on buying theatre tickets. I must contrive to return his kindness.'

'I have a little money, Tim.'

'No, not from you, Alice. I have Miss Charlotte's bounty which must suffice. Most of it will go on fees, and I must school myself against other attractions. Professor Bernardt is keeping a tight rein. He allows me a pound a week which means that I must make do and mend. My clothes, shirts, even shoes are all out. But I don't want to sponge on you. I'll be all right.' He was passionately sincere. 'I must pay you for my stay here. I can, you know. You owe me nothing, Alice. Rather the reverse, don't you think?'

She pouted. 'That doesn't come into it at all. You are my guest and you must look at it that way or I shall be cross.' She smiled suddenly, her teeth startling white. 'We mustn't quarrel, Tim, not you and I, ever.'

Tim busied himself in the garden for the next few weeks, chatting with old Dibbern who could scarcely walk, and seeking his advice about matters of horticulture. In the evenings he pored over his books, revising and subjecting himself to the professor's questionnaires.

For Alice he bought a silk scarf out of his precious shillings, and took her to the Melchester theatre where they watched with delight the episodes of a thrilling drama.

New term came round all too soon and the girl was

surprisingly tearful as she waited at the station with him for the train which was already ten minutes late.

He kissed her goodbye, a brief fleeting movement of his lips which stirred her deeply and then, complete with books and battered suitcase, he took his seat in the carriage. The train chugged its way out of the station. He waved frantically and then was swallowed up in the huge tunnel which burrowed under Melchester's main street.

Once back at Queen's he was eager to start work but Neil McAlister, lounging in the worn armchair by the open study window, was not in the least bit keen. Kiledin had apparently provided him with amusement that he had been loathe to leave. As for revision, he horrified Tim by admitting that he'd not done any.

'Old Hepplewhite will relish this. He'll skin you.'

This profound observation stirred Neil to the sudden feverish haste of turning out all his books willy-nilly in a vain attempt to make up for his laziness. He did not succeed.

In the first week of lectures, the Professors' Hepplewhite, Robertson and Dickens reduced Mr Neil McAlister to shamed confusion, and then to a lesser extent did the same with Tim Farley and each one of the other members of the class. And so the term wore on, cramming, cramming, cramming until even Neil's ruddy complexion had taken on a yellowish tinge.

Third and fourth term merged, with the exception of a week's break between, and there was no time for family visits. The intensified studies became exhausting and Tim, remembering Professor Bernardt's warning, took up squash for exercise. He was now beginning to think in the way that it was intended that he should. His arm, as he struck a flying shuttlecock, was no longer just an arm – it had become Humerus, Ulna, radius, Carpus, Metacarpus and phalanges, covered by biceps, triceps, supinator longus, and flexor carpor radialis for muscular co-ordination. He thought and breathed anatomy.

The year rushed on. Tim spent Christmas with Alice, lavishly spending his tiny store of pocket money, and then he was plunged into fifth term at Queen's. The college professors calmly and methodically steered the course, and then the desperate revision for a month.

The term's leave was a week away before Tim was aware of it.

'You must come to Kilendin this hol,' Neil insisted. 'I'm depending on you. The exams are on the doorstep and I'm scared. You know that I need someone around to keep me at it. We can do revision together and the air's good and sweet with the sea less than a hundred yards away. The weather is warm, too, and we can keep fit swimming and walking. There's nowhere like Kiledin in the spring, and I have a tendency to dissipate my time at Blairgowie when I should do better to keep away. It's urgent now, Tim, that I don't slip back. You're more of a sticker than I am. Will you?'

The reasoning was so sound that Tim with refusal on his lips checked himself. Neil had been a good friend to him.

'All right then, I'll come.'

'That's fine. We'll dine on grouse every day.' Neil stopped suddenly. 'Do you think that Alice and the others will mind too much?'

'I'll write and explain. Alice will understand. It will be in my own interests too, because we can arrange oral checks which are a big help and I don't want to fail. I couldn't fail.' He was anxious.

Neil smiled kindly. 'You won't fail,' he said reassuringly. He looked at the shapeless tweed jacket, the too short trousers, the large knotted tie. 'No,' he said again. 'You won't fail'.

The last week fled and Queen's poured out its jaded students for the term recess. Tim, clutching the worn suitcase which contained more books than anything else, hurried down the drive with his friend, desperate to catch the Elgin train which offered the only connection to Blairgowie.

Tim stood at the bottom of a steep rise gazing up at Kiledin's battlements, fast fading as the first purples of night closed in. The countryside was wild with vast clumps of gorse bush and heather. Appreciatively he sniffed the perfumes of the evening.

'So that is Kiledin,' he said.

'That is she. Home of lairds, victim of seiges and still impregnable.' Neil was proud of it.

They climbed the hill and then Tim could see the grey breakers which came almost to the walls.

'Tide's in,' said Neil. 'When it goes out again there's a beach and rocks. You'll like it.'

'Yes, I'll like it all right. Thank you for inviting me.'

'Come on now. We'll beard the lion in his den.'

A maidservant opened the door to them and then Tim's arm was being pumped by Mordrake McAlister.

'Heard a lot about ye. Neil says you're special and so you are.' He was hearty and affable.

'Where's Stella?' Neil asked.

'Out.'

'Mercer Grant, I suppose?'

'Aye, he's still around.' He shrugged. 'Annie will show ye your room, young Tim, and then we'll all have a wee drappie.'

Tim's room was vast and solid with huge timbers and carpeted floors. Three latticed windows overlooked the crashing sea and a fourth gave view to the moors. He unpacked his precious books and hung his Melchester suit in the wardrobe. Towel and soap were provided and he washed in cold water from the decorated china ewer. Refreshed, he made his way down the winding stone steps and so into the drawing room where Neil was pouring whisky.

'This'll warm ye,' said Mordrake, handing him a good measure.

'I'm not cold, thank you.'

'It'll warm ye anyway. Tip it down, lad.'

Tim saw Neil empty his glass in a single gulp and hesitantly attempted to do likewise. A second later he was coughing and choking, his face crimson.

'I said it would warm ye.' Neil's father was in a frivolous mood.

'Welcome to the prodigal son!' said a gay voice and then Stella McAlister was in the room, dark eyes travelling swiftly over the newcomer.

'Hullo, Stella,' Neil greeted her. 'This is Tim Farley from Queen's.'

'How do you do?' she held out a slim hand.

'How do you do.' His eyes locked with hers for a fleeting instant and he felt an uneasy sensation race down his spine. So this was Neil's sister. He had heard about her but he hadn't expected to see anyone so wildly beautiful.

'I hope you'll like Kiledin.' She was speaking to him again.

'I'm sure I shall, thank you.' His reply was polite, formal.

'Have a nip, lassie,' Mordrake said expansively. 'We've almost choked our friend here.'

Stella shook her head. 'Not for me, thanks.' She crossed the room with light step, the grace of her body feline.

'She's wonderful,' Tim thought, his mind enraptured. 'And she dislikes me.'

The next days were spent in leisure. Tim combed the gloomy passage-ways of Kiledin, stood on the battlements, thrilled at the vast panorama flung out before him in greens, browns and purple. The glinting sheen of the sea, now peaceful, spread to meet the smooth turquoise expanse of sky.

Neil taught him to ride a horse and they chased over the countryside, calling at Blairgowie for bacon and kidney grills with glasses of cool home brewed Scottish ale.

Towards evening they pored over their books and discussed the hazards of the future. Tim saw little of Stella who, even in their infrequent meetings, hurt him with her indifference.

Neil was quick to observe his friend's discomfort, just as he was aware of its source.

'Don't worry too much about Stella,' he said one morning as they were climbing the rocks on the shore. 'She can be a cruel little devil when she wishes.'

'And apparently she wishes.'

Neil shrugged. 'I wouldn't say that exactly. She's hostile at the moment but I expect she'll come round. Forget all about it and if she goes out of her way to be awkward ignore her or give her a piece of your mind. She'll respect you for it.'

Tim smiled, unable to imagine himself giving Stella 'a piece of his mind' as Neil so glibly termed it. 'I'll remember,' he said, sagely.

When they got back to Kiledin, Mercer Grant was there and reluctantly Neil introduced Tim. Mercer took his hand limply, his eyes examining him insolently. Tim flushed under the scrutiny and Neil's mouth tightened.

'Ah, another tyro!' sneered Mercer. 'I'm sure that with two of you among us we need never fear cough, cold or chill.'

Stella laughed and Neil turned on Mercer furiously.

'Shut up,' he snapped. 'Farley happens to be a friend of mine. If that's to be the talk damn well stay away from Kiledin. For two pins I'd pitch you out neck and crop now.'

'Now children,' Stella chided and Tim, looking with astonishment at Neil and Mercer, saw by their eyes just how much they hated each other.

'I said the wrong thing perhaps,' Mercer apologised casually.

'You did,' Neil growled. 'And don't say any more wrong things or else – ' He left the threat unfinished.

The incident delighted the girl, who chuckled again, while Mercer scowled.

'I amuse you, Stella, perhaps?'

'At the moment yes. I find the whole thing very very funny.'

Mercer swallowed his next remark and looked angrily at Tim, who for some obscure reason suddenly laughed too.

Mercer's fist were clenched as he moved to within an inch of him.

'Shut up!' he snarled, white with rage. 'Bloody well shut up!'

Tim, suddenly feeling the violence of the old Scottish lairds of Kiledin take hold of him, brought up his fist and punched Mercer on the nose. Mercer toppled to the floor with a crash.

There was a short hurtful silence and then Neil said, 'Good shot!' and the tension broke.

Timothy moved back to give Mercer room to stand up and braced himself for attack.

Mercer rose slowly, shaking his head, a thin trickle of blood seeping from his nostrils and then, face pale, eyes burning, he turned on his heel and walked from the room. The front door closed with a slam.

'He's yellow,' Neil said. 'I always knew that he was.' He grinned suddenly. 'There goes your latest beau, Stella. It's a pity the old man had to be out and miss it all.'

Stella shrugged and Tim stood waiting for her anger, but she didn't mention the incident further.

'What made you hit him?' Neil was frankly curious.

'I don't know,' Tim shook his head. 'I get fed up with people constantly having a down on me, I suppose. I'm sorry anyway. If you want me to leave just say so.'

'Leave!' Neil was incredulous. 'It's the best thing that could have happened so far as I'm concerned, but Stella will brood over it, won't you?' He turned to her.

'Shall I?' The girl shrugged her slim shoulders.

'Yes, not because he's any loss to you, but because he

106

hadn't the guts to hit back and you hate gutless people. But you'd see him again out of sheer perversity, wouldn't you?'

'Oh, shut up! You're always nagging.'

Another quarrel was imminent when Tim suggested, 'Let's go for a ride and all cool off.'

'I'm on,' Neil agreed readily, 'and Stella's sure to come now that she has nothing to do.'

'I'll not ride with either of you. I'll ride alone, thank you.' She turned her back on them and gazed stonily through the window.

'You'll get used to it,' her brother remarked as they went to saddle the horses. 'Her pride's wounded because her champion wouldn't fight, but watch out for her, Tim, she's a queer kid and she'll remember.'

They rode leisurely to suit Timothy's lack of experience, when with crashing hooves and no sign of recognition, Stella passed them on the moors, her face frowning, crimson lashed into her cheeks by the exertion.

Next day Neil went into Blairgowie alone and by evening he hadn't returned.

It was a warm night with a full moon and the sea nestled the beach placidly. Tim stood on the rocks inhaling the invigorating air when Stella suddenly appeared and came towards him.

'I'm sorry I was so bad tempered yesterday,' she said unexpectedly. 'I move in fits and starts you know. Are you enjoying it at Kiledin?'

'Very much, thank you.' It was the first time that she had ever approached him in conversation and he was surprised.

'Can I walk with you?'

'I'd like you to.' He smiled shyly and she smiled back, her teeth a white flash in the scarlet curtain of her mouth.

It was light enough by the moon for him to see the grace of her in the thin linen frock she wore, and he was both alarmed and enchanted.

They walked for some time and then came to a little bay of silvery sand. She was very close to him as they approached a huge rock split and worn by the sea which stood almost in the centre of the beach, and he could smell the expensive perfume she used.

'Like to swim? It's wonderful just here.' The question startled him.

'I don't swim well, but that won't matter, I suppose. How long will it take for us to go back for costumes?'

'There isn't any need, is there? You use one side of the rock and I'll use the other.' Her dark eyes mirrored his and he saw a glimmer of something that frightened him.

'If you like,' he gulped, 'I'll run back for the costumes while you wait here.'

'You're afraid,' she accused scornfully. 'I thought that you were studying to be a doctor. Is there anything to be ashamed of?' Her mouth was suddenly laughing, her eyes filled with merriment, daring him.

'N-no, I suppose not.' He looked at her quickly and then looked away again. 'All right, I'm game,' he agreed, watching the moonlight flicker in her tawny hair. She was breathlessly desirable and he strove desperately to stifle the strange emotion which suddenly possessed him.

It left him as quickly as it had come and he felt detached and remote. He gazed at the curved precision of her calmly.

'Which side of the rock do you want?' he asked.

'I'll take here.' She vanished from sight round the far side and with deliberation he began to undress himself.

She was wearing little and in less than a minute he heard her call 'I'm going,' and then he saw the shadowy white length of her slip from behind the rock and run full speed into the sea.

'It's deliciously warm,' she called to him, and then taking off the last of his garments he enjoyed the sensation of the warm night air brushing gently over his skin.

Still with the same deliberation he walked casually over

108

the moonlit stretch of sand and into the water. It was deep quickly, and he swam slowly towards where Stella was performing skilful roll dives which sent the water eddying in glinting lanes.

She was a powerful swimmer, with a crawl stroke which cleaved a lane in the placid sea. She veered towards him, slipped easily beneath the surface and then bobbed up at his side.

'What do you think?' she asked teasingly.

'Nice, warm and terribly scandalising.'

'I love it.' He could see that she did, her eyes shone with pleasure and her cascade of hair, soaking wet, floated on the surface of the water round her neck and clung to her face.

'Why didn't you tie your hair up with a handkerchief?'

'I forgot, but who cares? I'll race you.'

'And win, I expect.'

She won with practised ease and a strength which made it possible for her to swim in seas that were rough and dangerous.

They cruised in the calm water for almost half an hour, Tim floating on his back to conserve his energy, Stella at full rip all the time.

'I'm going out now,' he said. 'I'm getting tired.'

'Wait – I'm coming with you.'

She swam up to him and after a few yards their feet touched bottom. They stood facing each other waist deep in the green fluorescence and Tim looked deeply into her challenging eyes, cat-like in the moonlight. Her hair hung wetly to the honey richness of her shoulders. Her breasts were upswept and swung gently as she breathed. She was adorable and desirable and yet no shock touched him – his resolution as solid as the rocks. He felt removed from the situation. Mammae, areola, lymphatics, lobulles, ampullae, he thought to himself. The glands lymphatic he knew were connected to the axillaries of the armpit . . . then suddenly his mind went blank and refused to work.

'How shall we dry off?' he asked, wading forward towards the beach. 'I have nothing save a handkerchief.'

'That'll have to do!' she laughed.

They were clear of the water, Stella close beside him and he stared fixedly ahead. Never once did he bring his glance down to look at her, not even turning his head as he spoke.

'You're afraid of me, aren't you?' Her voice was soft and gently coaxing.

He smiled then, and his grey eyes lit up so that she was puzzled.

'Am I?' he said. 'I wonder.'

'Sit here.' She indicated a spot on the beach. He shivered, but sat down beside her. 'I'm not usually a moody person but you did annoy me over that business at the house.'

'And this is your revenge. You wanted to shock me?'

'In an abstract sort of way, yes. I thought you a bit of a fuddy duddy. I'm no post-Victorian woman you see, Mr Tim Farley, who intends to be slave to some male chauvinist. I'm me, Stella McAlister.' She looked at him thoughtfully, a half smile on her face.

'You sound chauvinistic yourself,' he defended.

'Oh, no I'm not,' she countered. 'I'm not an aggressive sort of person. Neither am I shameless. I don't deliberately try to shock, but the trappings of the post-war period are, for women, almost as bad as those endured at the time of the suffragettes.'

She suddenly held his hand. 'You know that I've decided that I quite like you?' she said. 'At least you're not self-opinionated like so many men.'

'No. I quite definitely am not,' he replied firmly. 'But let's stop fencing, Stella shall we? You know, it's a strange thing but until a few years ago I had never seen a woman undressed.' He suddenly squeezed the hand which was holding his. 'Seeing you bathed in moonlight and so exquisitely and beautifully formed reminds me very much

110

of that occasion. Then it was an accident – but this was stage-managed, Stella McAlister my wild Scottish lassie.' He suddenly rolled over until he lay close beside her, his face only inches from hers. 'And what have you got to say to that, then?'

Momentarily her eyes widened and then she laughed. 'My breasts are as two roes that are twins. My lips are a scarlet thread,' she quoted from the *Song of Solomon*. 'And I've had sex before, even if it was only with Mercer Grant.'

'Oh Stella, Stella,' he breathed, moving away from her. 'I had no intention. No thought.' He suddenly began to tremble, and she reached out and hugged his nakedness to her.

'You see how I have regained the advantage,' she chided. 'And now you are really shocked, aren't you?'

'Yes. No. Well it was a bit unexpected.' He stirred slightly, and then impulsively, recklessly covered her body with his own.

'You're a great surprise to me, Tim Farley,' Stella conceded and then she was quietened as, bracing his forearms in the soft sand, he kissed her gently and then more forcefully, until she suddenly felt an indefinable thread of magnetism reach out to her like an extra heartbeat.

'God,' she murmured. 'What has happened to me? Where has my independence gone? Nothing has ever been like this before. Nothing.'

She lifted her slimly elegant hand and placed it gently over her breast. He could feel the shape of her fragile femininity, her pulse that spoke to him like an endearment. Suddenly he knew from the little tremors rippling over her that she was in tears.

'Oh, my dearest dear, my dearest dear,' he said, scooping her up and hugging her close to him, crushing her breasts and biting gently at her neck.

'This has all gone wrong,' she sniffled, holding him

111

tightly. 'You should be subjugated by now and eating out of the palm of my hand.'

They laughed together then, the moonlight reflecting the whiteness of their teeth, the tidal water lapping lazily near to their feet.

The girl stood up, the pale lunar light sculpting her body.

Timothy, enchanted by the visual perfection of her, reached out a hand and held the calf of her leg in light fingers. It was as though a power supply had been switched on. She caught her breath, her body suddenly erect.

'I love you, Stella,' he said, releasing his hand.

She kneeled in the sand and kissed him, pressing his face between her perfumed breasts and then laughing, a trifle wildly, she was off running down the beach, her long and perfect legs striding with the elegance of a gazelle.

He chased after her and together they rolled into the sand in a flurry of entwined limbs.

'Stella, Stella, Stella,' he panted, thoroughly out of breath but cradling her to him once more.

Finally they lay back and looked at the brightness of the stars. There was a silence between them that went on and on and on. Only the faint sigh of the wind trespassed on their stillness, and the occasional cry of a late gull. No mention was made of the fact that he had said that he loved her.

'I'm getting cold,' she murmured, suddenly shivering slightly.

'We'd better get dressed,' he suggested. 'We must return to Kiledin. It's getting late. Neil will be back and probably is already wondering whether anything has happened to us.'

She nodded.

'And, Stella,' he began.

She looked up at him.

'Thank you for your delightful company and for – for' he stumbled over the words 'for just being you.'

Quickly they returned to their arbour and dressed.

He took her hand in his and together they walked across the beach and turned in the direction of the towering battlements of Kiledin.

3

Tim was up early next morning and went down to the shore for a before-breakfast walk.

His mind was a turmoil of conflicting emotions, blotting out everything save Stella McAlister. The image of her was with him as he walked: the vivid recollection of her beauty, her wildness, the passion he had stirred within her even as he himself had become inflamed. Initially she had intended to embarrass him but then she had loved him honestly. She had crossed the narrow bridge which could divide hate from love.

Tim came to the silver bay with its huge crag of rock, and looking out to sea he knew that despite his resolution not to be involved, not to be diverted, he was so already.

Stella had completely bowled him over. What remained of the calm, clear thinking he needed for the tasks ahead? What of the need for single-mindedness? There had been no place in his curriculum for love; but now it seemed that there could be no place in his love for the curriculum.

He thought with unease of Alice. He was a traitor, a renegade. He had betrayed his past – he who had no rights at all. He was charity's child fighting for a place in the world.

He cursed aloud and with bitterness. He would never be able to concentrate again, never. The weakness of man

113

and the warning words of Professor Bernardt crashed in his ears.

He stumbled away towards Kiledin where Neil met him on the flagged terrace.

'You feel all right?' he said at once. 'You're pale and there's fever in your eyes.'

'And in my brain too.' Tim's voice had an unusual harshness. 'No, I'm all right, a bit upset, that's all. Forget it.'

Neil looked at him curiously for a few seconds more, and then made no further reference to the matter.

'Breakfast's ready. Millie asked me to call you, she saw you slip out.'

The thought of breakfast sickened Tim but he said, 'ready when you are.'

They ate in silence, just the two of them. Bacon and eggs, hot rolls, coffee.

'Any ideas for this morning?' Neil asked.

Tim had no ideas but he said, 'we could lock ourselves away somewhere and carry on with the revision. We're way ahead but we can't do too much I suppose.'

After breakfast they plugged for two hours on the brain; Pons Varolii, Medulla Oblongata, Cerebellum, Cerebrum, Pituitary Body, Optic, Olfactory, Frontal Lobe. Sweat broke out on Tim's face in his vain effort to concentrate. In the centre of the brain diagram Stella's picture kept appearing – always without clothes.

'Mind if I pack up now?' he asked suddenly. 'I don't feel up to it just at the moment, I'm sorry Neil.'

The Scot was amazed.

'This is one thing I never would have believed Tim. I'm lazy, I have to drive myself but I never thought to see you call a halt.'

'I'm a bit mixed up today. I'll straighten things out by tomorrow.'

'You're in love with Stella, aren't you? Don't answer if you don't want to.'

114

Tim looked at him. 'Yes,' he said quite deliberately. 'I'm in love with Stella.'

Neil's expression didn't change. 'I'm sorry,' he said. 'She's very attractive I know, too attractive. Try and forget it, Tim. You're young, you'll soon get over it and if you'd rather leave Kiledin I'll know why. Everyone falls for Stella, but I didn't think that you would.'

For a moment a smile lifted the edges of Tim's mouth.

'You're making a mistake, Neil,' he said. 'You think that I'm loving hopelessly, don't you? But I'm sure Stella loves me too. That's what makes it so bad.'

Neil's eyes widened incredulously and his mouth dropped. He recovered himself with an effort. 'Has she told you so?' he asked shrewdly. 'She's ignored you to the point of rudeness until yesterday, don't forget.'

'She hasn't told me in so many words, but I know.' His mouth was puckered, furrows suddenly etching into his brow.

'If that little bitch is foxing you, toying with you, I'll . . .' Neil stood up, his face very red, and Tim heard his feet hurrying down the corridor. He called to him once but Neil didn't heed.

Stella was playing with her spaniels, Pancho and Jan, in the lee of the stables when Neil found her. His grip on her arm made her wince.

'Look, Stella,' his voice was tight with anger. 'You know why Tim came to Kiledin, don't you? You know the special reasons. That snivelling whelp Mercer Grant will be back this afternoon – use your wiles on him but leave my friend alone. Do you understand?'

'What has Tim told you?' She was suddenly scared at his ill-concealed rage.

'That he loves you and that you love him. What's more the silly young idiot believes it.'

'I'm sorry. I don't want him to worry, but I think that I do love him. It's true, you see.'

'What?' Neil's arm dropped limply. 'What game are you trying to play, Stella? Don't spoil his chances. Call it quits, you've sunk him as low as the sea bed as it is. Aren't you satisfied with that?'

'Neil,' she said, her voice surprisingly gentle. 'I love Tim. I can't help it. I love him, don't you understand? It happened yesterday, I don't know how or why, but it happened. He has this – charisma and it . . . it seemed to reach out, and envelop me. Before I knew where I was it had taken me over. Who is he, Neil? What is he?' And then she was suddenly crying, while Neil, utterly shocked, utterly confounded, held her in his arms.

When he returned to the study he was dazed and confused.

'Well?' Tim said from the casement.

Neil dropped into an armchair and lit a cigarette.

'Yes, you were right,' he said softly. 'But don't forget, Tim, Stella changes like the four winds. She honestly means it now but . . .'

'She might change.'

'Yes, Tim, she might.'

'That's something I must chance. I didn't want this to happen, Neil. I'd never even considered it. You know about me, I have nothing to offer, nothing.'

'There's your mind, Tim, and your honesty.'

'Oh, hell – let's go down to Blairgowie and have a drink.'

Tim avoided Stella all next day, locked in with Neil, striving for composure and concentration. They studied hard and neither by word nor sign did the girl interfere.

As time passed so Tim slipped back into the routine, and he found that he could absorb his work without Stella trespassing too much on his thoughts.

In the evening he wrote lengthily to Alice describing Kiledin, but he did not mention Stella. He had received no word from Alice despite his own two letters and he wondered if anything could be wrong at the house.

116

Soon the holiday was half over and they had covered a tremendous amount of work.

Stella and he spoke to each other formally, making polite conversation, which Neil endured with a pained expression. Mordrake served out his whisky liberally and occasionally Neil and Tim went into Blairgowie.

The bright warm weather broke on the third week, and torrential rain swept Kiledin. Angry seas roared and threshed up the shingle.

'Come on, let's watch the sea in the rain,' Stella suggested in an invitation which did not include Neil, and in heavy black mackintoshes she and Tim went out into the pouring rain and climbed the headland overlooking the sea.

The rain lashed down ceaselessly and a grey blur obliterated the horizon. The sky, lead-coloured, seemed to dip down right into the ocean. Giant whitecaps roared furiously, beating the rocks with savage hands. The hiss of the rushing water echoed above the storm and Stella's delighted laughter was soundless in the raging elements.

They walked carefully to the tip of the headland, the drenching rain beating on their uncovered heads. Stella's hair lay wetly against her face, shining drops of water clinging to her lashes and rolling down her cheeks like tears.

'You're a mad, wild girl to come out on a night like this,' Tim cried. He shook his head vigorously so that the rain whirled in a fine spray from his streaming hair. He felt warm and comfortable inside the thick mackintosh, and his senses were alert and responsive to the thresh of the torrent and drumming of the surging water.

'I like it,' Stella laughed. 'I like to be close to the power and pleasure of nature. It shocks the senses and brings other pleasures – the feel of a warm towel, the nice friendliness of a crackling fire. Kiss me.' She held up her wet mouth, and Tim kissing her briefly tasted the salt of the spray mixed with the rain.

117

'Where will it all end?' he thought as he held her cold hand. This dangerous, maddening girl whom he loved helplessly. Why must he love her when it was so essential that he should have no such restrictions?

'Do you love me?' she asked, as if reading his thoughts.

'Yes,' he said. 'Yes, I do – but I shouldn't, Stella, I shouldn't.'

'Kiss me again,' she said.

She held him this time and her restless mouth, dewy with rain, awoke him to the desire for her that he knew he must fight. Her love was inescapable, whole, burning and without any boundaries. She wanted him all the time, recklessly, daringly, with no thought of the consequence.

'God, but I love you.' She choked and the despair in her voice told him that she was fighting against her own feelings – and was losing.

His neck had grown hot and the pouring rain did nothing to cool it. Her kisses were like a torch on dry timber, spreading quickly, consuming him so that he was weak with carnal lust, which ashamed him but which he could not fight.

'We must go back,' he said hoarsely. 'Now, before the rain gets any worse.' He almost laughed at the stupidity of the remark. The rain couldn't possibly get any worse and anyway, they had come out into it voluntarily.

'Kiss me again,' she insisted. 'Kiss me again.' This time she held on so hard with her arms locked around him that he slipped, and they rolled on to the sopping wet earth together.

Her eyes were flaring into his as he struggled to get to his feet and she held him down. He felt as weak as a child and then, jumping to her feet, she hauled him up with her extended arms.

'I'm sorry,' she said. 'Forgive me.'

Her mouth near to his ear laughed gaily and her strong

teeth suddenly bit into his neck. 'That's because I love you,' she said. 'Come on now, a bath and hot whisky. Doubtless Neil is already thinking the worst.'

He was unsteady as they fought their way back to Kiledin in the high wind, and the light as the maid opened the door made him blink. Neil was in the big hall talking to Soames the manservant, and he looked up grinning.

'You'll be as wild as she is,' he called to Tim. 'Take off your things and come and have some cream of the Highlands.'

'Afterwards,' Tim shouted halfway up the stairs. 'I want a rubdown first and I'm dripping water.'

'It's raining outside,' Neil mocked. 'Or hadn't you noticed it particularly?' But Tim with Stella on his heels had vanished round the curve of the stairway.

He was back a quarter of an hour later, pink and ruddy, eyes glowing.

'By God!' Neil remarked, pouring him a stiff glass. 'This rain and romance mixture had something to recommend it. What have you been up to?' He was frankly curious.

Tim shrugged. 'Just watching the sea.'

'And getting wet,' Stella said, gliding into the room. 'Some for me, Neil, please. See what I told you about pleasures?' she said, turning to Tim. 'Nice, nice fire.' She held out her hands to the blaze and the flames etched her with darting bronze shadows.

The rest of the holiday fled. They rode horses, raced the barking, excited dogs, bathed in the cool sea and loved passionately.

Neil and Tim sweated over their books and charts for almost four hours every day – and drank more of Mordrake's Highland cream than was good for them.

On the evening before departure Stella crept noiselessly into Tim's bedroom as he was packing, and wound her soft arms about him.

'I shall miss you,' she said, tears glinting in her eyes. 'I shall miss you terribly. Promise to come back soon.'

'I promise.' There was a lump in his throat. 'But it's not right that I should live on you like this, like a damned parasite.'

'Don't be ridiculous!'

'I – I – ' He didn't go on but he thought guiltily of Alice and the professor. They depended on him, and he had behaved so unlike himself. 'Stella, is this meant to be, you and I? Is it, or have we been insane?'

'Could you stay away from me, forget me?' Her dark eyes locked with his.

'No, I know that I couldn't.' He groaned and then her perfumed mouth, soft and warm, silenced him.

'But if we go on like this it will be madness,' he said as she broke away. 'Just madness.'

'Let it be. You cannot deny me, you cannot. Let it be madness so long as we love.'

He slept badly, troubled by dreams, and in the morning he was pale and dark eyed.

Stella accompanied them in the dog cart to the station, and waved with a tiny handkerchief until the train was out of sight.

Their journey was uneventful, and back at Queen's all was hurry and bustle as the students returned full of their holiday experiences.

Grim routine soon quelled their loquaciousness and before long they were busily sweating out last term quarter. This was the final part of the past eighteen months of arduous training – still only a stepping stone towards the ultimate goal.

Tim received a letter from Alice apologising for not having written him at Kiledin. He knew a peculiar shame as he read the missive, and settling himself at the study desk wrote a long narrative back to her.

Next day he was startled to receive a letter from Nancy

Weston. It was very formal and yet he knew that she must somehow have become curious about him. He wrote back at some length telling her about the progress of his career. She was doubtless groomed by now for the role her mother wanted her to play. Tim didn't expect to hear from her again. There didn't seem much point really. He had been a good friend to her in childhood, but it all seemed so long ago that it might never even have happened.

The first mail he received from Stella amazed him. She had poured into it the whole of her passion so that it was almost as though she had stepped out of the envelope herself, vibrant, reckless, dangerous. He would never be able to write like that, never. He read the letter again. He didn't dare show it to Neil.

The atmosphere in the lecture rooms became intense as the examination time crept round. Nerves became ragged, tempers short as quietly, insistently, the professors put the final touches to their handiwork.

Faces were grave as the students trooped into the main lecture room for the commencement of the examinations. Rules were strict and the initial talking subdued; the first papers came out and the silence became tomblike. Then came a thin rustle of sound as each student pored over the questions.

Tim's stomach wobbled as he read the first. His mind was a complete blank. He knew nothing – nothing at all. Eighteen months of back-breaking work and he couldn't even begin to write. He counted ten and took a firm grip of himself.

The first question read: *With illustrations of the visual area say how the cerebral cortex and its functions have been investigated.* Picking up his pen he wrote smoothly and fluidly. All outside noises were shut away from his mind. There was nothing to worry about, nothing to fear. He wrote a thousand words, two thousand, and then went on to the next question.

The examinations occupied the best part of five days, with five written papers, three practicals and two 'vivas'. The climax of the ordeal was the Anatomy viva in which Timothy with amazing calm suffered Professor Hepplewhite and a visiting examiner to question him rapidly for almost an hour.

And then it was all over.

Life at Queen's College was now over for Tim Farley. He arrived at Melchester by an early train and Alice met him on the platform. She was pleased to see him but there was a change in her. Her face was grave and unsmiling.

'How long will it be before you know the examination results?' she asked.

'About a month, I expect. Whatever happens, Alice, I tried.'

'Yes, I know, Tim, I know. Tim, there's something happened since you've been away. It will shock you, but it was his own wish that you should not be told. Tim, Professor Bernardt is dead. A stroke.'

There was a silence, long lasting so that it seemed that Tim would never speak.

'We'll walk back, Tim, it will be best. The air's fresh in the lanes, you'll be able to think.' Alice held his arm.

'When did it happen?' he asked in a quiet level voice which gave nothing away; but the muscles of his face had sagged and he was white.

'When you were at Kiledin. He was able to speak for a while and forbade that you should be informed in case your work suffered. The professor left no money, Tim, but you have his blessing. Your affairs are now in the hand of the solicitor.'

'Yes . . . I shan't cry, Alice.' He looked into her eyes. 'He's happy now, he's with Charlotte.'

'That's how I looked at it, but it upset me. He was a strange man, Tim, but I had affection for him.'

'How did Dibbern take it?'

'They were never friends, but it upset the old man. *He'll* go on for ever, although his rheumatism is a worry.'

'You had all the responsibility, Alice, and you never told me.' He felt deceitful. Alice had had to bear all the trouble alone whilst he was making passionate love to Stella McAlister. He choked down the lump in his throat. 'I wish you had written to me, Alice.'

'The last words he ever spoke were that you should not be told until after the exams.'

'I didn't deserve that.' He all but told her of Stella. He had stabs of conscience, because he knew that Alice thought so much of him, perhaps too much. He was not equal to her respect, her hopes for him.

The lawns of the Georgian house were still shaved, for they had become old Dibbern's pet pride. The front beds, too, were well stocked and weedless – but Tim saw the ruin of the other gardens and the half empty glasshouses. Alice had taken on the rose garden, and early buds were ripening for their first burst of colour. It was tranquil here and Tim thought of his headlong love for Stella McAlister. 'I love Alice too,' he thought, 'but in a different kind of way.' He squeezed her arm affectionately, and she suddenly wanted to hold him, to tell him how she felt towards him; but her will was strong. Like her tears, she cried from within, holding everything inside, shutting off her mind. Tim seemed so mature now, so worldly.

'Where was the professor buried?' he asked.

'With Miss Charlotte. I thought it would be nice, I'm so horribly sentimental.'

Tim lazed for a month, during which time he heard almost daily from Stella, urging him to go to Kiledin.

He lied to Alice about the letters, saying that they were from Neil. Then he did receive one from Neil which confused matters so that the one lie turned into two; he said that the second letter was from Neil's father inviting him to Kiledin again.

In her heart Alice didn't want him to go but she said that he must; and then on the next day a long narrow envelope arrived.

Tim knew what it was and with beating heart tore the flap open. He read quickly and his face lighted up. He had passed second MB and had to report on the following Monday to the Leystone City General Hospital for further training towards his finals.

He wrote the news to Neil and Stella, excusing himself for not visiting them, lying that it was because Alice needed him at the house. Within, he knew that he was afraid, that Stella's wild inescapable love would destroy his control, obliviate everything save the desperate incredible intimacy which left him so helpless.

He heard almost by return of post that Neil had been successful and was going to a hospital in Aberdeen, which would be handy for Kiledin. Stella, whilst offering congratulations, promised to come immediately if he did not visit her at the very next available opportunity. He wrote at length that he adored her, that he could think of no one else – and then he thought of gentle loving Alice and felt miserable.

He departed on the Monday for Leystone in Yorkshire, still in the same worn suit which Alice had carefully pressed for him. There was a new suit in his case, new shoes and an expensive silk shirt and tie which the girl, with characteristic generosity, had given to him.

Brownstone pillars shadowed the main entrance of Leystone City General. Tim sniffed the odour of carbolic and anaesthetic with misgiving, adjusted his tie with its too large knot, and reported. Three years of clinical study lay before him.

For the next three months he worked away in the casualty department, learning the elements of diagnosis and the practice of simple anaesthetics. He was responsible to the resident medical officer who became to him a

124

sort of god, and from whom he learned much. He learned also from the Casualty Officer and the surgery sister – and secretly enjoyed having the patients address him as doctor.

The courses of lectures in Medicine, Surgery and Pathology progressed quickly and for a time Tim fell into a state of utter confusion. He pored over his text books and learned quickly the cardinal signs of *tumor, dolor, rubor, calor* and *functio laesa*. He made friends with a young student named Kennedy, and discussed prospects. Both decided to take the MB, BS degree and the diplomas of the Royal Colleges. Tim came to his decision over Conjoint despite the extra examination fees involved, because of the second chance it would give him should he fail in the major finals.

He wrote regular news of his activities to Neil, who replied in like vein. His letters to Stella in response to her impassioned narratives were severe and carefully worded. Alice, not a good letter writer, corresponded infrequently but with a simplicity which touched him.

Leystone was almost two hundred miles nearer to Kiledin than was Melchester, and on his first week's holiday he gave in to Stella's pleas and threats and went to Kiledin. Neil's own arrangements would not permit him to visit Kiledin at the same time, and Tim was disappointed and a little scared at having to contend with Stella alone.

She was waiting for him with the inevitable dog cart – gay, laughing, more beautiful than he had ever before seen her.

'Darling,' she kissed him quickly, holding his hands and looking up into his face.

Touching her lightly, he knew that the turmoil would start all over again. Even to see her increased his pulse rate, and her lips, smiling and provocative, tempted him to crush her to him, to kiss her and to go on kissing her until he was exhausted.

'You're bad for me, Stella,' he said as they started for

Kiledin. 'I love you to the point of foolishness, but where can it end? I cannot offer you marriage, I have so much work before me and so little time.' He shrugged. 'I have no money either.'

She laughed with curving mouth, eyes shining.

'You're here, Tim, that's all that matters. My father would accept you and put a settlement on you, but I know better than to suggest it.'

Tim bit his lip vexedly. 'I never would, you know that.'

She clung to him then, and the horse made its own way. 'Oh Tim, Tim, promise to love me always.'

His lips touched her brow. 'Always,' he said. 'Always.'

The battlements of Kiledin rose from the top of the hill to meet them, towering and growing as they approached. A bulwark of huge grey granite, timeless, fearless, looking down on them cautiously as though they were strangers.

It happened on the Thursday. They spent the early part of the week wildly riding on the moors, bathing in seas that for Tim's capabilities as a swimmer were dangerous. They walked under the stars at night, stood on Kiledin's battlements looking to the grey turgid water and vowing eternal love. Then the climax broke over his head, rolling him before its tempest helplessly.

They were sitting in the lee of a hill sheltered from a high wind and the first cold splashes of rain, arms linked, lazily at ease and listening to the cry of the gulls, and the rising howl of the gale.

'It will be rough tonight,' the girl said with expert knowledge. 'This is the forerunner of a storm.'

He held her cradled in his arms, the perfumed smell of her hair teasing his nostrils. Gently he bent and kissed her ear and she twisted in his arms, her mouth red and glistening. He crushed her to him, his mind fighting the wild turmoil of his bodily desire. 'Oh, my dear!' His voice was husky. 'When I am away I feel so safe, so secure, but when I am near you I am helpless. What is there about you, Stella, that drives a man so wretchedly insane?'

She smiled provocatively, her eyes alive, her lips curling inches from him, tempting him. Her slim hand lay on the waxen paleness of his cheeks – and the throaty growl of the gale increased to a thundering tempo.

She turned to him fully, pressing him back with her red mouth, pressing him back and down, levering her virile young body against him so that the nearness of her set his desire flaring. His breath shuddered, and his fine hands clutched at her so that her dress tore, leaving the whiteness of her shoulders gleaming in the thickening gloom.

He kissed her cheek, her ear, her throat, unable to restrain himself, and then her soft mouth covered his in dangerous, insistent urgency.

With a decisive twist of her own hand she ripped her dress from top to bottom. She was completely naked beneath, with her tawny hair lying in rich cascades between the firm contours of her breasts.

'Oh my love, my love,' he said holding her tightly. 'You terrify me and enchant me at one and the same time, but I cannot live without you.'

He pressed her into the cold wet earth and held her in a caress that knew neither time nor place.

The rain lashed fiercely but they were oblivious to its urgency, the magic of their being together the only thing that mattered in the whole world.

They lay for an hour clinging and exhausted, squeezing every precious drop from the incredible intimacy which they had generated, whilst thunder crashed in the dark sky as though contemptuous of Timothy's surrender to this bewitchingly beautiful girl.

4

There followed a year of 'General Firms', at the hospital. Each group was composed of six students, four courses a year alternating medical and surgical, taught by the honorary physicians and surgeons of the staff.

Tim was allocated patients in a ward and went the rounds with the Honorary and his Registrar. He had to know everything about his patients – the diagnosis, drugs, case history, and treatment.

The lectures each week were stepped up to eight, with practical classes in bacteriology and pathology. Tim studied fat text books on haematology, clinical biochemistry, orthopaedic surgery and forensic medicine.

Some of the students lived out but he was lucky enough to be allotted a tiny room on the premises where he lived amid the smell of ether and carbolic.

On the surgical 'firm', Tim, now almost twenty-two, was not only allocated patients in the ward but attended operations in the theatres. When his own particular case came up for operation, he put on sterile mask, gown and rubbers and assisted the surgeon as dresser.

He did special 'firms' in midwifery and Gynaecology, delivering some ten babies. He covered diseases of children, and anaesthetics, pathology, vaccination, fevers and spent eleven weeks in the opthalmic and skin departments.

He wrote long letters to Alice and Stella as the months dragged by. He drove himself hard, exercising very little, tiring his brain and body, eager in his thirst for knowledge. Never once did he leave Leystone. Neil wrote him an invitation but he refused. Then Stella, in desperation at his absence, came to visit him.

He felt the old desire burn as soon as he saw her.

'I don't like you any more, Tim Farley,' she said with concern as they walked the hospital grounds together. 'What on earth's the matter? I haven't seen you for weeks.'

'There's nothing the matter,' he replied. 'Nothing at all, but I do have my medical finals soon. As I explained in my letters, there's only a little while left to prepare.'

'Yes, and the little whiles seem like an eternity.'

'They do to me, too,' he said regarding her gravely. 'I have kept away deliberately and you know why. You affect me in such an extraordinary way that when I am with you I don't care about anything else. There is also the possibility that if we carry on as we are I shall make you pregnant sooner or later.'

She laughed at this. 'Good,' she said cheerfully. 'Make it sooner then rather than later because I don't mind in the least.'

Tim slipped his arm around her waist and squeezed her affectionately. 'What am I going to do with you?' he asked in mock despair.

She looked up at him smiling. 'That's easily answered,' she replied. 'We'll take a room and spend the night endeavouring for you to get me pregnant.'

At Stella's insistence they finally booked into a local hotel, an old-fashioned little place which smelled faintly of beeswax and cigar smoke.

They ate an early supper, and later as they undressed together in their bedroom Tim was conscious of the fact that if he didn't get her back to Kiledin soon, the exams would be lost for ever. Stella slipped off her clothes with incredible rapidity: in an instant she was naked, and so alluring that Tim could feel the instant trembling of his desire.

'Damn the exams,' he muttered – and then she was laughing in his arms as he scooped her up.

During the night the end fell off the bed with a crash, so great were the convulsions of their intercourse, and a worried voice on the landing shouted through the door: 'is all well inside?'

'Yes,' Stella gurgled artfully in reply.

'Very well inside, thank you.'

After their hectic night together Tim resolutely shut out everything from his mind save his work, and then he took his finals. Afterwards he did not dare face poor neglected Alice, nor did he visit Kiledin. He took cheap lodgings in Leystone while he waited for the results, and half starved on his tiny weekly allowance. He was thin to the point of emaciation: face gaunt, eyes large and luminous. Finally the envelope arrived – and he was Timothy Farley, Bachelor of Medicine, Bachelor of Surgery.

He was a qualified doctor now and he smiled as he savoured the fruits of his efforts. Doctor Timothy Farley, one of the Farleys of Bath. Would anyone recognise Tim Swaine, cottager's son, now? Tim thought of his childhood that seemed so long ago, of Tom and Mary Swaine, Miss Grosvenor the schoolmistress and his childhood friend, Nancy Weston. What was she doing now? Married, perhaps, to some aristocrat, as her mother wanted. He thought too of Charlotte Bemmington. It had been her wish that he should become a doctor, and he knew with inner conviction, just as Professor Bernardt had told him, that he must go further. He must be a surgeon.

He was tired, his head ached, but he read the letter again. He had done well at the examinations, exceptionally well: there was the offer of a house job at the hospital. A house job, what achievement! He lay face downwards on the bed and was suddenly weeping, and then he slept. He slept for hours as though his whole body was relaxing after the years of living on his nerves. He slept without dreaming, his face placid, a little smile hovering at the corners of his mouth. When the sun at its zenith spilled liquid gold into the mean room it lit his face in a kind of ethereal splendour, and etched the long sensitive fingers of his hands in bright relief against the coarse blankets covering the narrow bed.

It was dark outside when he awoke, his head aching. He washed in cold water and put on his clean shirt and best suit. He felt as though he didn't want anyone's company just then so he went out, alone, and walked for a long time thinking and planning his future. The house job at the hospital wouldn't pay much, but he could never afford a private practice: the last letter he had received from Charlotte's solicitors left him in no doubts as to that. There was a little over a hundred pounds remaining. So he would have to earn his keep at the hospital. He would at least have a decent room of his own in the living quarters in which he could concentrate on the surgical primary.

He stopped at a little old-fashioned inn, drank a glass of beer and smoked two cigarettes and then returned to his lodgings. He wrote a long letter to Alice and one to Neil McAlister. Then he wrote a shorter one to Stella.

Alice replied quickly – congratulating him, urging him to carry on with his work, longing to see him: her secret love and pain could not have been clearer to him had she written with her own tears.

Neil's reply came speeding on the wings of success. He had qualified – conjoint, nothing great – but Mordrake was buying him a practice. Doctor Neil McAlister, it sounded impressive, a certain loquacious dignity was suggested in the name.

Stella's letter of congratulation overflowed with her own joy and enthusiasm. She insisted that he come at once to Kiledin – and Tim was in no mood to argue. He left for Scotland that same day.

* * *

131

Neil was appalled to see Tim's paleness and the thinness of his body. 'You're not well, Tim,' he said seriously. 'You've been overdoing it.'

'Thanks for the diagnosis,' Tim mocked good-humouredly. 'I was afraid to relax in case something went wrong at the exams. I was lucky. I did well enough to get a house job. I shan't starve at any rate, and the next hurdle is already decided.'

'The Fellowship primary, of course. Can you never have enough?'

'I must do it, Neil, I must.'

'Yes, I know, old chap. Stella will be in soon, she had to visit Blairgowie. You two are hitting it off well, aren't you? Must say I'm surprised. Here comes my father.'

The door opened and Mordrake, his face florid as ever, came over to Tim and wrung his hand.

'Congratulations,' he boomed. 'Kiledin is already taking on the atmosphere of a hospital with all the new doctors around.' He beamed. He was proud of Neil's success.

Tim grinned back. 'How do you like having a doctor son?' he asked.

'I like it. My boy's done well. He had no need to study the way he did. I'm proud of him. I'm proud of you, too, and Stella tells me ye might become son-in-law to the laird of Kiledin. That would be two doctors in the family, and bonnie too. Tim lad, ye can have a practice like Neil. My little Stella wants it and anything she wants – ' His shrug indicated that anything Stella asked for he would provide.

Tim couldn't say anything, he was so filled with emotion and confusion. Neil saw how it was with him and clapped a friendly hand on his shoulder.

'Tim is ambitious, father,' he said protectively. 'There are other honours to be won. And now, how about a little drop of whisky, Tim? The best, of course.'

Mordrake smacked his lips in anticipation.

'Angus McGregor – the doctor in Blairgowie – says I'm

to have nae more. It's ma blood pressure, but with two doctors at hand I can take the risk. Ye'll know what to do if anything goes wrong.' He grinned lazily, enjoying himself.

Suddenly they heard a door banging; the sound of dogs barking excitely and feet running.

'Good afternoon, Doctor Farley!' cried a familiar voice – and then Stella was in his arms, unconcerned by the presence of Neil and her father. She was gay and laughing, her lips warm with love, her eyes welcoming him. 'My Tim,' she said, 'My Tim.'

'Stella. Stella darling,' he whispered, 'how I have missed you.'

Later that evening Tim and Stella walked up to the battlements, alone.

'You didn't get me pregnant after all!' Stella laughed. 'I think the shock of the end falling off that bed disturbed my hormones!'

Tim grinned at her audacity. 'You're delicious. You know that I am going to marry you, don't you?' he announced.

'I should think so, too. Who has a better claim?' He knew that she was laughing at him, but he loved every minute of being with her.

'You probably know that your father has offered to set me up in practice, at the same time as Neil?'

'Good. That's settled then.'

'Not quite.' He knew that she was still laughing at him. 'You know it's not?'

'Oh darling, darling of course I know. Neil never stops talking about your plans. You will take the post at the City General and eventually qualify for the surgical Fellowship. Won't you?'

'I must.'

'Of course you must. We will marry when it is convenient to your career and not before.'

'I am delighted to hear that you think as you do.'

'I shall enjoy being a doctor's wife – provided, of course, that you are the doctor. In any case a ring and a church ceremony won't make any difference to us.'

'No, I suppose not.' He paused, considering her implication for a moment. 'I'm sorry I couldn't accept your father's offer, but I don't want the help of other people. Not now, not any more.' His eyes suddenly clouded, and then he poured out the whole story of his life.

He told her of the Farleys of Bath.

'I've never even been to Bath,' he observed drily. 'Apparently my father was a sort of black sheep because he broke away from the family and married a housemaid. That was my mother. She died before I was old enough to remember, and my father was killed at Mafeking.'

'I wonder why Charlotte Bemmington wanted you to be a doctor?' Stella asked shrewdly.

'I've often thought about that myself,' replied Tim. 'But now that I am finally qualified I feel that it is only the beginning. There seems to be so much more that I have to do, so much more that I have to achieve. I hope that you can understand?'

Stella looked at him kindly, her eyes bright with her love for him. An inexplicable something bound her to him. Stella could have had any one of a hundred men, but Tim Farley had made her feel as she had never felt before.

That night Tim slept badly, his mind clicking mutinously, his thoughts a jumble. Somewhere at the back of his head a little voice was speaking to him. Telling him that no matter what, he must finish his task. It was as though his destiny was being revealed to him. 'A great surgeon,' the voice said. 'The power of God is in your hands, the power of God. A great surgeon, a great surgeon.' Dreams, dreams. He turned restlessly, twisting first to one side and then to the other, and always the voice was there speaking to him. He shuddered in his sleep and woke sweating, his fingers tearing at the coverlet as though a monster was trying to strangle him. The room was still dark, and he heard the crash of the sea in the distance, and the voice slowly receding as though it had entered a long narrow tunnel.

He listened but there was nothing further.

'Hallucinations,' he thought. 'Damned hallucinations. I need a sedative.' And then he laughed. 'Diagnosing myself. What I actually need is good food, fresh air and exercise, and rest for my mind. It's ticking like a dynamo.'

He slid out of bed and stood looking through the window high up near the battlements. The black clouds rolled to one side and a sliver of watery moon appeared, its pale silver light filling the room with a ghostly gloom. He glanced at the clock on the bedside table. It was half-past four. Suddenly he heard a creak, and spun round as the door opened quietly. Then Stella was standing at his side, a silk dressing-gown tied loosely about her. Her hand touched his cheek and he slipped his arm around her slender waist. For some reason he thought of the voice of his imaginings. Had it been a sign? a warning? He shook his head reproachfully, but his senses were relaxing in the fragrance which came from the girl. Everything went from his head at her nearness. Beneath the silken gown he knew that she was naked.

She laid her head on his shoulder and her perfume enveloped him.

'What wickedness,' he murmured. 'I don't applaud my action beneath your father's roof.' He picked her up and laid her on the rumpled bed. As he did so the sky darkened. There was a gutteral snarl of thunder, a flash of lightning and the rain began to hiss in torrents.

5

The car pulled slowly into the white winding drive leading to the large country house, carefully navigated the sweeping curve between the landscaped gardens, and drew to a standstill a few feet from the gloomy porchway of the front door.

A short dumpy little man climbed out, adjusted the tilt of his smart, grey trilby hat and ran lightly up the three steps of the porch. Adjusting his hat again he banged heavily on the brass knocker, which he was just able to reach by standing on tip-toe.

He waited expectantly for long seconds, and had impatiently checked his wrist watch twice before the door finally swung open to reveal an old gnarled butler, with grey feathery side whiskers and a bald pate, regarding him with ill-veiled curiosity.

'Good afternoon, sir,' the butler observed mildly. 'You wish to see Sir William?'

'Yes I do.' Obviously the visitor did not like to be kept waiting. 'My name is Farjeon. Doctor Henry Farjeon. Please ask Sir William if he can spare a few moments.'

'Come inside, Doctor Farjeon. I'll tell Sir William you are here. Your name is familiar, sir.'

'I'm an old friend of Sir William,' Farjeon said, following the butler inside and taking off his hat and coat.

'Henry!' boomed a deep voice. 'What the devil brings you down here?' Sir William Gadsby walked from the drawing room with long strides and began to pump Doctor

Farjeon's hand. 'I thought it was your voice I heard. This is a pleasant surprise. Come into the den, my dear chap, and have a toddy. Take Doctor Farjeon's things, Matthew, he'll be staying to dinner.'

Sir William clasped an affectionate arm around Henry Farjeon's shoulder and led him into his private den.

When they were comfortably seated and had sampled the whisky liqueur, Sir William cocked his head on one side. He was a big man in his late fifties with thick black hair and an unwrinkled, long jawed face. His eyes, icy blue, were keen and intelligent and even sitting he made plump, grey-haired Henry Farjeon look absurdly small. 'Is this a purely social call, Henry, or strictly business?' he asked curiously.

Farjeon smiled. 'A little of both. It's nice to see you again, William, of course – but there's a motive.'

'I thought so,' Gadsby gestured knowingly. 'I hardly expected you to come all this way just for the pleasure of seeing me. How's your wife?'

'Well, thank you, and yours?'

'Tolerably well. Mustn't complain I suppose. Hospital keeping you busy?'

'Too much so, too much so.' Farjeon shook his head regretfully.

They were amiable and at ease; life-long friends who had seen little of each other during the past years. Both busy men – Doctor Farjeon chief of the Leystone City General and William Gadsby knighted and one of the world's leading surgeons – and both clever men. Sir William was so exceptionally brilliant that he had brought himself great honour and respect. But now, they were just two men, friends in a room who had known each other since student days.

Henry Farjeon slipped out a pigskin cigar case and offered it to Sir William. They trimmed the cigars and lit up contentedly. Soon the room was hazed with blue fronds of swirling smoke and filled with a pleasant aromatic odour.

137

'And now, Henry, in your own good time tell me what it's all about?' Sir William crossed his long legs and looked at Farjeon with twinkling eyes. He knew that it must be something special, because Henry rarely called just to pass the time of day. He looked at the sparkling cut glass decanter on the Queen Anne table near to the door, and waited.

'We've known each other a long time, William, you and I,' began Farjeon in his precise crisp voice. 'I respect you and I like to think that you respect me.'

'That goes without saying, but I won't interrupt. Carry on Henry.'

Farjeon tipped the ash from his cigar into the tray at his side.

'Remember, William, two or three years ago when you called to see me at the City General and have a look round. You mentioned at the time that you were keen on finding an assistant – someone to follow you, someone prepared to work solely for the love of it, someone who had something to give and feel that he must give it, abundantly, selflessly and go on giving. I said at the time that no such person existed and you agreed with me.'

'Yes, I remember,' Sir William nodded his head. 'I was inspired watching your chaps rushing about. I used to do the same, feeling so important, so useful, until I fell into the trap of the money lure. Yes, I remember well enough. I have my large house, my servants, friends who aren't worth a fig some of them, that is. I'm what you might call a fashionable surgeon now, aren't I?' he grinned, and Henry Farjeon smiled at the self deprecation.

'Seriously, William,' Henry went on, 'I've found your man; he's only just taken his primary but is amazingly capable of major ops. He's exceptional – a youngster, about twenty-seven and untidy as a scarecrow. You wouldn't believe it and – ' Henry Farjeon's eyes narrowed, 'there's something special about his hands. I don't

138

know what, nor do any of my colleagues. He himself is unconscious of anything peculiar, but it's there all right. I've never known anything so weird before. The nurses are scared of him. We had a cerebral tumour – a bad business, absolutely no chance at all – but something urged me to let this young man do it. I told him to carry on and the theatre sister looked at me as though I had gone mad. I watched his every move meticulously. He went to work with a speed and precision that bewildered me. He never spoke once except to the theatre sister and his eyes were lit like two bloody Christmas tree candles. The patient lived and the op time was the fastest I'd ever seen done. It floored me absolutely. I've watched him since and it's been the same every time. There's nothing he can't handle and he's never lost a patient. Theoretically, of course, I do the ops but it's not my doing – it's his. A month ago he did a palliative on a hopeless case. It was deep tissue and he could only guess at the penetration, but he went right ahead and so far the patient is fine, just fine.' Farjeon suddenly realised that he was sweating and began to dab his forehead with a pocket handkerchief. 'Excuse me,' he said.

'And you think that this young miracle man is the one I've been looking for?'

'Could be. He wants to go in for Orthopaedics, and no one knows more about it than do you.'

'It's a queer business, Henry, but coming from you I know that it can be nothing but true. What is this youngster's name?'

'Farley, Timothy Farley. There's no question, of course, about the Fellowship – he'll eat it. He fascinates me, damn him – and those hands, they're not ordinary hands. I'd never noticed before, but they're almost too perfect. They're the sort of hands you'd expect to find on an exquisite sculpture. But he's an unhandsome little beggar, and if you saw him you'd think he'd been down a mine or behind a plough. Absolutely no idea of looking the part.'

'I'm very curious, Henry, and I thank you for telling me.

Henry you're a fine surgeon.' Sir William sipped his drink meditatively. 'You know things, don't you? A hundred and more tricky ops a year, a man of vast experience, respected, listened to, and my friend – my real friend. I want you to bring Farley to the Royal Elizabeth, Henry, one day next month. I'll let you know the exact date. I shan't take any risks, mind. I'd like it better if he had already won the Fellowship but I'll watch him as you did, and I think that I can stake my reputation on your word. In fact, I know I can.' A smile played at the corners of his handsome mouth. 'Never did I think to see the practical, staid, experienced Henry Farjeon so much impressed – disturbed I might even say – by an apprentice.' He was jocular. 'Come, Henry, another cigar.' He proffered a cedarwood box of Coronas. 'I feel almost excited.'

The Royal Elizabeth Orthopaedic Hospital at Kimberley was world famous in 1926, and Sir William Gadsby recognised as one of the best known surgeons of the century. His exceptionally brilliant work had earned for him an early knighthood, and in private practice he had made a fair sized personal fortune, though it had given him little joy either in the making or since. For three years after the war his particular skill had been available free of charge for the needs of the wounded, maimed and crippled. His name was held in the highest regard by people who had cause to know, and by those others who knew just as they would know the status of a particularly outstanding sportsman. It was common knowledge.

The Royal Elizabeth had a pleasant location in the centre of a verdant piece of countryside, flanked liberally with majestic woodland and providing recreational facilities of the finest kind. The buildings themselves were long structures of pleasant blue and white stone, surrounded by glass-covered verandahs on which the patients sunned themselves. There were some very good doctors and surgeons on the staff, and the pick of the nursing profession.

Sir William Gadsby was proud of the Royal Elizabeth, a pride justified by the large number of successful treatments for twisted bones and limbs, and deformities of children.

It was Wednesday and Gadsby, seated in a comfortable armchair in his office, briefly turned the pages of a new surgical text book. He looked up as the door opened and smiled as Elaine Watson, his theatre supervisor, entered with her diary.

'I see you have young Joyce Smith booked for today, Sir William. Any time in particular, or will you tell me when you have seen the charts?'

'I saw them this morning. She'll be all right. Prepare the theatre and let me know.' Gadsby lit a cigarette. 'By the way, Elaine, you once nursed at the Leystone City General, didn't you?'

Elaine Watson nodded. 'Three years,' she answered, wondering what was coming next.

'You'd know Doctor Farjeon, Henry Farjeon, wouldn't you?' He looked at Elaine calculatingly and she nodded.

'Good man, would you say?' Gadsby looked at her again.

'Very good. Why do you ask?'

'He's coming along today. I know you're a fine girl, Elaine, and I wanted to see how you'd react to my question. You see, Doctor Farjeon is a life-long friend of mine, and he's been telling me about a young surgeon he has at the City General, a Mr Farley. Gave him a very fine name, so good in fact that I thought maybe – well, you know.'

Elaine smiled. 'Doctor Farjeon would be quite confident of what he was talking about, I can assure you.'

'I'm glad that you have as much faith in him as I have. It's nice to know that somebody's on my side. I shall give young Farley Joyce Smith's talipes calcaneus to do. Tell

141

me what you think, Elaine, and don't worry – I shall be in overall charge.' He tapped the ash from his cigarette into the tray. 'And now be off with you, and see that everything is all right in the theatre. Don't want it looking like a recreation room with visitors coming.' He smiled at Elaine's obvious disgust that her operating theatre should be compared with anything but an operating theatre.

As Sir William stubbed out the last inch of his cigarette he heard the squeal of wheels on the red cinders of the drive outside and, looking through the window, saw Henry Farjeon's car draw to a standstill. He hurried from the room to meet him.

'You're early, Henry,' he said. 'Come inside and have a warm. There's a bite to the air, enough to freeze you in that dreadnought contraption you choose to drive about in.'

He skipped up the steps like a youngster and Henry Farjeon and Tim followed.

'This, of course, must be Mr Farley,' Gadsby said once they were in his room. 'How do you do.' He held out a strong brown hand. 'I've heard a lot about you from Farjeon here. He speaks very highly of you.' Gadsby watched the flush creep into the young man's thin cheeks.

'I'm sure I don't deserve it,' Tim said softly. 'And I'm very pleased to meet you, Sir William.' Their eyes met and Gadsby saw the muted spark in the grey level gaze of the young man.

'Farjeon's right,' he mused. 'He does look untidy but there's something about him.'

He motioned to a chair. 'Sit down and make yourself comfortable. We'll have a whisky later on and I'll show you round my hospital, which no doubt will bore Henry,' he chuckled.

'You know that's not right,' Farjeon protested. 'True, most of the thrill has gone, but then I'm getting old.'

'Had a good trip down?' Gadsby asked him.

'Fair. I stiffen up after the first twenty miles or so. A definite sign of age, I suppose.'

142

'Nonsense, nonsense.' Sir William dismissed the suggestion with a wave of his hand. 'I don't want to rush you, gentlemen, but my theatre sister is preparing for one of my patients. A young girl, talipes calcaneus, quite bad, but I think we can put her right. Ever seen a talipo, Doctor Farley?' He looked at Timothy shrewdly.

Tim shook his head.

'Know how it's done?'

'Theoretically, yes,' Tim answered. 'Depends, of course, on just how bad; but in any case I should need to make an examination before I could say more.'

'Well, you'll be in the theatre with me so you'll have every opportunity. In fact you can come with me to see her now. I'll show you the X-ray plates too.'

The children's ward was beautifully constructed with long sun windows, radiation heating and animals painted on the cream glazed walls. It was spotless and fresh smelling, with the gay chatter of patients who were not bodily ill and did not quite realise the seriousness of their being there.

Joyce Smith sat up in bed as she saw Sir William enter in company with the ward sister and Tim. Henry Farjeon had stayed behind, warming himself at Sir William's fire and contemplating the arduous journey they had to face on their return.

Joyce was seven and was very pleased with the pink rabbit she had for a bed companion. She smiled at Tim who smiled back reassuringly. 'She's had a soother,' Sir William informed him. 'That's why Nurse has put her to bed. Kids frighten easily when they see the inside of the operating theatre. I've brought a new doctor to see you, Joyce.' He sat on the edge of the bed and held the little girl's hand. 'Show him that foot of yours, the one with the funny little bend in it.'

Joyce obediently poked her foot from beneath the blankets, while the ward sister stood by and wondered what this was all about. What could an obviously young

143

doctor possibly have to say that Sir William did not know already?

Gadsby watched Timothy handle the child's leg. He took special note of the young doctor's beautifully shaped hands, the confident way he held the limb, and the sudden flexing of the strong fingers which moved as though wanted to caress the deformed foot into its correct shape.

Tim knew he was being tested, and felt suddenly scared. 'It's not so serious as some,' he said in a low voice. 'Your plates probably show need for removal of parts of the tarsus and metatarsus: possibly an adjustment is required in the oscalcis.'

Sir William nodded. 'I'll show you the plates,' he said. 'And you'll see how right you were. Ready, Elaine?' He turned to Sister Watson as she walked in.

'Ready, Sir William.'

'Righto, we'll be down at once. Come Farley.' Tim followed him downstairs where they were rejoined by Dr Farjeon. 'Wash up, gentlemen, and I'll show you the best op room in the whole country.'

Masked, gowned, and with tight-fitting rubber gloves casing his fingers, Timothy stood next to Sir William at the operating table. Joyce Smith's eyes had closed in sleep and the anaesthetist held her pulse between thumb and forefinger. The child's leg protruded from beneath the sheet. Dr Farjeon glanced at his pupil for signs of agitation. There were none.

Sir William weighed up in his mind where Timothy should incise the foot. He had gone over it with him beforehand on a chart to be quite sure. Farley had been superb in his reasoning. He passed over the scalpel and Timothy held it lightly.

'Show me where you will incise?'

All eyes were on Timothy as he went over the incisions with light gestures.

Sir William smiled. 'I have faith in you,' he said. 'I will not touch your hand. Carry on.'

The atmosphere was tense as Tim went to work. He performed capably and cooly, passing and repassing instruments, cracking bone with a little chromium hammer and dividing tendons with measured skill. Gadsby watched his sure movements with respect. Once he looked at the intense grey eyes, the little flame burning. He didn't speak.

Timothy looked at the anaesthetist for assurance, then he swabbed out the incision. His mind was tight with concentration because he wanted to be successful, and yet he did not care whether he impressed Sir William Gadsby or not. He thought of Stella: beautiful, wonderful Stella. She was perfect; she'd never need to lie on an operating table and have twisted limbs straightened.

His fingers moved lithely. The time had gone quickly, conversation had been brief. He was aware of Mr Farjeon and Sir William Gadsby watching his hands; he was aware of the blue-eyed look of the theatre supervisor. He ligatured and sutured, and then arranged the elastic tension strip and the plaster to support the changed bone structure while the scalpel incisions healed. More treatment would have to follow – massage and foot exercises – but he knew that he had given little Joyce Smith a new foot.

They were drinking whisky in Sir William's den as soon as they had cleaned up after the operation. Tim refused a cigar, but had developed a liking for the smooth golden liquid ever since his regular visits to Kiledin. From half closed eyes he watched the strong-jawed face of Sir William Gadsby: the master surgeon, a physician and surgeon better than the best; a man revered all over the world for his great professional skill. He was the man whose disciple Tim would like to be.

Henry Farjeon blew out a cloud of sweet-smelling cigar

smoke which climbed slowly ceilingwards, and clung in side eddies to the cut glass whisky decanter which sparkled in the firelight. There was a hint of snow in the air outside, and he looked anxiously at his big gold watch.

'How would you like to work with me, young Farley?' Sir William asked, breaking the silence. 'Here in Orthopaedic. Doctor Farjeon assures me that you need have no fear of the Fellowship. I'll brush you up on general surgery too, but orthopaedics are my strong line.'

Timothy blinked his eyes open. He knew that he'd done well in the theatre, but he hadn't quite expected this.

'Without being more highly qualified, you mean?' He was astounded. Sir William Gadsby nodded. 'It's not usual, I know, but you have it in you, Farley, in your hands, and in your mind. It's been born with you, I can tell. You're no ordinary person. I thought that Henry was biased in his praise of your ability; but I know it to be true now that I have seen you at work.'

Timothy looked at Doctor Farjeon.

'Come, what do you say?' pursued Sir William.

'I can't think of anything I'd like better, sir. I hope that I'll not let you down. It rather overwhelms me.'

'It's a wonderful opportunity, my boy,' said Farjeon. 'And next year I am quite certain that you will get your Fellowship with ease.' He smiled, and Timothy suddenly recalled the very beginning of it all, when he and Neil McAlister had struggled with elementary medicine and physiology, often despairing and looking towards the finish of their training as they would to a road which had no ending. The surgical Fellowship itself now stood pinpointed as the unattainable shining star. But the brilliant Doctor Farjeon had just assured him that he would pass with honours – and next year, too!

'When you have taken the last hurdle,' Sir William broke in on his thoughts, 'there will be other work that I shall want you to undertake on your own – work that I haven't time for. I am neglecting my private practice already. If all goes as I want it to, Farley – and that depends on you, of course – you will follow in my footsteps. You will be the second Gadsby.' He smiled wryly. 'How would you like that?'

'I want no personal honour, sir,' Timothy assured him earnestly. 'But I want so much to perform the miracles that I know you have performed.'

Gadsby narrowed his eyes. 'Miracles, Mr Farley, miracles?'

'I think so.'

'You have the miracle hands if any of us do, Farley.' He stopped and pondered, looking at Timothy with keen eyes. 'I wonder.' His brow creased into a frown. 'Ridiculous,' he murmured, and then he turned abruptly to Henry Farjeon who had raised himself stiffly from his armchair.

'Time we were off, William. Long way to go, you know.'

'Nonsense, you can't go without staying to lunch. We shall go to the George Hotel in Kimberly, and I'll not hear a word against it. Come on now, no shilly-shallying. You're always worrying about pushing off, Henry,' Gadsby accused in vexed tones. 'We shall be having roast duckling with all the trimmings, and more whisky, I can assure you.

'No, no,' Farjeon protested. 'No more whisky. Remember I have to drive the car.'

'Oh well, perhaps you're right – but you will have lunch, and another cigar. We'll go down to the George in that old boneshaker of yours at once.' He grinned at Timothy, who smiled back in appreciation. To dine with Sir William Gadsby was more than flattering. This would make news for Stella, marvellous news.

6

Under Sir William Gadsby's expert and meticulous guidance Tim's knowledge prospered, and for a tyro surgeon he was held in high esteem by the staff at the Royal Elizabeth Hospital.

He wrote Stella and Alice glowing letters telling of his extremely good fortune and of the unusual opportunity he had been offered. Buoyed up and keen he grew thinner than ever, living off nervous energy. Gadsby had to send him away from the hospital altogether at each month end. He spent most of his time at Kiledin, loving the delightful Stella with passion and sincerity. Then he finally went to visit Alice. He felt that he owed her much more than just a casual call. He knew that the time was well overdue to face facts as they were, and to tell Alice about Stella. His cowardice could no longer be tolerated. He realised, albeit late in the day, that he should have told her before, long before.

When he arrived at Charlotte Bemmington's old house the tranquillity surrounding it enveloped him like a glove. All was placid and serene. Old Dibbern welcomed him with obvious pleasure, and Alice herself held him so close that her perfumed skin enraptured his senses.

'My dearest, dearest, Tim.' She greeted him softly and her eyes were brimming with tears as she clung to him.

'Hello, Alice,' he said with a wry smile. 'How are you, and how is the old place?'

'Fine, Tim, just fine.' She linked arms with him as they walked to the shadowed entrance of the house. 'You're doing very well then, Tim. I've kept all your letters. Charlotte would have been so proud.'

'I've been lucky, Alice. Sir William is a fine tutor, probably the best there is.'

She lifted his hand, spreading the slender fingers with her own and pressing her lips gently to the palm. 'You've earned it, Tim. You deserve it.'

Her lips touching his hand sparked off her old tenderness for him, but not with the slightest indication did she betray her feelings. She longed for his arms and his love, but never had he shown anything more than a brotherly fondness for her. She had many times wept over him, but that had certainly not helped. How long was this visit to be, she wondered. Just a single day – or perhaps two?

'I can stay for a week if you will have me,' Tim ventured, as if in answer to her unspoken question.

'Of course you can stay. I am always delighted when you are here.' She smiled at him, her face showing its pleasure.

They spent their time poking about in the garden with occasional visits to the shops. Alice was a superb cook and she excelled herself for Tim. Her apple pies melted deliciously in his mouth, and as he looked fondly at this handsome, trim girl with her earnestly bent head he wondered at his good fortune in knowing both Alice and Stella. He could never love anyone like he loved Stella, but he loved Alice in a different kind of way. All the more reason then, he told himself, to give Alice a completely honest picture of his life as it was. After all, had he not come for that very purpose?

One evening they were crossing the meadow at the side of the house, arms linked and laughing gaily.

'You haven't said much about Neil McAlister on this visit, Tim,' Alice remarked, unconsciously giving him an opening so that he could get onto the subject of the McAlisters.

149

'There's not much to tell,' he said. 'He's in practice, and I go up to Kiledin from time to time. His sister, Stella is very well too. I have mentioned Stella to you before, I think.'

'Fleetingly,' the girl acknowledged, wondering what was coming next.

'Ah! Yes, well.' Tim felt himself stumbling over the words. 'Stella and I have developed a kind of relationship.' It tumbled out not at all in the way that he had intended to say it.

Alice looked at his flushed and confused face. She felt as though a knife had penetrated her breast. The hurt was such that she almost stopped breathing, but outwardly she remained calm and unruffled.

'What you do, Tim, is your own affair,' she said quietly. 'I am always here if you need me, but I'd rather not hear any more about it, if you don't mind.'

And that, as far as Alice was concerned, concluded the matter. Tim couldn't think of anything more to say. The whole confrontation had been a mess, and he felt dishonest, ashamed and embarrassed.

Over the next few days Alice appeared not to have changed towards Tim in any way, despite his pronouncement. She was still obviously pleased that he was with her, and her face was placid and untroubled. When the time finally came for him to take his leave, her farewells were as sincere as ever: the light brushing of her lips upon his cheek a caress which came straight from her heart. It was a troubled Tim Farley indeed who that day caught the train back to the hospital.

As Tim progressed with his work so Sir William Gadsby grew more and more mystified. He saw life as it was governed by the laws and explanations of science. Tim Farley, he knew, would become an outstanding surgeon; but his ability even now was such that defied all the laws of probability. Even a genius couldn't be expected to make the progress that Timothy was making. Already there was gossip and rumour circulating amongst the sisters and nurses. Other doctors, good men with keen analytical minds, were discussing the amazing work of young Farley.

Sir William looked at the wall clock. It was time he went home – there were friends coming to dinner. He had just made up his mind to leave when there was a knock at the door.

'Come in!'

'Sorry to disturb you, Sir William,' said consultant surgeon Vincent Godfrey apologetically as he opened the door. 'I'd like a few words with you, sir, if I may. It's about young Farley.'

'Sit down, Godfrey. Drink? Smoke?'

Godfrey shook his head. Gadsby looked at him carefully. Vincent Godfrey was one of the best honorary surgeons at the hospital: a likeable, dependable and very clever man who, despite a rich private practice, put in many hours of unpaid work.

'What's on your mind, Vincent, or can I guess? You mentioned Farley's name, I think?'

'Yes, I did. He's been assisting me in the theatre all morning. He asked you if he might, if you remember.'

'I remember,' Gadsby nodded his head. 'The Porterman girl, your special case. Everything all right?'

'I think so. Farley did the op.'

'Mmm, you surprise me. I thought that was your own little pet.'

'It was, and then for no reason at all I told Farley to go ahead.'

'And?' Gadsby waited.

'We're men of science, Sir William, you and I. In fact, so are all of us here. I've been thinking about Farley: reasoning with myself, seeking explanations. How can Farley operate so quickly and without a mistake on complaints of which he can have no possible knowledge, except in theory? The theatre sisters have nick-named him

"Miracle Hands". I've heard the expression before – it signifies very little, of course, but in Farley's case – ' He paused. 'I've seen him operate many times, Sir William, and so have you. There's something about him that's quite uncanny, don't you think?'

Sir William allowed his eyes to flicker to the ceiling. It was yellowing, needed a coat of whitewash he thought. Then he looked back at Godfrey.

'He is uncanny, Vincent,' he said quietly. 'I, too, have wondered and looked for explanations, but there are none that I can think of at the moment. Last week in number three, Mattson, the chappie with the smashed legs – intelligent, mature, thirty years of age – asked me where Farley was. He was concerned at his absence. You know why?'

'No.' Godfrey leaned forward with interest.

'Mattson gets severe pain in his legs, and he told me with all sincerity that when Farley touched his legs during examination the pain vanished – as though Farley's hands had removed the cause. I laughed, of course.' Sir William looked at the ceiling again. 'But I part believed the story: enough, in fact, to test the statement. I used three patients, all suffering pain, and I instructed Farley to carry out routine examinations on progress. Afterwards I questioned the patients closely. All, mark you, intelligent people. All said that the pain vanished when Farley touched them. It's quite unbelievable.'

'Yes, it is.' Godfrey was nonplussed. 'Miracle hands, eh? I won't believe it.'

'Have you ever looked closely at Farley's hands?'

'Yes, I have, and they are rather fine.'

'They're beautiful hands, Godfrey, wonderful hands. In fact, never before have I seen hands so sensitive and well balanced. They are perfection. Tell me, Godfrey, which of your patients suffers pain badly.'

Godfrey shrugged. 'I have a spinal in number one who needs morphine occasionally.'

'Right. You can witness this experiment yourself. I had intended to hurry away, but I'm as interested as a schoolboy. Let's go and look at this spinal.'

Ward number one was a women's on the ground floor – an airy spacious room with long sun windows and waxed parquet floor. They met the ward sister at the door, who looked at them in surprise.

'Sorry to call on you at this time,' Sir William apologised, 'but we're rather interested in a spinal you have. Sister, please be good enough to send Doctor Farley along. He was in the theatre half an hour or so ago. You'll probably find him in the library.'

The sister nodded and went away silently. Vincent Godfrey led Sir William past the rows of beds where patients were sitting chatting or dozing while two nurses busied themselves with the tea trolleys.

They stopped at the end bed. A young woman paused in her reading to look at them.

'Good afternoon, Miss Lorrimer,' Godfrey said in a friendly voice, picking up the chart secured at the bottom of the bed. 'This is Sir William Gadsby: he's very interested in you, and we may have another doctor, Doctor Farley, coming along to see you too.' He sat casually on the end of the bed.

'How's the pain, Miss Lorrimer?'

The girl shrugged and smiled wryly. 'No worse,' she said. 'Perhaps a little better.'

But Sir William saw that her eyes belied her. They were large and smoky with pain and there were the tell-tale blue shadows. He felt her pulse. It was a little fast. She was a good looking girl of about twenty-three, and even without make-up she had a natural loveliness. Her features were good, although she had thinned to the point where her cheek bones were prominent. Gadsby could see that she had suffered and was suffering.

He beckoned unobtrusively to Godfrey and they step-

153

ped away from the bed. 'Have the nurses put some screens round, Godfrey, there's a good chap.'

Godfrey instructed the nurses, one of whom was standing nearby in case anything was required. It was unusual for any of the doctors or surgeons to call in the ward at this hour except in emergency. She wondered what was amiss.

'This Lorrimer girl,' Sir William said. 'What's the trouble?'

'I'm not sure yet. Two lots of X-rays have shown negative; but I'm almost certain that there has been some sort of injury to the spinal cord. She came here from the Cottage Hospital. There has been no injury or heavy blow that she can remember, but I am convinced that there has been a spinal rupture.'

'And no paralysis?'

'That's the queer part of it,' Godfrey frowned. 'The middle of her back is fastened in fabricated elastic. I didn't use plaster, there is no evidence of its being necessary. Here comes Farley now.' He gestured towards the door which Tim has just opened.

'Here is Doctor Farley,' the ward sister was panting. 'I had the dickens own job finding him. Anything I can do?' Her eyes wandered to the red screen.

'Yes please, Sister,' Godfrey said. 'Get Miss Lorrimer ready for an examination. Take off all the strapping. When did she have morphine last?'

'First thing after your round this morning. She's in pain again now, I know, but you explicitly instructed me not to give her any more today.'

'Yes, that's quite all right. I'm sorry that we've upset you like this.'

'Well, it is rather a surprise.'

'Sir William's idea.' He turned to Gadsby, who was explaining the case quietly to Timothy.

The Sister and one of the nurses disappeared behind the screen, and began to prepare the patient.

'I thought you might be keen to see this case, Farley,'

Sir William said. 'It's one of Mr Godfrey's, but since you're under my wing there's no reason why you shouldn't give an opinion. Godfrey hasn't made a diagnosis yet but the patient is in great pain. In fact, morphine is being administered from time to time. All right, Vincent, let's have a look at her.'

The three men went behind the screen and the sister stood by waiting, while the nurse wheeled up a console of instruments.

Janice Lorrimer lay face downwards on the bed, the sheet peeled back to her waist.

'You said that the pain was a little better a few minutes ago, Miss Lorrimer,' Sir William began. 'Actually you meant that you'd like to think it was better, but it's still bad, isn't it?'

'Yes, I'm afraid so.' The voice came muffled from the pillow.

'I should like your views on this, Doctor Farley,' Sir William remarked very seriously. 'I've explained to you most of the details.'

'My views?' Tim's eyebrows shot up and then he recovered himself.

'Yes, Sir William, of course, sir.' It was quite unethical to give the patient cause for alarm by appearing anything but confident.

He looked down intently at the smooth expanse of Janice Lorrimer's back. There was no visual sign of damage, no inflammation, no misplaced vertebrae and the shocking thing was that Sir William had said that the X-ray plates revealed nothing. Very carefully he touched her back with his long sensitive fingers. Gently he pressed the spine and the girl shuddered, muscles standing suddenly rigid. The seat of pain was under his fingertips now, midway in the small of her back.

'Miss Lorrimer,' he said. 'Does my touching you lightly like this increase the symptoms of pain much?'

'Yes,' she was gasping. 'It's at its worst now.'

He took his hands away and then placed them at a short distance from the vertebrae, using a little pressure.

'No pain there,' he said.

'None.'

He felt carefully with his hands around the seat of the suspected injury. He was at a loss for diagnosis or explanation. There were no outward signs, and according to the X-rays no internal. There was no paralysis which would result from injury to the spinal chord. He checked over the possibilities in his mind and then, suddenly, Janice Lorrimer's head screwed round and she smiled at Tim gratefully. Sir William and Godfrey moved a step closer, eyes narrowed. Sir William's hand touched Godfrey's arm. Neither spoke.

'The pain's going, doctor,' the girl said, almost gaily. 'You must have straightened something.'

'Perhaps,' Tim smiled at her.

Godfrey opened his mouth to speak and then closed it again, saying nothing.

Tim pressed the vertebrae where the girl had actually complained of fierce pain.

'Does that hurt?' he asked.

'No, it does not. The pain's gone, all of it.'

Tim frowned in perplexity, unable to provide a reason. He pressed again, harder.

'Quite sure?'

'Quite, quite sure.'

'I can't understand it,' he muttered to himself. He tested her pulse, looking at his watch. It was quite normal. He picked up the bed card. The pulse had been fast for the last twenty-four hours. He looked first at Sir William, and then at Godfrey. He placed his hands on Janice's back again and manipulated the vertebrae with his fingers.

'Any pain, Miss Lorrimer?'

'No pain,' she said cheerfully. 'It feels wonderful.'

Timothy straightened himself. 'I don't think we'll bother with the strapping for the time being,' he said.

'Thank you, doctor.' Janice Lorrimer rolled over onto her back, her eyes suddenly filling with tears.

Tim signalled the ward sister and then turned to Sir William and Vincent Godfrey.

The three of them walked round the screens and into the centre of the ward.

'Well,' said Sir William, 'what did you make of it?'

'Nothing,' Timothy shook his head. 'You heard her say that the pain had gone.'

'I saw her eyes and knew that it had gone.'

'I made no diagnosis,' said Tim. 'I suggest a possible corruption of the articular surfaces of the Vertebrae pressuring a major nerve. My examination may by unforeseen accident have set this to right.'

Vincent Godfrey nodded assent. 'Possible,' he said. 'Possible.' Godfrey was prepared for any explanation other than the one he had discussed with Sir William. 'We'll see how she's progressing when I do my round in the morning.'

Timothy nodded. 'If you'll excuse me then, I have some case histories to get through.'

He left them and Godfrey and Sir William returned to the latter's room. Neither spoke for some time.

Gadsby eased himself into a leather armchair, and sliced the end of a Corona. He pushed the box over to Godfrey.

'Your move, Godfrey,' he said. 'You know as well as I do that there's no explanation. She'll have the pain back in the morning, and if Farley lays his hands on her again it will vanish.'

'I don't want to believe it,' Godfrey said. 'I just don't. What you're suggesting is that he has Divine guidance, the hands of God. You said so yourself. When he lays his hands on her, the healer lays his hands.' Godfrey pulled furiously at his cigar.

'It confirms only what I myself have already seen and investigated,' Sir William observed. 'We shall say nothing.

There may be an explanation and there may not. The whole thing may simply be a series of colossal coincidences. If ever our suspicion was voiced to the media the whole damn hospital would be swarming with people demanding to be cured by the man with the hands of God. The bloody awful thing about it is that he suspects nothing of this power himself, and I know well enough that he's still worried about his final for the Fellowship.' He laughed drily. 'After your ward check-up tomorrow, Vincent, report to me. I have two majors which I shall give to Farley. If I'm wrong about him there will be two deaths on my hands. It's a lean chance that I myself can perform the ops successfully, but for anyone else it's almost an impossibility.'

'Except Farley.'

'Except Farley – and there's someone higher up than we shall ever be, pushing Farley, and you know whom I'm suggesting.'

'Yes, I know. From now onwards we shall be witnessing miracles, the suggestion of which on previous occasions we have treated with contempt.'

'I daren't reply to you, Vincent. I just daren't. I'm as mixed up as a kid who has just started medical school. I must get off now. See me in the morning.' He threw away his half-burned cigar. 'Stay and finish yours,' he said. 'Relax and think. We may have missed an essential point.' But he knew they hadn't.

When Sir William arrived at his home his wife's guests had already been waiting for half an hour. He made his apologies hurriedly and raced upstairs to change.

After dinner they played bridge, gossiped over unimportant things, smoked expensive cigars and drank Scotch.

Sir William's irritation was ill-concealed, and although he strove to master it, it became so obvious that the guests left early.

At last he sat alone in his study, one window open, the

cool night air creeping steadily into the room. His wife had gone to bed. Carefully he considered the phenomenon of Timothy Farley.

Of Timothy's private life he knew nothing, but quite obviously he had sprung from humble surroundings. He lived on his small salary by careful budgeting. He dressed shabbily and unfashionably; in fact he seemed not to care about anything save his work. Sir William wondered where he went to on his free weekends. There had been the name of a girl mentioned, Stella somebody or other, somewhere in Scotland. He shrugged – none of his business, anyway. What did concern him was the fact that there was dynamite at the Royal Elizabeth, dynamite in the shape of Timothy Farley. He was eager to drop in at the hospital in the morning and find out just how Godfrey's patient, Miss Lorrimer, was progressing. He stood up, yawned and closed the windows carefully. No good ringing for the butler to lock up. He'd gone to bed: he remembered his wife mentioning that she had given him permission. He poured himself a small brandy and sniffed the liquid appreciatively. He knew that he was growing too fond of the stuff, that and whisky. He emptied the glass, checked the doors, and went to bed. But he did not sleep well. There were too many things for him to think about. Next morning he breakfasted early and went for a walk in the lanes, afterwards driving to the hospital in his car.

He was checking over his reference books on the two major operations he had for the day when Vincent Godfrey came in.

'Morning, Sir William. Miss Lorrimer has no pain this morning. She swears that she is cured. She says that something inside keeps telling her so. Maybe Farley just happened to strike the right spot after all.'

'Maybe. It's possible, I suppose; but what of our other medical evidence. Do you honestly think in your own mind that he just touched a spot, as you say?'

Godfrey considered the question and then shrugged his shoulders. 'No,' he said. 'No, I don't. Damned if I know what the hell to think.'

Later in the morning Timothy, under the supervision of Sir William and Vincent Godfrey, performed the major. In the afternoon he did the second one. An hour afterwards Sir William said to Godfrey, 'Well, Vincent, what now?'

'I have nothing to say. I could tell by the look in the theatre sister's eyes that she knows, and after what we've just witnessed the whole hospital will know.'

Sir William nodded his head. 'It looks conclusive enough. I shall have to mention it to the Board, of course.' He examined his hands briefly. 'The Board won't believe me, but that will probably be for the best. We don't want demonstrations and public performances. I like the man; he has a life to lead. He's in an honourable profession, not a freak to be followed and chased by every damn crank in the country. I'm going downstairs. Can I drop you somewhere?'

Godfrey nodded assent and the two left the building.

The train rocked steadily and the lilting clatter of the wheels made Timothy feel drowsy. His head started to sag forward, but he recovered himself with a jerk and glanced sleepily through the window. Telegraph poles flickered by, and vistas of meadowland stretched out in its richest green. Here and there he caught the silver glint of water, the yellow of a haystack and dappled cows ambling sedately to the shade of a favourite tree. It was a brilliant spring day, and the carriage was hot. Carefully he lowered the window a notch, fearful lest he disturb his fellow passengers, all of whom had their eyes closed save the girl in the corner who was amusing herself with a pile of magazines.

Timothy Farley, MB, BS, FRCS. There had been no

difficulty with the surgical Fellowship after all. He could hardly wait to reach Kiledin and share his joy with Stella. Carefully he adjusted the crease of his trousers and sniffed appreciatively at the cool air which blew in from the part open window.

He was wearing a new suit, a blue mohair which made him feel self-conscious. His shoes, shirt and tie were new, and the overcoat lying on the rack above his head was also new. Despite this, however, there was still an untidy air about him, as though regardless of effort he would never be able to look smart and debonair.

He looked at the girl in the corner. She was neatly dressed and wore a huge diamond ring on her engagement finger. It was funny, he thought, the idea had never occurred to him to buy Stella a ring. He half regretted it now, but he would make it up to her as soon as possible. He had good prospects: Sir William Gadsby had offered to take him on in his private practice, besides the honorary work. He didn't care for the idea much but he must have money if he was to marry Stella – and this was what he was on his way to do now. He felt strangely guilty about this. In his pocket was a half finished letter he had begun to write to Alice, but which he had been quite unable to finish. It lay like a firebrand, constantly reminding him that he had never been entirely honest with the girl, although it had not been his intention to be otherwise. When he talked with her his intended words of explanation had always died away unsaid.

Only once had he ever tried to talk about Stella, and the wounded hurt he had seen in Alice's expressive eyes had silenced him. Even now, trying to write as he had done in an attempt to clear up the matter without ambiguity, his pen had crawled to a halt. The unfinished letter left him still with the problem of finding a satisfactory solution.

'Would you like a magazine to look at?' It was the girl in the corner. She was smiling at him.

'Thank you.' He took the glossy picture magazine from

161

her extended hand and began to turn the pages. It was a society magazine, liberal with photographs of all the fashionable weddings. He was half way through when the pictures in the centre page suddenly leaped at him. Nancy Weston, lovely, unsmiling, in an ivory wedding dress; a man considerably older than herself, silk hat in hand, standing at her side. *Miss Nancy Weston and Anthony Rupert Alexander Fitzgerald, Sixth Earl of Pemley*. Nancy Weston married to an Earl! Her mother had had her wish then. He looked at the groups, picking out her father and mother without hesitation. Douglas Weston looked his age but Mrs Weston was ageless, beautiful as ever, exquisitely dressed and smiling in triumph. Timothy examined the picture of Nancy again and felt his heart beating a little rapidly.

He allowed his mind to slip back to the intimate memories of their childhood. He'd known happiness then, brief because of the sadness which had come later, but all the more cherished because of its brevity. He looked through the rest of the magazine quickly and handed it back with murmured thanks.

Watching the glint of diamonds in the ring of the girl opposite he suddenly hated himself for not having thought of a ring for Stella; he wished he hadn't ever seen this girl and then the fevered beat of the rushing train grew subdued and they slipped into Elgin where a hoarse voice shouted 'All change! All change!'

Tim swung himself from the carriage, thinking of the diamond ring which had awakened in him the selfishness of his shortcomings. He felt inclined to purchase a ring in Elgin with what money he had. But an indicator board with the name Blairgowie on it, and two minutes to go on the time clock, changed his mind for him and he ran towards the little engine with its two bare carriages.

It started almost at once, and his mind turned from rings to one thought only: beloved Stella.

* * *

It was still light, with the sun well up in the sky, when finally he climbed stiffly onto the tiny platform of Blairgo-wie. He almost fell over a milk churn in his eagerness – and then he saw a half familiar figure hurrying towards him.

He was surprised to see that it was Mercer Grant, and still more surprised to hear him panting from exertion as he came up to him, a line of perspiration on his forehead.

'Tim, I –'

'Hello, Mercer.'

'There's no time for that now. You must hurry. Thank goodness the train was on time. Neil sent me. There's been an accident. Stella . . .' he gasped to get his words out.

'What's happened?' Tim's voice was suddenly harsh. 'Tell me – quick – what's happened to Stella?'

'Her horse threw her less than half an hour ago. I don't want to frighten you. Neil's with her. He arrived last night. He's worried, I can tell you, and knowing the time of the train and that you were on it, he asked me to meet you. I happened to be at Kiledin, you know how it is. My car's outside. Come on, you must hurry.'

Tim fumbled for his ticket, dropped it, retrieved it again and thrust it at the ticket collector. He was in a fever of impatience. Mercer's bull-nosed car stood with steaming radiator outside the station. He swept open the door for Tim, turned on the ignition and swung the starting handle. The engine snapped to life with a savage cough, steadied, faded for a second and then began to throb rhythmically.

Mercer jumped in, engaged the gears with a crash and the car jolted away. 'Drive your fastest,' Tim said in a choked voice. 'Don't bother to talk if it will delay us and – and thanks for coming.'

Mercer nodded without speaking. His lips were tight, his face green.

The grey sun-lit battlements of Kiledin appeared and the car groaned up the hill as Mercer stamped the

163

accelerator down hard until the gears began to scream. Water was boiling from the radiator when finally they drew to a halt in front of the massive doors. Tim jumped out and pounded on the big brass knocker.

The door was opened almost at once by a maid, her face crumpled in fright. Timothy brushed past her, Mercer Grant at his heels.

'Upstairs – you know the bedroom.'

Tim nodded and looking up, saw Mordrake, his face ashen, gazing down at him from the first landing.

'I'm right glad ye've come, laddie. It's a nasty business. Ma son's with her and Doctor McGregor from Blairgowie. It looks bad, Tim boy, aye bad.'

Tim felt the cold hand of fear touch him. The big man had gone all to pieces. He hurried on, leaving Mordrake and Mercer Grant on the landing. He knew the room well and, without knocking, opened the door.

Neil McAlister looked up as he entered and came over to greet him.

'Hullo, Tim,' he said softly. 'I wish it hadn't been like this.' He gripped Tim's hand quickly. 'This is Doctor McGregor.'

Tim shook hands briefly with the bespectacled little man with the mild blue eyes. They had Stella laid out on a table padded with blankets, a hard pillow beneath her head. The room seemed chill and cold and overquiet, although the day was warm and sunlight still poured through the open windows. Tim looked at the still form of his beloved, her face a white mask, long-lashed eyes closed. 'What have you made of it?' he asked, his voice harsh and unnatural.

McGregor answered, 'Fracture of the skull, seemingly, and something's got to be done at once. There's no telephone here, and in any case the nearest hospital is at Elgin – two hours away, and she can't be moved. It will be fatal to delay any longer. I'm a GP. This is out of my category and Neil can't handle it. We've been praying that you'd caught the early train. Well, you're here now. Better check my examination. There's been blood from the ears.'

Tim nodded. He knew that this was not of particular consequence – it might be a serious indicator, might not. A small vessel could have been ruptured. He checked Stella's pulse and pursed his lips.

'I've got a standard surgical kit with me,' McGregor said.

Neil groaned. No X-rays, no arc lamps, very little of anything. 'Better cut as much of her hair off as possible,' Tim said.

McGregor nodded and opened the stiff black case standing at the side of the table.

Tim walked to the window and looked out. Below he could see the sea, calm and unruffled. Neil came over to him and gripped his arm momentarily.

'Are you going to do it?'

'It's for your father to say, when I've concluded my examination, and if I agree with McGregor's diagnosis. At the moment I think he's right, but I wish we could get hold of somebody else. It's upset me to see her – and God, I don't want to fail.'

'You won't. You've had skull fractures before?' It was a question.

'Several, depressed, comminuted, all successful.'

'Good.' Neil's face was grave, he made no further comment.

Tim turned round and saw that the little Scots doctor had cut off Stella's tawny hair. It lay discarded on the floor. Angus McGregor was a practical man. Tim felt a sudden lump form in his throat.

'Better get some shaving soap and a good razor, Neil,' McGregor said. 'I'll shave the scalp as much as possible, then we shall be all set.'

Neil nodded without speaking and went out.

Tim stood looking at Stella, his face drawn. Her breathing came harshly and he saw the specks of blood forming in her dainty ears. He could see the wound and the bruise, an ugly gash with swollen purple surrounds, but he didn't touch it.

McGregor left him looking and poured antiseptic into a basin and produced a pile of handkerchiefs from a drawer. Then he began to tear up a sheet.

'Have a look at the kit,' he said and Tim, his heart pounding, opened the bag and examined the instruments. They were complete to a trephine, which surprised him. McGregor apparently was shrewdly prepared for anything.

Neil returned with shaving soap and razor, handing them to McGregor. 'My father says it's all right for you to go ahead if you think it necessary. I've told him the risks: his word is sufficient. You don't need a written statement.'

'I must have one. Get it later.'

'Very well then.'

Tim watched McGregor shave Stella's scalp quickly. The removal of hair had changed her features completely, but she still looked beautiful. Selecting a probe Tim examined Stella's injury with great care, manipulating the probe gently. A groan escaped the girl's closed lips and her eyelids flickered. Tim took five minutes over his examination, his face pinched and grave.

'Yes, it's a fracture,' he said after what to Neil seemed hours of waiting. 'There's pressure and we must operate without delay.' He bit his lip. 'Get the maid to bring plenty of hot water, Neil, and improvise handkerchiefs as masks. Can't be helped there aren't any gloves, but McGregor has plenty of antiseptic wash ready.' He began to pace the room.

'We shall have to use chloroform, Doctor McGregor. Let's get started.'

He seemed glad that he'd made the decision. The responsibility now was his, solely his. He tested the steady beat of Stella's heart.

Neil dashed off to arrange for the water and McGregor

unstoppered the bottle of chloroform. Very soon the sickly odour was creeping into the room.

Neil came back almost at once, slopping the steaming water on to the carpet. He arranged the two enamel buckets near to the wall and all three washed hands and arms thoroughly, tying handkerchiefs sprinkled with antiseptic over the lower parts of their faces. McGregor poured chloroform on to a pad of lint: he was a keen worker and anxious now to get the business over.

'Hold it away from her face for a short while,' Tim said. 'Let plenty of air mix with it.' He spread a sheet over Stella's body from the neck downwards, while Neil first sterilised and then laid out the instruments on a small table and unwrapped rolls of cotton wool. They had to be their own nurses.

'All set,' McGregor said. He held Stella's pulse between thumb and forefinger. 'She's away now.'

Tim passed his finger along the wound and examined the bone. He could feel the loose fragments and the depression of the bone below its level: he raised it with the point of an elevator, using the instrument as a lever. The aperture was not quite large enough and he used the Heys saw. His early lectures flashed through his mind. *The incision for the operation should be carefully and properly planned so as to give sufficient space with as little mutilation as possible. Pay due attention to the resistance of tissue and ligature all bleeding vessels.*

Quite suddenly he felt himself beginning to sweat. It startled him because he had never sweated in an operation before. He felt McGregor's eyes on him. Neil looked sickly.

'Pulse,' he said briefly to McGregor.

'Quite good.'

Tim frowned. That was no answer. He wondered why he had begun to sweat. He'd done so many operations, and with such confidence and such success. But this was Stella he was working on. Stella.

The inner table was splintered considerably, he observed.

'Trephine,' he said to Neil without looking at him.

He applied the instrument so that exactly half of its circle was situated upon the edge overhanging the depressed bone, and removed a portion of the undepressed cranium. He took out the splinters revealed. There was no particular extravasation of blood, with the vascular network of the brain quite undisturbed. He pointed this out to Neil and McGregor. It looked a straightforward enough job. He laid down the scalp flaps and applied sutures.

'Cold water dress it for the time being,' he said to Neil. 'And rigorous antiphlogistic. I think it will be all right.'

'My congratulations,' McGregor said. 'As neat a bit of surgery as I've ever seen.'

'Thank you.' He hoped there wouldn't be complications, shock, or haemorrhage. He'd operated to perfection, he knew, with nothing overlooked, nothing chanced. The conditions had been bad but he'd had two doctors with him, one a very experienced man in his own particular line.

The floor was covered with bloody waste, and he felt sticky with the unaccustomed sweat.

'She mightn't come to for hours,' McGregor said. 'Even after the chloroform has worn off.'

'Yes, I know. Better tell your father, Neil, that it's over. Don't give him any reassurances yet.' He checked Stella's pulse. It was coming strongly. He felt better. 'We can put her to bed now.' He pulled down the sheet. 'Cut off her clothes, Doctor McGregor. She'll be safe to move to the bed.'

Angus McGregor did as he was asked. They got hold of hot water bottles and then moved Stella to the bed and covered her with blankets.

'I'll get the maid to clean up,' Neil said. 'If she can face it.'

The heavy smell of chloroform was sickly in the room.

Tim pushed the windows wider and McGregor began to wash his instruments. Tim scrubbed in the bucket and helped McGregor to pack up.

'It's been a bad day for you, Farley,' he said. 'But I think you've won.'

'I hope so.' He was glad that McGregor couldn't read his thoughts. The emotional turmoil and the terrific shock churned in him. He felt sudden nausea.

'Let's go downstairs for a whisky,' he suggested. 'I could do with one – a large one.'

They passed a scared maid on their way downstairs. Tim nodded to her as she went by, pan and brush in her hand to clean up the room.

Neil had a whisky waiting for them. His own ruddy colour was beginning to seep back into his face. His father and Mercer Grant were nowhere to be seen. Suddenly, it began to grow dark.

Tim had his whisky glass half way to his lips when the first sullen grunt of thunder rolled in from the hills. The liquid hit his stomach like a ball of fire just as McGregor said, 'Storm blowing up. That's queer for the time of season, and the day so tranquil too.'

Forked lightning pitched across the sky in ragged tongues, black clouds banked hurriedly and the thunder roared. Even as Tim set the glass down on the polished table the rain rushed down in swishing torrents, and Neil hurried to close the casements.

'The windows in Stella's room,' Tim said. 'I'll go up and shut them.'

He hurried away and ran up the stone staircase. Opening the door of Stella's room, he saw with some surprise that the maid hadn't even been in there: and then, suddenly, his heart stopped beating.

A cry escaped him, long drawn, like an animal in pain, and then he was bending over Stella, touching her face, her hands, and knowing all the time that she was dead. He dropped to his knees sobbing wildly, shuddering racking cries which tore at his body. He leaned over the still white form of her, his tears dropping on her lovely face with the soft glitter of falling wax. He held her wrist in his hand, feeling for the pulse, denying to himself that she was dead, but he knew that she had left him, left Kiledin – this wonderful girl with whom he had known such joy: the gay, wildly loving, irresistible Stella, his to possess, to love and be loved.

He struggled to take hold of himself but his control had gone completely. He kissed the cold lips which he had known so warm, so vibrant and utterly living. The full realisation of her death had not penetrated his mind and all the time he sobbed over her, the rain lashed heedlessly through the open windows, forming shallow pools of water on the floor and wetting the furniture. Cold, storm rain pouring over Kiledin in unexpected torrents. The portent of it suddenly stirred in Tim's mind so that his heaving, sobbing body became tense and still. Those subconscious voices he had heard. The signs and omens. Always to the tumult of thunder-riven storm. He had loved Stella with abandon, but there had been no sin, no shame. Their consummation had been so enriched that once in each others' arms the universe seemed timeless.

And now he had had his first failure, when failure seemed impossible. It was as though hands other than his own had intervened. He felt suddenly cold and afraid. He crossed swiftly to the windows and hurled them to, with a crash that echoed back across the room in eddies of harsh sound to die away, suddenly leaving everything dark and quiet. And then, as if to confuse him further, the rain stopped, the thunder ceased its savage roar and the sun broke through the thick clouds, filtering its yellow fingers into the room to settle on the still face of Stella. He looked at the wonder of her just once, and then with bowed head stumbled through the door, his eyes wet with tears, his shoulders crouched: and thus it was that he walked into the room below.

170

Neil, seeing him, dropped the whisky glass on to the table with a bang. He knew just by looking what had happened.

'It's Stella, isn't it?' he said, his voice suddenly husky.

'She's dead.' Tim took a deep, hurtful breath. Neil went pale. McGregor wanted to say 'Not your fault, old chap, you did everything possible,' but he said nothing. This, he knew, was the wrong time to say anything.

Tim slumped into a chair and poured himself a half tumbler full of whisky. He felt slightly drunk after he had swallowed it. There was Mordrake to be told – he felt suddenly sick inside.

'Where's your father?' he asked Neil.

'I don't know. Down at the stables, maybe. I'd better go and look for him, tell him.' There was a suspicious moistness about his eyes. 'It's hard for you, Tim, but not your fault. Never think of it like that.' His lips quivered suddenly. 'I'll go out and find my father. I think he half expected it, that's why he went out. He was afraid.'

'The old man's heart is not good,' McGregor said after Neil had gone. 'I hope this doesn't upset him too much. I'd best be going. This is no time for you to have me around.' He seemed suddenly anxious to leave, and Tim was glad for him to go. He felt as though he didn't want to see anybody or face anybody. He thought of Stella, the living Stella who had been so vital that every time he'd operated at the Royal Elizabeth the comparison of Stella and the unfortunate patient always flitted through his mind.

After McGregor had gone, he groaned as if in pain and then went upstairs again.

Neil found him sitting by her, his eyes tragic and far away as though he did not belong any more, as though something inside him had died with her. Neil touched his arm gently but Tim did not turn or move, just sat there motionless, looking at her as though she were not dead. As though she were just asleep.

THREE

1

During summer the lane was beautiful with horse chestnut in full leaf, and the hedgerows alive with the quickening thrust of nature anxious not to lose a second.

At the far end of the lane on the left hand side, the wall began. It was an ugly wall of old red brick and lichen-covered cement which had receded well inside the level of the facing. On top of the brickwork were iron staples, with rusty iron brackets and barbed wire running in triple strands for what seemed an endless distance. The wall went along for almost a mile, interspaced once by a massive pair of gilded, wrought iron gates with an enamelled crest in the centre and stone lions atop each of the pillars. Next to the gates was a small wooden door let into the wall, and farther along a similar door, both painted a fresh green.

Inside the wrought iron gates stood a neat keeper's lodge, with a red gravel drive cutting through dark woodland and curving like a gay crimson thread into vast landscape gardens. The house, towering behind, was of the size and grandeur of a palace, with fitted French windows opening onto outside balconies and clipped box trees standing like sentinel dwarfs beneath the huge casements of the ground floor.

Above the arch of the doorway the plaster effigy of a hawk brooded down at the two gleaming Rolls Royces parked outside. A gardener with bent back forked the rich brown earth between the chrysanthemums, and a young girl in a blue dress led a fat waddling corgi across the lawn. Over the tall spires of this ancestral building the sun shone brilliantly, picking out the cracks in the brown stone, throwing long shadows to the front and across the lawns in dark wedges. This was Wendover Court, built at the time of Richard the Lionheart and occupied by descendants of one family ever since.

In the great drawing room an old lady sat erectly, in a carved wooden chair, eyes half closed, one gnarled hand tapping the arm of the chair impatiently. Suddenly she pulled a plush bell rope and a liveried footman appeared on silent feet.

'Send Jules in with my milk and brandy in fifteen minutes time,' she commanded.

'Very good, madame.' The sleek head of the footman bowed.

The old lady looked briefly through the casement window and saw her grandchild playing with the overfed corgi on the lawn. She sniffed contemptuously. They neither had looks nor could they breed, her sons and daughters. She felt her inside tighten with shame, and for the second time that morning she opened the *London News* and read the thick black headlines of the letterpress: *His Majesty the King has bestowed a knighthood in the New Year's list of honours on one of the nation's youngest and most distinguished surgeons, Sir Timothy Farley.* There was a photograph too. It was Jonathon's son all right – she could tell by the eyes. It was time he was accepted at Wendover: he would help grace it with the tradition that seemed to be on the wane this last generation, with the brood and second brood running loose at the present time. Oh, yes, she'd made Johnathon's progeny suffer – not a word, not a penny – but she must forget a little of the past, just enough to make him acceptable. He was a nationally known figure and Wendover needed him.

* * *

The thick, blue, expensive-looking envelope lay at the left hand side of the bread and butter plate, and Timothy glanced at it curiously. He usually ate breakfast before bothering with the mail, but seized by sudden curiosity at the altogether unfamiliar appearance of the envelope, tore open the flap.

The well-penned handwriting made strange reading and he puckered his face into a frown. Again he read the contents of the letter, and then smiled bitterly. The Farleys of Bath had at last recognised him: his father's people were actually asking him to visit them at Wendover Court. He read the missive again, very slowly, and then with great care he refolded the expensive blue notepaper, slipped it into the thick crested envelope, turned in his chair and tossed it on to the fire. He commenced to eat his grapefruit.

After breakfast he sat examining a report received from another surgeon at a big London hospital. He perused the memorandum carefully, made a few pencilled notes and then placed the sheaf of papers inside his briefcase. He sat looking into the fire and thinking about the letter from his grandmother.

He was thirty-six now, but looked slightly older. His house was a small detached villa, and he had for house-keeper the worthy Mrs Muffin who mothered him affectionately. Because of his brilliance he had been knighted, an honour which had not affected him in any way although he knew that this social reward was the only reason for the invitation from Wendover. Greatest of his friends was Sir William Gadsby, but he had many scattered the length and breadth of the country. He was a busy man, busy all day and often all night, and the strain could be seen in his face. Patients sought his aid all over the world, and yet he could never reconcile himself to his position. Somewhere he knew there was a tiny part of himself not at ease. Occasionally he found time to visit Kiledin. Neil McAlister had given up his practice in Edinburgh. The urge for

177

medicine had gone and he had become a gentleman of leisure. Mordrake McAlister had died of a heart seizure and Neil had inherited Kiledin and Mordrake's fortune. He had married a daughter of the Camerons of Logowrie and they were intensely happy with their two children, a boy Ian, and a girl Stella. Tim thought of the other Stella. The Stella who had become more shadowy, more distant as time slowly removed her from his mind – but too slowly. Life had given him success which he accepted in a matter-of-fact fashion. He worked harder now than he had ever done before, and he had fulfilled the hopes that other people had seen in him: Professor Bernardt, Charlotte Bemmington, Alice, Henry Farjeon, Sir William Gadsby. Alice was still unshakeable, kind. He remembered he hadn't seen her for several months and hadn't heard from her for almost five weeks. He must make a point of visiting her, he must find the time. Time had almost become his master: he must learn to control it, take a week off, a fortnight, or even a month. He could fit it in with Gadsby quite easily. He must get himself a secretary to control his business. There was so much of it and he lost so much time keeping his own records. Time, time – it was relentless, slow to pass in youth, moving so much more quickly as one grew older, putting life behind it hour by hour, minute by minute. There were two operations for today and Gadsby wanted him to do one of his private patients tomorrow. He yawned again, and when Mrs Muffin came in she found him asleep in the chair. She didn't disturb him, the hospital would ring if they wanted him. He woke with a start half an hour later and began to examine the big leather-covered diary on the bookshelf. He would be in London for a week; there were three visits to the north; an American patient was being flown over to see him at the Royal Elizabeth on Friday. Time, time, he would never fit it all in.

* * *

A fortnight elapsed: a fortnight of rush and dash which many a man of his position would not have accepted so gracefully. He had little money and yet with a private practice he could have amassed a fortune. His hospital stipend provided him with his ordinary needs and for items above those needs he had no wish. The cheques that were sent to him in recognition of his prowess he gave to the Royal Elizabeth for extra beds, and extra equipment, and the snobberies which had once crawled under his skin he dismissed with curtness and an arrogance which was peculiar to himself. In the medical world he was treated with respect and admiration alike, and sometimes with a strange fear as other doctors saw him at work, and observed him do the impossible.

The plump, elderly little man who waited for him at the bottom of the steps at the Royal Elizabeth ran forward eagerly and doffed his hat.

'Sir Timothy Farley?' he said in question.

Timothy looked at him in surprise. 'Yes,' he said, 'I'm Farley.'

'How do you do. I'm Francis.'

Timothy looked at him in puzzlement and then looked at the chauffeur-driven Rolls Royce drawn up in the hospital grounds.

'Yes, what can I do for you?'

'You don't know me then. Of course you wouldn't. How silly of me. You've never seen me before. I'm Francis Farley, your father's brother.'

'Oh yes.' If Timothy felt surprise he did not show it. 'I had your letter. At least, I presume it was your letter.'

'I wrote you a fortnight ago on behalf of my mother – a blue envelope.'

'That was it.'

'You didn't answer.' The voice was reproachful.

'I didn't think that the letter called for an answer. After all, it's thirty-six years too late. I threw it onto the fire.'

'Oh!' Francis Farley's face fell. 'Perhaps we could have a chat about it.'

Timothy looked at him through narrowed eyes. 'There isn't much to talk about, is there? Come along inside.'

He had made no offer to shake hands, nor did he do so now. He led the way to his hospital quarters, observing Francis's obvious distaste for hospitals. The plump little man was quite relieved when the door of the private den finally closed.

'Whisky?' asked Timothy.

'Er, no, thank you.'

'Cigar or cigarette?'

'No, thank you.'

Tim shrugged, poured himself a small whisky and lit a cigarette. 'Sit down, Francis, I shan't eat you.' He spoke to the elder man as he would to a child. 'This is a great occasion for me. I must treat it as such.' The irony was quite lost on his uncle.

'You wouldn't remember your father, of course, Timothy,' Francis said as though imparting a great secret. 'A fine fellow, Johnathan. It was unfortunate that he left us under such unfavourable circumstances.'

'Was it?' Timothy wondered if his father had been anything like Francis. He chose to think not. 'Why have you come to see me, Francis Farley?' he asked. 'Or do I know the answer?'

'Your grandmother wishes to see you.'

'I have no grandmother. Let us talk in terms of names rather than of relations.'

Francis could see that this was going to be difficult, and a fine line of perspiration broke out on his forehead. Timothy smiled wryly. He didn't think much of his grandmother's emissary.

'I'll be quite frank with you, Timothy. My mother is a very hard woman: dour, rigid in her views. She kept us all down even more so than did my father before his death. There is James, my brother, and my sisters, Cecilia and

Rosamunde. All of us married, although no one in the eyes of my mother was ever any good. Johnathan, the youngest, and your father, escaped her. She never forgave him and she knew of your movements up to the time that you were fourteen, holding you up as an example of what would happen to any of us dare we rebel. I suppose that under this inquisition we grew up soft and timid, as I admit that we are. We all depend on her utterly.' Timothy suddenly felt a little sorry for him. 'I must confess that I no longer have the courage to argue with her.'

'And why does she want to see me after so long?'

'I'm not sure. I'm not sure of anything any more, but I think that the prestige of you being her grandson would please her. She is a country woman, a society leader and she sets great store by the power of position. Your name is on everybody's tongue: you have been knighted at an early age; brought honour to the country; received the personal congratulations of the King. These things are the breath of life to her – family power as it was in the old days of the Farleys.'

'And yet my father – your brother – an officer in the British Army, was killed at Mafeking without the shedding of a tear. My mother died immediately afterwards. I was reared by cottage people and didn't even know my identity for years – not that it was important – but my grandmother made no provision, nor did she intend to. I could have starved for all that she cared, although it seems that she went to some pains to keep check of my early movements as a means to blackmail yourself and the rest of the family. What do I owe to this woman of whom you speak? Had I not risen as I have risen, would she have bothered with me then? I think not.'

'It is true.' Francis shook his head sadly. 'You are quite right, but I shall be terrified to go back and say that you will not come. She was furious when you did not answer the letter. She took it as a personal affront.'

'It was intended to be.'

'Yes, I suppose you had every right.'

'I think so.'

'She is very rich, you know.' He looked at Timothy for the effect of this, but was disappointed.

'You set a high value on your mother's riches then, Francis?'

'She provides for us and we are the descendants, you and I, and the others.'

'I'm not a descendant, Francis. You're the heir, the eldest son. I'm the disowned grandson, remember.' He felt like saying, 'and if you're a specimen of the Farleys I like to think that what gifts I have come from my mother.' What pity he had had for his uncle dissolved. He saw him as a cringing, sponging, fat little man who sat waiting to inherit the Farley fortune.

'You won't visit us, then, that is your final word?' Francis moistened his lips. 'After all she *is* your grandmother.'

'So you have already said. I'm a busy man, Francis, too busy to waste time on trivialities, and I admit that I had intended to ignore the Farley family as I believe that they deserve to be ignored. I must confess, however, to being intrigued by the thought that women actually do exist who are as hard as my grandmother appears to be. Yes, you know, on reflection I think that I will see her, if only to satisfy my undeniable curiosity.'

Francis did not hesitate to conceal his relief.

'Oh, good,' he said, his nervous tension dissolving. He was anxious now to conclude matters, to tie Timothy down. 'That's settled then. When shall we expect you?' Thoughts of his mother's disapproval obviously unsettled him. 'Perhaps soon,' he urged.

Timothy considered the question at length. 'I'll try to call sometime during next Sunday,' he said eventually. 'Don't depend upon it, in case I am unable to come. Are there any special directions to reach Wendover?'

'Once you are in Bath, ask any policeman. It's quite

well known you know. Everyone is familiar with the Farleys of Bath.'

Timothy suddenly hated his smugness, his condescension.

Francis picked up his hat. 'I'll be off now, Mama will be pleased that you are coming. Thank you for your courtesy.'

With frowning brow Timothy escorted him along the white tiled corridor, and then stood for a few moments watching the Rolls as it moved smoothly down the drive.

2

Looking through the window, Nancy watched the nervous winging flight of the birds and envied them. The trees were a dark mass at the bottom of the bright green streamers of lawn, and as she watched the rise and fall of the plump black bodies, the outstretched points of shining wings, she felt very sad. Once she had been happy, she remembered, when she'd been a young girl; but not now, not any more. Yes, it had all seemed so pleasant – pictures in the society magazines, important callers, the sixth Earl of Pemley and she Lady Anthony Fitzgerald of Pemley, no longer plain Nancy Weston, but Lady Fitzgerald of Pemley.

Her husband's ancestral home had been in such a chronic state of disrepair that after their marriage it had seemed inadvisable to spend the fabulous sum of money required to put it right. They had stayed here at her father's home at Worley until Tony arranged to get

somewhere, but the temporary stay soon became permanent because the sixth Earl of Pemley had not only been
penniless but badly in debt too.

Her father had paid Tony's debts – a gesture which the
sixth Earl took for granted, and once tied to the Weston
fortune he was not long in revealing his true chemistry.
Blessed with more than the average share of man's
cunning, Tony saw his ally in Clare, Nancy's mother, and
toadied to her. She, in turn, realised that if nothing else he
had the right connections. That, for Clare, was sufficient.

Barely three months after their marriage, Nancy had
caught him with his first mistress, and from thence onwards denied him all contact with herself. There followed
unhappiness and hatred, while Tony's miserable life
developed into a series of mistresses. At intervals he
would plead with her, but she steadfastly refused to have
anything to do with him. Her pride sustained the theoreti-
cal relationship and her mother, even though guessing the
truth, still saw in Tony the fulfilment of her dreams for her
daughter. The marriage moved from one catastrophe to
another, but in the eyes of Clare Weston the sixth Earl of
Pemley could do no wrong.

Nancy watched two thrushes with speckled waistcoats
hop across the lawn. The doctor had been a long time
upstairs. She wondered why. She considered half
hopefully that perhaps Tony was dead. She imagined her
mother coming into the room and saying 'Tony is dead.'
What would have been her reaction – no tears, no regrets,
a little flutter of hope in her heart perhaps?

She could hear only faint sounds from above, but then
of course the rooms were so large, the ceilings so high.
What would the sounds indicate, anyway, the movements
of the doctor or her mother? Tony wouldn't move: she
hoped that he never would move again. It seemed justice
to her own reasoning that it had happened the way it had.
Another of Tony's girl friends could be found at the
bottom of this episode – two o'clock in the morning,

drunk, and driving drunk so that he had struck one of the stone pillars at the end of the drive. Even then he had only sustained a broken leg. She smiled humourlessly at that. A crash like Tony had had, and then to get away with nothing more than a broken leg – the fates hadn't been kind to her then. But now, how about now? With the leg cased in plaster, hobbling here, hobbling there, he had chosen to come into her bedroom, his breath reeking of whisky.

'Nancy, for God's sake, Nancy?' She had turned her back on him with all the contempt that had bred inside her, and then he had reached for her and ripped her dress from top to bottom. The marks of her fingers as she slapped his face had jumped into his cheeks like sudden daubs of red paint, and then he had come after her, half hobbling, half running. To evade him was easy and then he had fallen down the stairs with a terrific crash; all the way from the first step to the last of a long, winding flight of stairs.

At the bottom he was unconscious, the marks of her fingers still on his cheeks. There had been foam on his mouth and the plaster had broken from his leg as though a china vase had dropped and smashed. The servants got him to bed, moaning, whining with pain, and she had been glad, glad.

Her mother, in hysteria, screamed for her to call the doctor and she had done so slowly, reluctantly. She shrugged at the memory, and then the door opened.

'Hello, Daddy,' she said as her father came into the room.

Douglas Weston had lost his old zealous fire. He was an aged man now, shrunken, the top of his head smoothly shining and quite hairless.

'What's this I hear about Anthony?'

'He fell downstairs.'

'Hurt much?'

'I don't know yet, the doctor and mother are with him.'

185

She almost said that she didn't care, but in front of her father the words stuck in her throat.

Mr Weston laid his hand gently on his daughter's shoulders. 'I know how it is, my dear,' he said, quietly. 'And to think that your mother could do this to you.'

He saw the quick tears suddenly well in her eyes, but he knew as she knew that the tears were not for her husband. They were tears for herself, tears which showed that her resistance was on the point of crumbling, and tears which showed that she hoped – hoped for the worst.

'Don't think that way, my child – not like that.'

'No, Daddy.' She hung her head a little to hide the tears but she had no shame because of his knowledge. She knew now that he knew and was glad.

They heard the sound of footsteps, the murmur of voices and then her mother and Doctor Percival were suddenly with them, Percival grave of face, her mother, even in her fifties well preserved, waving her hands in distress.

'Oh, Nancy my child, my poor child!' She lavished her scant affection on her daughter in a sudden hug which Nancy received coldly. 'Tell her, doctor, tell her.'

Doctor Percival looked at the white, over-calm face. 'Your husband, Lady Fitzgerald, is in a very serious condition,' he said quietly. 'He should go to hospital at once but I fear that it will be impossible to move him.' Her face, he saw, was still serene: she was a lovely woman, thirty-four at least, but could get away with twenty-four, took after her mother . . . He recollected himself. 'So far as I am able to determine, Lady Fitzgerald, your husband has broken his neck and probably has two fractures of the spine. He's quite unconscious and I've done my best to make him comfortable.' Momentarily he held his chin. 'The setting of his leg, of course, has broken again, but that is of comparative unimportance in view of the other dangerous injuries.' Doctor Percival watched the sudden quick flight of a bird winging past the partly-opened windows. His client did not seem to be particularly upset at the grave news he was imparting. 'Your husband, Lady Fitzgerald, is very near to death.' Did he observe a spark of hope in her eyes, hope that this should be so? 'He must have specialist attention and quickly, very quickly. I cannot accept the responsibility for him.'

'Doctor Percival has suggested Sir William Gadsby,' Clare Weston said breathlessly. 'We must have him at once.'

'Gadsby is one of the finest in the country,' Percival emphasised. 'He's expensive, of course, but I think that you should have him. He would be here by tomorrow if I telephoned at once.'

'Yes, do so, doctor, right away.' Clare wrung her hands. 'We must do all we can, all we can.'

'Very well then: and I think that I had better stay on for a while in case there is any change.' The doctor looked at Nancy but she was still as stone.

'I'll show you where the phone is,' Douglas Weston said. 'Have you Gadsby's number?'

'We shall have to get it from the exchange. They're sure to know.'

'Very well.'

As they went through the door, Clare turned to Nancy.

'You don't seem very upset, my dear.'

'I'm not.' Turning her back on her mother, she walked with long strides in the wake of her father and Doctor Percival.

Sir William Gadsby arrived early next morning. He had travelled during the night, and without wasting time on formalities was ushered by Dr Percival into the patient's bedroom.

Gadsby was there for a long, long time, and when finally he had completed his examination Percival took him downstairs and introduced him to Nancy, Clare and Douglas Weston.

He shook hands formally and his keen eyes flickered round the expensively ornate room. He wondered why, in the whole of this household, only Clare Weston showed any particular concern.

'May I sit down?' he asked quietly.

'Please do.' Douglas Weston stood up, his face flushing at his bad manners. 'I beg your pardon. Can I get you anything – brandy, whisky, a cigar?'

'I'll have a whisky please, a small one, plenty of soda.' Sir William sat down.

'Cigar? Havana, conditioned.' Douglas Weston proffered the slim box.

'Excellent.' Gadsby smiled his appreciation, and taking one tested the crackle of the leaf against his ear.

Nancy watched with fascination this tall man with the alive eyes and long jaw. She felt the power of him, as though he were connected by short-wave. He oozed confidence and capability.

'Lady Fitzgerald,' he suddenly turned to her, ignoring her mother. 'I expect you are wondering what I have to say on the condition of the Earl of Pemley.' He did not wait for an answer. 'I have conducted a very thorough examination on your husband who, as you are probably aware, is still in a coma.'

'I was not aware.'

Gadsby's frosty look said 'Well, you should have been', but he ignored her remark.

'My findings are perfectly accurate, of that you may be certain. The bone of the leg which was in the plaster cast is fractured again. That I have put right, but your husband has a broken neck and no less than three fractures of the spine. One alone is serious enough but in the whole of my experience I have never met with anyone who has survived so grave an injury. Your husband is paralysed from below the highest point of fracture and I'm afraid that there is little or anything I can do for him. Moving him is quite out of the question which, of course, sets limitations on X-ray facilities and so on. However, I want you to call in another opinion.'

'But I understood from Doctor Percival that you were the best.' Clare vigorously protested. 'Is that not so, Doctor?' she turned to Percival who shrugged and answered, 'That was purely a personal view of course, madam, but Sir William seems to think that there is one better.'

'Doctor Percival flattered me,' Gadsby said drily. 'Lady Fitzgerald,' he turned to Nancy again, 'your husband is a dying man. I suggest that nothing must be too much trouble for you, and I want you to give me permission to bring in Sir Timothy Farley. There will be no fee – Farley is an idealist, he does not make any charge. You have heard of Sir Timothy Farley of course?'

'No I – ' Nancy suddenly stopped and Gadsby saw more reaction in her than he had seen during the whole of the time that he had been at the house. Her hand went to her mouth suddenly and her lovely eyes opened wide.

'What did you say the name was?' she asked breathlessly, looking intensely at Gadsby waiting, waiting.

'Farley. Sir Timothy Farley.'

She opened her mouth to speak and then closed it again. Tim Farley – Tim Swaine? No – he'd be about thirty-six; he couldn't possibly have been knighted, or be a famous surgeon and one respected so highly by a man of Gadsby's calibre. It was a coincidence of names. Occasionally she had written to Tim years ago. He had been studying medicine then – but no, it couldn't be.

'How old is this Sir Timothy Farley of whom you speak?'

'Thirty-six or so. He's something of a prodigy.'

'Tim Farley.' Nancy's eyes suddenly became brilliantly alive. 'Yes, Sir William, you may certainly send for him.'

'You shall not. He won't set foot in this house.' Clare Weston stood up, lips trembling, cheeks slowly changing to scarlet as the blood surged up from her neck. The past suddenly rocketed back into her mind. That boy under the bed staring at her through the mirror whilst she was with Nigel Thorpe, all those many years ago. She couldn't bear the thought of it. 'There is no need to send for him, Sir William. You are quite capable.'

'I beg your pardon, madam. If I were quite capable I should not have mentioned Farley.'

'You will not send for him.'

'Clare!' Her husband protested, shocked himself by this revelation and knowing that conscience must be threatening to choke his wife.

'Send for him at once, Sir William.' Nancy drew herself up, eyes stormy in defiance of her mother. 'Those are my instructions and the Earl of Pemley happens to be my husband.'

'No!' Clare's voice was an agony.

'I will show you to the telephone, Sir William.' Nancy's red mouth curved in triumph.

3

It was remarkable, Timothy mused as he drove to Bath, how vivid and close memories were when one considered the past carefully. What had been five, ten, fifteen years ago seemed to have occurred only yesterday if the mind reflected upon each small detail. He remembered so clearly sitting for hours in his cramped bedroom as a child, wondering about the mysterious Farleys of Bath.

It seemed amusing, now that he had beheld a flesh and blood Farley. How disappointing, how ridiculously droll this little pudgy puppet of a man, Francis Farley, had been. A little man cringing before the threats of his mother, pompous in his own right and yet afraid – so afraid.

The day had turned out brilliantly, and Timothy was able to savour to the full the rare luxury of the country-side. He stopped several times to view distant hills, to smell the rich odour of field and meadow, to watch the measured flight of wild duck and the majestic pattern of two swans on wing.

Enquiring from a motor cyclist who had stopped by the roadside, Timothy was advised to by-pass the city of Bath itself and approach from the rear, thereby avoiding traffic and the unfamiliar turns and twists of the streets. And so he did not directly approach Aquae Sulis, nor see the concert room and pump room which Beau Nash had developed in the eighteenth century. Instead, he crossed the Avon at Greenemarsh, had a fleeting glimpse of the attractive squares and circuits of the city from behind the Saddlers, and then came up to Wendover from the end of the lane facing into and approaching the city. He stopped the car at the crested wrought iron gates and rang the bell to the lodge. He was admitted quickly, and driving his car slowly down the curving red drive peered into the dense trees for signs of animal life. The trunks of oak and beech were so close that the drive appeared to have been laid between the edges of two forests. Then without any warning the trees ended, and he saw the vastness of Wendover Court, the huge lay of the gardens, the silent Rolls Royces on the gleaming expanse of forecourt, and the twitch of a heavy drape as though hidden eyes had been watching for him through the lead-laced windows at the side of the cathedral-like entrance.

So this had been the home of his father. He stopped the car, stepped out and, hands in pockets, looked at the motionless hawk impressed in the archway, tense, pre-pared as though for its death dive on some helpless animal.

He did not hurry to make his presence officially known. Instead he walked a few steps to the right and then to the left, allowing his eyes to absorb the vast pillared structure spreading in ungainly fashion like some unfinished coliseum.

Charlotte Bemmington's Georgian manor would have been lost in any one corner of it – even the solid, buttressed fortress of Kiledin, towering on the shores of the Firth of Moray, seemed small by comparison. He looked at but could not see the whole of Wendover in one glance. The size of it was fantastic, and the fortune that maintained it must also have been fantastic.

Taking a deep breath he plunged up the stone steps, through the shadowed coolness of a colossal arch, and pulled determinedly on the brass bell knob.

No answering melody could be heard, but the bell had sounded, for the door suddenly swung open and a liveried footman looked at him enquiringly.

'I am Sir Timothy Farley. Mrs Farley Senior is expecting me, I believe.'

'Come inside, sir.' The footman inclined his head courteously, and Timothy followed him into the domed and massive hall.

A second footman took his hat and coat and then he was led to a side door, panelled in rich mahogany, whereon the footman knocked in warning before opening it.

'Sir Timothy Farley,' he announced, standing to one side so that the visitor could pass, and then Timothy stood face to face with his grandmother.

His impressions of all that he saw were brief. A fleeting glimpse of sparkling cut glass on the old dark woods of original furniture, the ornate Italian fireplace, the thick carpets, the single bearskin – and then the hard magnetic eyes of the aged woman held him.

She was alone, bejewelled, splendidly dressed, her true age indeterminate. Her hair white, braided and festooned with diamond clips, was thickly luxuriant, her cheeks of good colour, faint blue veins showing in the expanse of delicate forehead.

Timothy heard the click of the door as the servant withdrew. Now he was alone with her, and he felt the strength of her will reach to him.

'So you are Johnathan's boy.' She looked at him in disappointment. He was shabby – not shabby because his clothes were not good, but he looked shabby. Nor was he handsome, and yet something intrigued her. Then she saw his hands – capable, exquisitely shaped and still, like fine sculpture. The hands of an artist – an artist in surgery, the finest in England, who had been knighted by the King, and was respected throughout the world. And he was a Farley of Bath, grandson to the grande dame of Wendover.

'Sit down,' she said, waving a gnarled hand towards a comfortable hide chair. 'You're not afraid of me, are you?'

'Should I be?' Timothy half smiled despite himself. 'I have no fear, I do assure you.'

The old lady shrugged graciously. 'You did not come because it was my wish, did you? You were interested in seeing me, weren't you? Francis hinted as much.'

'I was curious, I must confess.' He opened his cigarette case. 'Do you mind if I smoke?'

'No. I'll have one, too.'

He walked to her with the open case, his experienced eyes looking at her more carefully as she selected a cigarette.

'Will I do?' she asked, grinning crookedly as the first fronds of tobacco smoke hazed ceilingwards.

'I don't know what you mean.' Timothy sat down again.

'You looked me over, my boy, I saw you, don't deny it. Have I any outward signs which will determine to you how much longer I have to live?' Her smile was sardonic, waspish.

'You appear to be in excellent health. You have your own doctor?'

'Quite. You do not consider me a gracious person?'

'I have never even considered you.'

'Nor I you.' She was blunt, forthright, her intuition advising her against a false approach. 'No, I confess that my disposition is a harsh one. I make no excuses – my upbringing was such, it is bred in me, not as with the present generation. I have a core of steel. All the Farleys had; but not any more. You saw Francis?'

'I did.'

'He's your uncle, of course, and the rest are like him. Perhaps your father was the pick of the bunch. He, at least, had the strength of his defiance. The Farley tradition must go on.'

'In the manner prescribed by yourself, with the hard inner core of which you are so proud?'

'Not necessarily, but with dignity, the dignity of position.'

'I have no dignity.'

'But you have position. You have distinction.'

'Not advanced by you or any other of the Farleys.'

'No, a mistake, a bad mistake on my part and one which I very much regret.' She shook her head, 'But for the sake of Wendover your prowess, your greatness must be related to this house – to the Farley name as respresented by this house. Wendover and the families of Wendover have a place in history, but there are shadows now, and soon there will be no one worthy to carry the name of Farley into the future unless you do. Alone, unaided by me who has so much wealth, you have made your own way, carved your own high place in life. I scorned you, spurned you, held you to ridicule, but you were greater than I. You have risen, pioneered, spurred to success by the Farley blood: blood that has been shed on all the battlefields of England since Richard the Lionheart – blood which made us what we are.'

'You are wrong.' Timothy leaned back and looked at the entwined seraphs on the moulded ceiling. 'Quite wrong. You know why, of course?'

'Yes, I know what you have in mind.' She drew a deep breath and her old hands became agitated so that the jewelled rings flashed and sparkled.

'You think that you would have your mother's blood: your mother whom I did not even know, never wanted to know. But you haven't, I tell you, you haven't. You have Farley blood.' Her voice grew shrill.

'Like Francis?'

'A throwback, all of them.' She spat the words out contemptuously and he saw the sudden hard anger blaze in her eyes. He had come to scorn her, perhaps abuse her, but he knew that he could not. Whatever she was, she believed implicitly in herself and the tradition of the Farleys. She was a Farley by marriage only, and yet she had been well picked and the tradition hammered into her until she was concerned with nothing save the propagation of the trust now in her hands: the furtherance of the Farleys not only as a name, but as a great name. And she had but one hope – the hope of Timothy accepting his birth.

'The trust of the Farley will,' she pursued, her voice dry, 'automatically contributes to the maintenance of Wendover and the descendants of Wendover, but over certain dispensations I have complete control. There is wealth here, more than you could ever use, and I am prepared to alter the will in your favour for the whole of this amount. More than that I cannot do. I can never bequeath the house, for instance, nor the fundamental expenditure that goes with the house, for those are sealed conditions of days gone by, but the rest – ' her face was a hard mask, her eyes burning, her will trying to force him to a decision.

'I want nothing,' he said. 'Nothing, do you understand?' He felt a sudden resentment for this woman who sought to

195

exercise her wishes on him. 'For over thirty years now I've done without the Farleys of Bath, and I shall continue to do so. I am not vindictive, but I cannot accept the hardness of your upbringing as a just excuse for anything that has occurred previously. Yesterday I longed for this moment, to meet you face to face, to hate you and tell you how much I hated; but I do not hate you, nor yet do I despise you. I know that you are trying to bargain with me, trying to bribe me into accepting Wendover so that you can claim me as a Farley of Wendover – a great man, a great Farley of Wendover. I am not great, believe me.' He paused momentarily for breath. 'I have no skills or ability inherited from a specific breed of people. Certainly I have a gift, but who gave me that gift? Was it you? Was it the Farleys? Was it God? People say that I have the hands of God. Such talk frightens the hell out of me, but there *is* something. I know it and I feel it, and whatever it is none of it comes from this house. Do you understand?'

'No, and I will not listen to this talk, this stupid, ridiculous talk.' She stamped her foot, eyes blazing with fire. 'You belong here, do you hear, you belong and I order you to stay – I command you.'

'I'm sorry.' He looked at her sternly. 'I respect you for what you are but I will never accept you nor the way of life you represent. When I leave here, I shall not come back again, ever.'

His words left her momentarily speechless, and then her anger poured over him. Words, pleas, threats – to all of which he shook his head, until becoming silent she froze rigid, her face and body stiff like wood, her lips a thin line, her eyes two narrowed orbs from the corners of which uncontrolled tears suddenly ran.

'I am not weeping for myself,' she said bitterly, her voice harsh with emotion. 'I am weeping for Wendover. Now get out. I never want to see you again.'

He was shocked by this sudden turn in her, the dismissal like the vicious cutting lash of a whip.

'I still do not hate you,' he said, standing and looking at her. 'Goodbye.' He turned, abruptly, opened the door himself and closed it quietly after him. The footman who handed him his coat regarded him curiously as he left the house and walked quickly towards his car.

In the room he had left, his grandmother sat weeping, a peculiar sound like the punctuated cracking of dry sticks. But of this Tim knew nothing. Three hours later he was back from where he had started, his mind wiped clear of the day's events.

Back at home he had barely finished his lunch when Gadsby was clamouring for him on the telephone. He was shocked to hear that his friend was at the Weston's house at Worley.

He felt sudden confusion. It seemed strange that circumstance had so arranged that he should visit the Westons again, that he would see Nancy after almost twenty years. What age would she be? Thirty-four or thereabouts surely, and still at the old squire's house at Worley. He remembered having seen her wedding photographs in the magazine he'd read on that fateful train journey to Kiledin. Married to the sixth Earl of Pemley. And now they had need of Tim: the Earl had triple spinal fracture, paralysis, and a broken neck. What could they expect? What could anyone expect?

The first trailing shadows of twilight were laying soft fingers on the countryside, and it was almost nine o'clock when he arrived. He would put up somewhere for the night and spend an hour or so in the vicinity, refreshing his memory, but not now. Now, he just wanted to get the business over and sleep.

A servant opened the door for him as he hammered impatiently, and he strode in to what had once been a familiar setting. The pictoglyph was still there on the wall, the dark timbers of the ceiling, the rugs, the waxed wood panelling. All this he took in at a glance as, black case in

197

hand, he walked the expanse of the hallway towards Sir William who was hurrying to meet him.

'Better come in and have a drink. You look washed up.'

'I'm tired.' Timothy yawned openly.

'Sorry I had to drag you all this way.'

'No need to be.'

Gadsby led him into a small room where Scotch and soda stood ready on a Sheraton table.

'I arranged that we should be alone like this. Business first, the family after.' Carefully he acquainted Timothy with the details of the case, not mentioning anything about the tension and bitterness that had been so apparent in the family.

'We don't want anybody under our feet.' Gadsby pursued. 'As soon as you feel ready we'll take a look at the patient.'

'I think soap and hot water wouldn't come amiss,' Tim said. 'Stimulate my nerve ends.'

'Of course. There's a bathroom on the landing. Plenty of towels available. You go up. I'll see you in twenty minutes or so.'

Half an hour later a refreshed Tim rejoined forces with Gadsby, and they went off to consider what could best be done for Anthony Fitzgerald, Earl of Pemley.

It was a long deliberation, and even longer in its application.

It was well after midnight when the two orthopaedic surgeons finally left the bedroom and went downstairs. Their clothes reeked with the cloying odour of anaesthetic.

'In here,' Gadsby said, pushing open the heavy door of the drawing room.

Timothy followed, and then Nancy was rushing to meet him. She shook his hand warmly, but she was embarrassed and a slow scarlet flush crept into her cheeks.

'Hello, Tim,' she said softly. 'It's been a long time, hasn't it?'

'Yes, it's been a long time.' He looked at the startling mature beauty of her, the smooth skin faintly golden and the slightly full red lips. He forgot the room, forgot Gadsby and the Earl of Pemley on whose crushed backbone he had worked miracles for the past three relentless hours. Gadsby watched curiously and then Nancy, suddenly becoming aware of the tension and her own embarrassment, turned away with a little laugh.

'You remember Daddy, of course,' she said and her father, who had been waiting, came over to Timothy and pumped him warmly by the hand.

Tim was surprised at the amazing change in Douglas Weston. He could not remember Nancy's father with overmuch clarity, but he saw that however he had been, he was an old man now, old not so much in years as in the physical failure of his body, for he was wrinkled and emaciated.

'I never thought to see you in this house again, Tim,' Weston said. 'Especially under such circumstances. I'm proud to renew my acquaintance with you, very proud.'

'Thank you.'

'Quite a reunion,' Gadsby remarked drily. 'Now if we all make ourselves comfortable, I will take it upon myself to say a few things about your husband, Lady Fitzgerald.'

'Very well,' Nancy suddenly became cold and arrogant.

'My colleague, Sir Timothy Farley, who quite obviously is an old acquaintance of yours, has performed within the limitations afforded by the bedroom, several feats of extraordinary skilful surgery. We think that your husband has a chance of recovery, Lady Fitzgerald. Tomorrow, or is it today?' He looked at his watch. It was fifty minutes past midnight. 'Today, later on today, that is, I shall return to the Royal Elizabeth, which is my resident hospital, and arrange for the construction of a special steel frame which it will be necessary for your husband to have fastened to him. We've fixed him up temporarily with improvisation but it will, of course, be imperative to have

199

this frame as soon as possible. A great deal of further supervision will be required and several X-ray plates are needed. As soon as the frame is fitted we shall remove him to the Royal Elizabeth. There will be little danger involved now, and it is vitally important for further progressive treatment, you understand.'

Nancy nodded. 'Anything you say, Sir William.'

Gadsby looked at her with hard eyes. 'Your husband's injuries are of great interest to me, Lady Fitzgerald: had it not been for Timothy I doubt if he would be alive now. It is an extraordinary case, and one which will cause much controversy if he survives. When Doctor Percival looks in later this morning, much later I hope, I shall explain the position to him and then it will be up to you.'

'I understand.' Nancy nodded her head.

'I have to get back to the hospital as soon as I've had some sleep, and doubtless Tim will want to do so as well. The room upstairs, by the way, needs a clean up. We made rather a mess, but that couldn't be helped, of course.'

'Is Anthony conscious now?' Nancy's father asked.

'Not yet. He's still under the anaesthetic, and his body has suffered a good deal of shock, but Doctor Percival can handle that until we get him moved.'

Weston nodded. 'It's almost one,' he said. 'Time for a stinger.' He reached for the whisky. 'The servants are in bed, lucky beggars, and your chauffeur too, Sir William.' He filled the thin whisky tumblers. 'Say when.'

Timothy, half asleep in the chair, sipped the drink appreciatively. Nancy's father watched him through narrowed eyes. 'The superlative hands,' he mused. 'I always thought that there was something strange about him, even as a youngster.' He remembered Timothy's last visit over twenty years ago. It had not been a success, but one never knew about anyone. Who would have thought that young Tim from the village would have been knighted, and in his thirties too? Who would have thought that he would

200

become a surgeon so brilliant that even the famous William Gadsby respected him? Life was an amazing tangle of the unforeseen.

Nancy opened a box of fat Turkish cigarettes and handed them round. Soon the room was thick with the aromatic odour of burning Oriental tobacco. She watched Tim through the faintly purple haze. He hadn't changed a bit, she thought, he was still Tim Swaine of Worley to her, although he had earned such distinction. Not good looking, but calm and thoughtful, his eyes grave and with something about them that she liked. She remembered the pool, *his* pool and how she had fallen into it. She remembered her twisted ankle and how he had so gallantly struggled to get her home, and then she remembered with a start how, when he had touched her swollen ankle, the pain of the hurt had miraculously vanished. Miracle hands was what Sir William Gadsby had said, the man with miracle hands. Tim Swaine, Doctor Tim Farley, Sir Timothy Farley. No, it was too much to believe; but they had said that Tony would live, Tony with the frightful injuries to his back. Timothy had spent three hours with him and now he would live – when at heart she wanted him to die.

Timothy stifled a yawn. He didn't like the cigarette he was smoking, but he bore his distaste in silence. His eyes flicked from Douglas Weston, whom he observed drank his whisky greedily, to Nancy. There was strain about her, he could see by the faintly blue shadows beneath her eyes, and the nervous way she fluttered her hands, but she was quietly lovely. He held nothing against these people – Nancy had always been kind if a little arrogant, and her father smug, self-satisfied, self-important. Clare Weston he had only ever seen a few times in the whole of his life, but he knew that she was at the root of all unease in this house. He wondered about her – where was she now? – he wondered about Nancy, at the bitterness of her hate, only part hidden, that she had for her husband, Tony Fitzgerald.

Gadsby finished his glass and handed it back to Mr

Weston for replenishment. He too was wondering, needles of conjecture were alive in his brain. Why had Nancy been so pleased to see Tim Farley? How did Tim link up with the Weston history, and why had Mrs Weston hidden herself away? He shrugged, drew heavily on the Turkish cigarette and shrugged again. No business of his, anyway – it was time they were all in bed. Tim was almost asleep in his chair, his face white and lined with fatigue. He must suggest bed, or they would be up for the rest of the night. He must remember to have a last look at the patient, too. It was a special case even for the medical profession. There would be a good deal of surmise over this if Nancy's husband survived. He had watched Timothy at work with no X-ray guides and a minimum of equipment. It had not been the hands of an ordinary mortal who had eased these vertebrae together, straightened nerves, bent, broken and set again a locked neck. It had been the hands of God – the fabulous hands of Timothy Farley controlled by God. Too fantastic an idea for a man of science to contemplate – and yet he was unable to refute the fantasy . . . He yawned openly, shaking himself out of his reverie. 'Bed,' he said. 'How about bed for all of us?'

Clare Weston heard them climb the stairs. She heard Nancy's sudden light chatter and then her husband came into the bedroom. She feigned sleep, but she was not asleep. She had heard them in Tony's room, Gadsby and the other one, the one whom Nancy said was Tim Swaine who once had lived in the village. She remembered the burned letters, the hate and disgust she had nurtured against the little wretch, the quarrels with Douglas over him, the rows with Nancy over their writing – and now he had come back to embarrass her. She couldn't face him, she just couldn't. She'd heard them in the room talking, the crash of an overturned basin, the click of steel instruments, the sickly smell of chloroform which had crept into her own bedroom. They would be gone soon, and perhaps they'd been able to save Tony after all. Her uneasy mind brooded over Nancy's married life. She realised her mistake now, but it was too late, much too late. Then she fell asleep.

Tim slept heavily and did not wake until almost half-past ten the next morning. He had a big room overlooking the fir trees which formed a dark background to the yellow thatched stables. His eyes were still heavy with sleep as he bathed and changed, and he decided on a good walk, as soon as he had had breakfast, to freshen his jaded body.

Sir William was already up when he pushed open the door of the breakfast room.

'You're late,' Gadsby admonished mockingly. 'I've almost finished.' He spread a thin layer of marmalade onto the hot buttered toast.

The butler arranged a chair for Tim and poured coffee. There was no one else in the room.

'How's Pemley this morning? I haven't been in myself,' Tim asked.

'Showing signs of life. Percival has been and gone. He's arranging for a nurse to come in today.'

Tim nodded, finished off the iced grapefruit and savoured a hot grill of ham and kidneys. 'I shan't return today,' he said. 'I intend to have a look round – nostalgia you know. Worley was once my home.'

'Yes, so I believe.' Gadsby looked at him curiously. 'Look, Tim this is home country to you. If I were in your place I'd book a room at the best hotel you can find and have a week here. You need a rest. Just a week would help out – a month would be better, but that's beyond my powers of persuasion. Let me know before I go and I'll tell Mrs Muffin not to expect you.'

'I think that an excellent idea.' They both looked up as Nancy, in a smart summer dress, walked into the room. 'And you can stay here, Tim, no need to bother with stuffy hotels,' she added gaily.

Tim shook his head dubiously. 'It's nice of you to offer,

Nancy, but I don't know, I'm so busy.' He was surprised at her sudden insistence that he stay at the Gables, but it was a fine opportunity. He ached for a rest, and he could keep an eye on Fitzgerald while Sir William made arrangements at the hospital. 'I don't think your mother would approve very much,' he said with a sudden grin.

'Damn my mother!' Nancy said with venom. 'I should like you to stay, Tim.' Her eyes met his. 'Please, we have so much to talk about.'

'All right with you, William? Will you take my patients for a few days?'

'Pleasure! And you know as well as I do that you need to relax or something will crack – and we don't want that to happen. You're too valuable.' He looked suddenly at Nancy. 'Look after him,' he said. 'Feed him up well and if he speaks of returning in anything less than a week, hit him with something hard. Persuade him to stay longer if you can.'

'I'll try,' the girl said, laughing.

Tim remembered the long slanting hill as, with Nancy at his side, he looked down into the valley. To the left lay the thick copse where as a boy he had treasured the knowledge of the whereabouts of birds' nests.

He was silent for some time and then, in response to Nancy's questions, he began to tell her about himself, his work, his hopes, and his vast interest in the mind, the body and the human spine. She, remembering him as a child, felt a great wonder at his achievements.

They walked on down the hill until Timothy saw the cottage where he had once lived. It had not changed, save that the thatch on the roof was new.

'Who lives there now?' he asked.

'I don't know. It was empty for quite some time but there's a big family there at present. Market gardeners, I think.'

Yes, it would always be the same Worley, a town of

market gardening, farming, remote and sheltered from industry, ancient in its beliefs and planning, its sanitation and public services crude and elementary. It would never change, sufficient unto its self, with its rolling meadows, the earth fresh and brown where plough and harrow had laid it bare.

'You are not happy, are you, Nancy?' he asked suddenly.

'Happy?' she shrugged. 'Perhaps I don't know what happiness is. Perhaps though having everything at hand, everything that I want, I have missed the finer side of life.'

He looked at her troubled frowning brow. 'You wouldn't really care if your husband were to die, would you?'

'No.' The defiant answer startled him.

'It's none of my business, I know, but it's all so obvious. Gadsby saw it, I have seen it. Would you care to tell me why?'

'Shall we walk into the copse and look at the pool? Your pool, remember.'

'Yes, I remember,' he laughed softly. 'My pool. Come on, I'm very eager to see it.' He held her hand suddenly, and then just as suddenly let go. This was no way to keep a clear perspective. He must never forget that trust in him was implicit.

It was cool and sweet smelling in the shadowed walk of the copse.

'Have you ever known hate, Timothy?' Nancy asked suddenly. 'Something that starts to build itself up inside, insidiously at first, and then growing, growing until it becomes the core of your being, controlled as much as you can control it by pride alone, afraid that if the pride goes you will do something desperate and hurtful?'

He looked at the strange remoteness which had suddenly crept into her face. 'I have never hated that much,' he said quietly. 'All this hinges back on your marriage, of course.'

She nodded. 'I hate Tony and I think, too, that I hate my mother whom I followed and listened too blindly. From my marriage onwards my life slowly crumbled round me. Tony was unfaithful, and there were so many other things that I just don't care anymore now. If he dies I shall be glad, glad so that I can savour freedom once more. I shall leave Worley altogether – the pride of the aristocrats.' She laughed bitterly.

Tim was pensive, thinking about her: Fitzgerald would have died had he not come along, but he must not consider that. He must not think that he had saved Fitzgerald at the expense of Nancy's happiness. He had remade a smashed body, that was all. He must not think about personages; he must not set himself up as a judge and decide whether the death of a person would be beneficial to the community, that it would be a blessing were he to let that person die. He had no powers of life and death. He was a surgeon, a healer, and foremost in his mind must be the saving of life, all life.

The weather remained glorious, with bright sunshine and warm air fragrant with the smells peculiar to untouched countryside. Tim phoned Gadsby once with a half promise that he would stay for a week longer than he had anticipated. On the Friday, Tony Fitzgerald, sixth Earl of Pemley, conscious and alive, was removed to the Royal Elizabeth Orthopaedic Hospital for prolonged observation and treatment, and on the same day Timothy ran into Nancy's mother who had made her intention of avoiding him very obvious.

He had been reading a volume of Shelley in the extensive library, and was on his way to the music room where he heard Nancy playing the minuet suite, when he was suddenly face to face with Clare and she had no possible chance of avoiding him.

'Good morning,' he said after a quick startled pause. 'You're Nancy's mother, of course?'

She stood motionless and afraid like a hunted fawn, her eyes large and pleading.

'Yes, you must be Mr Farley. How do you do.' She held out a slim uncertain hand which he shook gravely. She was quite beautiful still, he saw, and looked at least ten years younger than her age, which he estimated must be in the middle fifties. He smiled suddenly at the way she had called him Mr Farley, and at her obvious effort to be casual, as though meeting someone completely new, someone whom she had never before met or knew nothing about.

'I'm glad that you were able to stay,' she said. 'Nancy mentioned that you would probably be our guest. I'm very pleased.'

'I am, too.' He bore her no grudge, no malice. Why should she assume this attitude, he thought, why should she? The past was over, done with.

'There will be a few people in at the weekend,' Clare Weston said. 'I am sure they will be anxious to meet you.' She did not mention her son-in-law, but deep in her lovely eyes he could see the merest shadow of something in her mind – regret, sorrow over her daughter, he would never know.

'I'm glad that you don't mind having me,' he said.

She laughed. 'The house is big enough, surely.'

'Yes, of course, but this is the first time that I have seen you since I arrived.'

'I'm sorry, but I have been quite busy, quite busy.'

'I have been busy, too. Let's stop fencing with each other, shall we? The past is over. I'm the little boy of whom you didn't approve, but please let us not be silly over the business. There is enough bitterness in this house without fomenting anymore. I'm Tim Farley, no one else. The past is buried and any mistakes that were to be made, have been made. Shall we be friends?' He held out his hand and she suddenly clasped it firmly.

'Thank you,' she said. And I'm grateful for all you have done and – and I'm sorry.'

'Don't be,' he said quickly. 'Everyone is entitled to their own beliefs. You're quite lovely, you know. I well remember the first time that I saw you.' She warmed to his flattery. This was the language she understood.

'I *was* lovely,' she admitted. 'Once upon a time, but then loveliness isn't everything, is it?' She shrugged slightly as though compelled to accept something which she could not now alter. There were no steps to retrace, there was no time to cancel, and no tears to shed which could wash out any of the past.

Tim could almost feel sorry for her, sorry for the utter dependence she had upon the one thread which sustained her, upon which she leaned the whole of her weight. Through her colossal vanity she had lost the love of her daughter and of her husband. She had built the fire, burning herself until the burns didn't hurt any more, until she was completely hardened. But one day – and not very far distant – her strength must collapse, and then she would be alone, utterly alone.

At the weekend there were several callers, some by invitation, others who just dropped by. Mostly they were county people and it was obvious to Timothy that Clare Weston's little knot of admirers had thinned since the old days.

On the Saturday afternoon they rode and although it was not strenuous, Timothy, always uneasy in the saddle, was glad when it was over. Nancy's mother no longer went to hounds for she was more careful of herself now that age had begun to overtake her, but nevertheless, she maintained herself perfectly astride and seemed just as well groomed after the ride as before.

In the evening they played bridge and later danced in the giant hall. Nancy's mother expanded further towards Timothy during the evening, becoming quite possessive when she introduced him to her friends. Douglas Weston kept pretty much to himself most of the time, putting away rapid whiskys without any seeming effect. Tim had

had as much to drink as was good for him, and Nancy a little more so. Despite protests, however, Nancy persuaded him to dance with her again and again, and he thought it strange that his awkwardness provoked no despairing comment from her. He had never learned to dance well, but she didn't seem to mind and coaxed him round with enthusiasm.

'Most of the people are staying,' she said as the music stopped and they walked into the drawing room. 'There will be tiresome sport tomorrow, usually my father conducts a gunshoot – pheasant and partridge and things.'

'I don't think I should care very much for that.' He shrugged expressively. 'I'd much prefer our usual walk. I'd like to have a look at my old schoolroom, if it's still there of course.'

'Oh, it's there all right. Worley makes a point of being non-progressive.'

'We could have a drink in the local and rub shoulders with the bar customers. I always find that quite exciting, they are such interesting people.'

'Very well, I'm game for anything.' She slipped her hand into his and moved closer so that the faint suggestion of perfume which clung to her was quite distinct. There was, too, a warm soft fragrance about her, a ripeness which he found suddenly very appealing.

'Too much to drink,' he thought. 'I must take it easy.'

'I'd better ring Gadsby on Monday and tell him not to expect me for another week,' he remarked. 'No doubt he'll be surprised after the years he's argued with me to take time off.'

'It just shows that I must be good for you.' She smiled, her teeth very white, her eyes alive as he had never seen them so before.

'How much have you had to drink?' he asked. 'Enough I should say.'

'No, not enough, not yet. Why do you ask?'

'Your eyes are too bright, pupils dilated.'

'Oh, you doctors.'

'Very well, I won't talk shop anymore, but let's not dance again.' The music had suddenly started. 'I've had as much as I can stand for one evening.'

'Tim.' She turned suddenly from the window through which she had been looking. 'I feel that I must talk to you before I go out of my head.' Her voice was little more than a whisper, although there was no one else in the room.

He nodded in understanding, and sat next to her as she moved to the deep cushioned settle beneath the window.

'People get older all the time don't they?' she said. 'They look back with pleasure on happy memories, pleasant events.' She sighed, deeply troubled. 'You can look back and feel the satisfaction of tremendous achievements. But what can I look back upon?' She sighed again, a tremulous almost despairing sound. 'My whole life has been so utterly pointless. I despise my husband and hate my mother. Everything seems so damned negative. I need some love, Tim. Someone who wants me for myself, and not for what I have.'

He saw the sadness in her eyes.

'That seems a fair summation of what it is that ails you,' he observed quietly. 'I'm no psychoanalyst, but the brooding in this house is apparent and so obvious. Your own unhappiness cries out for help in everything you say and do. But how can I assist? I haven't seen you since we were children together, and the current situation has been occasioned only by the merest of chances.'

'Fate, wouldn't you say?' She was eager.

'If you like.' He acquiesced comfortingly. 'But nevertheless you are still the wife of the Earl of Pemley.'

'Damn him. Damn him. Damn him,' she cried wretchedly.

'And even if you weren't,' Timothy pursued relentlessly, 'A brief and casual meeting between you and me constitutes very little in terms of a lasting relationship.

210

The cause of your unhappiness is obvious enough, and I see only the finality of divorce as a solution. But you must endeavour to broaden your outlook. Be taught by your own unhappy experiences. You need love, real love, but few of us have ever experienced real love, and fewer still lasting love.

'Have you ever experienced it?'

'Yes, I have.'

'I won't be hurtful and ask you to tell me about it.' She looked him squarely in the face. 'Could you love me?'

He was quite shaken by her question and his face said as much

'I cannot answer that,' he spoke quite deliberately. 'We are worlds apart, and under any circumstances my work always comes first.'

'But could you love me?' she insisted, and he heard the beginning of hysteria in her voice. 'Help me Timothy. Please help me.'

'I could love you sexually if that is what you want. There has always been a thread of understanding between us, even though it was years ago. But it's not the same as love. You desperately need a sexual relationship. But it must be a good sexual relationship, not a casual one. Love and sex are not the same thing. Not the same thing at all. Do you understand what I am trying to say?'

She sniffled a bit at his forthrightness.

'Now don't cry,' he admonished. 'I am trying to be helpful. I don't want to sound pompous. My own experience of love that I told you about was sexual, but so full of love that there was never anything else like it in the whole world. If you can find a relationship like that you will never look back.'

'What happened.'

'She – Stella died. We were to have married.'

'I'm sorry.'

He became very silent, very still. 'Fortunately I had my work. Without it I should have been in a padded cell.'

'There are questions I want to ask, but I won't. I can see that it has been painful.'

'Yes. I've never told anyone before how it was with me. You see, Nancy you are not the only one to have suffered, and there is still plenty of time for you to do something about your own problem.'

'Yes, I see.'

'Don't settle for anything less than you want. There has been unhappiness for you, but that unhappiness has now given you a clearly defined picture of what it is you need. A sexual relationship is not the answer, unless with the man you love and, more importantly, who really and truly loves you in return.'

She nodded and Timothy rose to his feet. 'I think that now would be as good a time as any to join the others. We have been away for long enough, and I think that perhaps both of us are just a little intoxicated.'

Sleep did not come easily to Timothy that night. He thought of the tragedy of Nancy, his childhood sweetheart. Her disenchantment with the decadent Earl of Pemley. He believed that he had given her sound advice. She must get out of the marriage now while there was still time to find some happiness. She was an extremely beautiful woman. She must disregard position. Forget the false teachings of her mother.

He dozed fitfully, half conscious of the path of the moon as it filtered through the part open window, and then he was wide away as he heard the light sound of footsteps and the gentle click of the door opening.

He knew that it was Nancy. He could hear her hurried, half scared breathing and smell the faint elusive perfume she wore.

Suddenly she was in bed with him, clinging to him, her body naked and warmly desirable.

'Nancy, for God's sake.' His muted protest was smothered as her mouth covered his. Her lips were soft and

212

trembling, her skin hot to his touch. 'This is not the way. Not the way,' he said, but he made no attempt to push her to one side. Instead he held her tightly and knew the pleasure of her closeness, the feel of her yielding breasts pressing in to him.

Very gently his hands comforted her quivering body. Neither spoke, although he knew that she was crying a little. Carefully he traced her body, feeling the pleasurable trembling he evoked within her. He broke the silence. 'Nancy – I.'

'Don't spoil anything,' she kissed him again. 'I want to speak so much but I don't know the words to use. The things to say.'

'You don't have to say anything. You've said it all without uttering a word.'

'How? How?'

'Your whole self is talking for you.' He caressed the long curves of her thighs. 'Not just talking, but positively shouting. When we were together earlier this evening I had not even considered the development of any kind of intimacy between us. I know how terribly frustrating your married life has been. But think about it, Nancy. You don't want a relationship with me, do you, that at best can only be a one off?'

She looked at him sombrely. 'I want you to show me what it is like. What it is that I have been missing. I know you are responding to me, I can feel you.'

'Of course you can.' He held her scented lips lightly with his own. She was utterly desirable, and stimulated to the full for a sexual encounter.

A profound shudder rippled through her and she was unable to contain herself. 'Oh my dear, my dear.' And then she was sighing her delight as slowly he brought her to an utterly fulfilling climax. The first she had ever known.

Briefly he thought of his tragic Stella. Theirs had been an incredible union. It had been good with Nancy, but not quite like Stella, for no one could ever replace Stella.

'You enjoyed it?' he asked, a trifle breathlessly.

'Oh yes. Yes. I've never experienced anything like it before in my whole life. It was marvellous, absolutely marvellous.'

'I enjoyed it, too. We were completely in harmony. It becomes a kind of therapy, then. You see how much you need a partner with whom the therapy can become a permanent and loving thing. You will find it utterly fulfilling.'

'You aren't going to send me away, are you Timothy?' Her voice was small and anxious.

He hugged her nakedness to him. 'No, I'll not send you away,' he assured her. 'But this is only an interlude. Good for both of us perhaps, but without the hope of enduring stability.'

She clung to him in sudden desperation as though fearful that he would vanish. Her kisses burned into him and he felt his desire for her quicken again.

'More,' she urged him. 'More.'

Through the haze which had crept into his mind he heard the distant growl of thunder, and his body suddenly went ice cold.

'No I can't any more,' he said abruptly and in some alarm. 'We have both looked into the time crystal. You know now what it is that you need to do, and I feel, too, that my own destiny is slowly taking shape.'

'I thought that I heard thunder,' Nancy observed, surprised at the sudden change in him.

'Yes, you did. I heard it, too.'

'It doesn't bother you, does it?' She sounded concerned.

'No, indeed not. But it is trying to say something.'

'It says something to me,' she laughed. 'Usually that a storm is on the way.'

He knew that she had misinterpreted him, as he had intended that she should, for the thunder meant far more to him than the symbolism he had claimed.

214

'It's time for you to go along,' he said. 'Back to your own bed.' There was finality in his voice. 'Perhaps we can talk some more in the morning.'

'I'd like that very much.' She kissed him hesitantly, and slipped from the bed, her nakedness a pale shadow as reluctantly she opened the door and vanished into the corridor.

4

Autumn brought with it early frost, and a warning of bitter weather to come. The first snows of November were followed by more snow in December and January, and far into March the freezing weather continued, so that Timothy gave up all hope of it ever being warm again. Spring was only a mark on the calendar and the blossom and early buds were late arriving, so deeply had winter dug in its icy fingers. And then, almost miraculously, the face of the earth changed. The winds became warm, the snow melted and the sun which had seemed permanently hidden behind flint grey clouds showed its face once again and all nature stirred.

During this period Timothy reconciled himself to the work of healing. The incident with his grandmother at Bath he erased from his mind completely. Nancy was just a pleasant memory. He felt that he had been warned by that threatening rumble of thunder, and he respected the warning. The Earl of Pemley had been despatched, cured, save for a slight dragging of his left leg, and he now had many more cases to occupy his mind. All his time was spent in his practice of medicine and surgery, the manipulation of his miraculous hands; but somewhere in the structure of his life there was a blank. A dark opaque spot which did not fit, which somehow seemed obvious and yet which he could not establish. Within himself he knew that he was a lonely man, despite his many friends and the firm bond which lay between himself and Sir William Gadsby. At night he would sometimes lie awake thinking, wondering, analysing himself in an effort to find a cure for what he felt to be a part of himself hopelessly out of tempo with the rest. He did not have the comradeship of women and yet he had mixed with women. He had loved passionately and he had attempted to recapture lost time with Nancy, only to find that time was his enemy and not his friend. The one love which had seemed the last link in the chain of his destiny, the love of Stella McAlister, he had lost tragically and frighteningly, and he had slipped into the habit of regarding women only with professional doctor's eyes. The powerful force that nature had provided, the allure, the provocativeness that was woman's by right, he had ceased to accept and looked only at the components inside, reducing surface qualities to the harsh terms of physiology, with the result that the normal desire which formed an essential part of man was fast leaving him. It was on a morning in June, when a glance through the windows left no doubt that summer had really come, that he suddenly knew what it was he missed. He knew at last what was intended of him, and cursed to think that he had been so long in making a decision. His destiny had been plotted and planned from the start and whenever he had attempted to move from the set path he was pushed back again, sometimes gently, sometimes with terrifying force.

It was now so clear, so obvious, and he in his blindness had ignored it. He dressed hurriedly, a fever of impatience suddenly gripping him. He might be too late, but he knew that he would not be. He knew that however long he had been he would never have been too late.

He phoned Gadsby at his private house. He packed a suitcase quickly and unskilfully and tossed it into the back of the car. To Mrs Muffin he gave last minute instructions, told her to phone the Royal Elizabeth and refer all his patients to Sir William, and then only writhing blue serpents of exhaust smoke were left to mark his hurried exit.

The roses in the garden made a splendid show. Bright golds and yellows vied with crimson and pink, orange and white. Tending the garden, she looked as beautiful as any bloom, any flower. Time had neither changed nor aged her. It seemed merely to have passed by without laying a finger on her. The soft glow of health and youth gleamed from under her skin like a newly opened bud and her eyes, startlingly blue, were calm and clear. Sadness she had known, but shrugged it off when in her rose garden because here was a tranquillity which soothed her troubled soul.

She heard the car approach, but she did not lift her head until there was the crunch of footsteps on the path behind her. Then she turned, and he was there. Timothy was there.

She did not move but her heart gladdened and her eyes brightened. How long had it been? She could not remember when last she had seen him, and even then his visits had been fleeting – even hurtful, so obviously had they seemed a duty.

'Hello, Tim.' Her voice was low. How long would he stay? An hour? A day? But she would be happy while he was with her, very happy.

There was a strange spark in his usually sombre grey eyes, and then suddenly he had walked right up to her and she was in his arms.

'Hello, Alice.' He said very softly and then he was kissing her. The shock of the unexpectedness changed to gladness, a feeling which grew inside her, suffusing her with joy she had rarely known.

217

'Oh, Tim. Oh, Tim.' Her eyes spilled tears and she was crying gently.

He held her tightly to him. 'My dearest,' he said breathlessly. 'It's taken me all this time, all this long time to know, to realise, I've been such a bloody fool.'

'No, no you haven't.' She looked into his face. 'I waited, Tim. You had so much to do, so much to accomplish. I just kept on hoping and hoping. There could never have been anyone else, ever.'

A weight seemed to lift from his shoulders. The blank spot, the part of him that he knew to be wrong was appeased. The loose ends of the chain were at last united and he felt a sudden peace as he held her in his arms, the sun shining, the vivid roses nodding their heads in the light breeze.

'Can there ever have been such a stupid man?'

'No, never.'

They laughed together and he kissed her again, feeling the softness of her pressing against him, aware of the calm beauty that lay in her face. For so long he had wondered, and all the time she had been waiting for him, waiting to fill the role which she knew was hers to fill.

They walked towards the house, arms linked, heads close together, each pensive, each filled with gladness. Dibbern the gardener, now old and wrinkled, hobbled forward to welcome him.

There was a quiet dignity about the house, a restfulness which he had not known for so long. This was his home, he remembered. Alice's now, by right, but his, too. He could feel the friendliness of it as though it were alive, as indeed it was alive with the memories of the past, as clear as though today was the final day after all the yesterdays. He thought with guilt of his neglect, of his fleeting scanty visits, of the aching heart that Alice had endured because of his unkindness. The hand that had guided him to success had been so diffident, so slow to lead him back home and yet the revelation had finally come to him. His task then had not been in vain. It had always been intended that he should come to her, for the whole of his destiny had been bound up with this house from the time he had first appeared as a hopeful gardener's boy.

He took her hand. 'I have so much to say, so much to talk about.'

'There will always be time.'

'Yes, of course.'

He pottered in the garden with Dibbern, who was now ninety-three years of age. He read the poets, slim elegant volumes hardly touched in the library. Twice he phoned Gadsby, who assured him that there was nothing at all for him to worry about, and then he settled back for a real holiday, a real rest.

Some three weeks later, just after he had finished an excellent lunch cooked and served by Alice, he heard the sound of a car pulling into the drive. He peered through the window as a short little man in a dark overcoat and black homburg, a stranger to him, walked up the steps and sounded the bell. He heard Alice cross the hallway, the low sounds of exchanged conversation and then she called him. He hurried out and looked at the dapper little stranger curiously.

'Sir Timothy Farley?' It was said as a question.

'Yes.'

'How do you do, sir.' The stranger held out his hand. 'My name's Warwick, of the firm Stevens and Warwick, solicitors. May we talk somewhere? My visit is of a somewhat private nature.'

Timothy was nonplussed. He had no knowledge of the firm Stevens and Warwick. 'Very well.' He nodded his head in assent, and led the visitor into the library.

'I've already been to the Royal Elizabeth,' said Warwick, settling himself down in a chair after having refused to take off his coat. 'I met Sir William Gadsby and he informed me of your whereabouts. Sir Timothy, when did you last see your grandmother?'

219

'My grandmother?' Timothy was startled. 'I've only ever seen her once, twelve months ago or more, and I wouldn't say that we were on particularly friendly terms. Has she issued a writ against me or something?'

Warwick laughed. 'Hardly,' he said, shifting one knee across the other. 'It's remarkable all the same.' He coughed. 'Sir Timothy, your grandmother died thirteen weeks ago. You were aware, of course?'

'Aware?' he was astonished. 'I certainly was not aware. She appeared to be in very good health when I visited her.'

'Well, you should know if anyone, but evidently there was something wrong, radically wrong.' He coughed again. 'Anyway there was a will, a perfectly normal and expected procedure, and Wendover and the equipage of Wendover is, of course, handed on to the next of kin; also a great deal of the family fortune which is a fixed condition of the will. There has, however, been an added provision, a new clause.' He paused dramatically. 'Grandmother Farley, Sir Timothy, has left to you personally and unconditionally, the sum of thirteen million pounds.' He paused to allow the effect of his words to sink in.

Timothy's jaw dropped. 'Thirteen million pounds! But I – ' He stopped suddenly.

'You did not expect it?'

'Expect it? I've never heard of such a sum, and you say that it has been left to me. Why me?'

Warwick spread his hands eloquently. 'Perhaps she thought that you could put it to good use?' he suggested.

'Thirteen million pounds,' Timothy said it softly to himself, as though to make sure that he could say it, half expecting Warwick to contradict him.

'Exactly.'

Timothy whistled in amazement.

'There are certain formalities, of course. You will have to visit me at my London office and so on.'

'I understand.' Timothy nodded his head slowly, his

right hand feeling automatically for his cigarette case. 'You'll stay to dinner?' he asked as an afterthought.

Warwick shook his head brusquely. 'I must be off: very busy, you know.'

'A drink then?'

Again a brisk shake of the head. 'No, thank you.' He held out his hand. 'I'm proud to have met you, Sir Timothy.'

Tim shook the proferred hand and escorted his visitor to the door, and then dashed off to acquaint Alice with the startling news.

It was too fabulous a sum, thirteen million pounds. He mulled over its potentialities for almost a week. It was lethal, that amount of money – deadly – and then, quite suddenly, he knew what he had to do with it. His course was set, the way clear and obvious.

He rushed off to London to see Warwick and finally settle matters, and then he toured Wales for a week, Alice with him, seeking, until finally he came to a hill which overlooked rolling pasture.

'This is the place,' he said to the girl who stood beside him, obviously worried at his strange agitation. 'I feel it. I know it.'

It was a beautiful strip of country, Alice was quick to acknowledge, carpet upon carpet of rich green grass, blue mountains far away like a haze of smoke on the skyline, and an exhilarating perfume in the air.

'It's very pretty,' she said, 'but I don't understand you, Timothy.'

'You will.' He squeezed her hand. 'Sit down and I'll explain.' He patted the grass, sitting down himself. When she had settled comfortably beside him, he linked his arm with hers and looked out over the wild green pasture land.

'Blue mountains,' he said. 'And such air, sniff it.' He held up his nose and sniffed loudly. 'Beautiful air, beautiful.' He pointed with his finger. 'Do you know what I see?' he asked.

'I shall be very pleased to know. You sound so awfully excited.'

'I am, I'm keyed up more than any student has ever been at his first op. I see lorries,' he said, 'Dozens of them. I see mixing machines and cement machines, I see scaffolding and hundreds of men working. I see foundations being dug, pipes being laid, bricks and mortar, granite and marble, and slowly I see it taking shape, slowly, slowly but it is there, my dream, my debt.'

'Well, anyway I know that it must be a building of some sort.'

'It is a building, the Charlotte Bemmington Orthopaedic Hospital and it will be built right here.'

'Oh, Timothy, how marvellous!' She clapped her hands and hugged him to her. 'Darling, it's a wonderful idea, just wonderful.'

'I think so, and Gran Farley's thirteen million should just about do it. It will be the finest hospital in the world, with the finest doctors and the finest nurses. And there'll be a portrait of Charlotte in the main hall.'

'And you must have a portrait of your grandmother, too.'

'Very well, then.'

'When will you start?'

'At once. I'll engage land agents to buy, architects to plan and engineers to build. Nothing will be too expensive – first class equipment, fine laboratories, grants for students.'

'But the upkeep will be tremendous, even with thirteen million pounds.'

'Many people are in my debt, and quite a number of them very rich. This will be a way for them to show their appreciation.'

'Yes, it will be a wonderful way.'

'I shall make the initial arrangements and then Warwick will have to handle the rest. He seems a capable enough chap. After that I must go back to the Royal Elizabeth.'

He saw her face fall. 'This time next week,' he said softly, 'we shall be married. Just a quiet wedding, Gadsby and a few others you know, and when the Charlotte Bemmington Hospital is built I shall make it my resident hospital. Charlotte said that you should never sell the manor, but she did not say that you could not move it. We'll have it taken down, brick by brick, and rebuilt here on this spot less than a mile from the hospital. How would you like that?'

'Do you think that Charlotte would mind?'

'Charlotte Bemmington, not she. This is her hospital, her spirit will come with the house. She'll be able to watch over it.'

'Yes, I think you're right.'

'I know that I'm right.'

They sat looking out over the green fields, each of them quietly thoughtful.

'We have the whole of our future together before us,' the girl remarked pensively. 'It will be good because I want it to be good.'

'So do I.' Timothy took her hand gently into his. 'But let's not talk too much about the future, Alice. Each tomorrow is the beginning of the end for some of us. The world can change overnight. Friends become enemies, and He whom none shall spurn may be spurned. Today is September 3rd 1938. I wonder what we shall be saying this time next year?'

'I know what I shall be saying.'

'You do?'

'That I will always love you.'

He smiled, and then with arms around each other they walked slowly towards the car, neither knowing nor suspecting that in exactly one year's time all the horrors of World War II would commence.